AUG 15

The Sweetness of Honey

**Center Point
Large Print**

Also by Alison Kent and available from
Center Point Large Print:

The Second Chance Café
Beneath the Patchwork Moon

**This Large Print Book carries the
Seal of Approval of N.A.V.H.**

The Sweetness of Honey

—A Hope Springs Novel—

ALISON KENT

CENTER POINT LARGE PRINT
THORNDIKE, MAINE

This Center Point Large Print edition is published
in the year 2015 by arrangement with
Amazon Publishing, www.apub.com.

This is a work of fiction. Names, characters,
organizations, places, events, and incidents
are either products of the author's
imagination or are used fictitiously.

The text of this Large Print edition
may vary from the original edition.
Printed in the United States of America
on permanent paper.
Set in 16-point Times New Roman type.

ISBN: 978-1-62899-661-6

Library of Congress Cataloging-in-Publication Data

Kent, Alison.
  The sweetness of honey : a Hope Springs novel / Alison Kent. —
Center Point Large Print edition.
  pages cm
  Summary: "Dark-haired beauty Indiana Keller buys a property in Hope
Springs, Texas, for three reasons: to expand her vegetable business, to
harvest and sell delicious honey from the property's established bee
colony, and to reunite with her estranged siblings. While Indiana tries to
reconnect with her brothers, two local men begin vying for her heart"
  —Provided by publisher.
  ISBN 978-1-62899-661-6 (library bindfing : alk. paper)
  1. Brothers and sisters—Fiction. 2. Missing persons—Fiction.
    3. Bee culture—Fiction. 4. Texas—Fiction. 5. Large type books.\
    I. Title.
  PS3561.E5155S94 2015
  813'.54—dc23
                                                    2015022007

To the readers who have fallen in love
with Hope Springs and the small town's
residents, and who e-mail, review,
and touch base on social media.

Thank you, thank you, thank you.

Chapter One

The bees were what had sold her. The bees and Hiram Glass. The lovely octogenarian had tended the hives for years, selling the honey at the same farmers markets where she sold root vegetables, and vine vegetables, and leafy greens—and, the years the weather cooperated, strawberries the size of her fist, but that didn't happen often.

She would leave untouched the section of the acreage where the busy hives thrived; these days, honeybees faced so many obstacles. Moving them would add unnecessary stress, and there was no need. Their location allowed more than enough room for the expansion of IJK Gardens—though the Hope Springs, Texas, property would be more of an annex; the farm in Buda that served as her bread and butter was forty miles away.

It was a nice bit of separation. The business of earning a living from the pleasure of getting her hands dirty for fun.

The annex would be her baby, her indulgence, the heirloom vegetables she'd grow here her specialty. They would cost more to cultivate, requiring higher prices, but the demand was equally high. Consumers determined to avoid genetically modified foods would pay for quality produce. And pay for the honey from her bees.

Her bees. The words made Indiana Keller smile. Even now, standing across Three Wishes Road from her property, in the driveway of the Caffey-Gatlin Academy, she could hear them. She had to close her eyes, and be very still, and hold her breath, and bow the muscles of her imagination, but the hum was there, a soft, busy vibration of work being done.

Work had been her life for years now. Work kept her sane. Work left her no time for a personal life. Work was her savior and most of the time her friend. An easy one to keep. Demanding yet constantly loyal, and in the end, she was the boss. That was the part she liked best. Calling the shots. Taking charge.

Doing so had gotten her through some very dark days. The darkest were gone now, and, vestigial family issues aside, she'd come through relatively unscathed; but she would never forget them, what going through them had cost her, what she'd made of herself, by herself, for herself, because of that cost. And now, with this new venture beckoning her . . .

She hugged herself tightly, shivering in awe that the gorgeously overgrown and scruffy fifteen acres across the street was hers, all hers, and there was absolutely no rush to get done the things she wanted to do. As long as her impatience didn't get in the way, she could take her time clearing the space for the greenhouses, and making over the cottage to live in, because first on her list was learning everything she needed to about taking care of the bees.

Just as the thought entertained her, a new sort of buzzing set up along her spine. Not one she heard, but felt. An awareness. A sense of impending change. A clear breach of her private communion. What she heard were footsteps crunching the driveway's gravel, and she flexed her fingers, then rubbed at her palms where her nails had dug deep.

The steps drew closer, and they were firm, heavy, most likely belonging to a man. Possibly Angelo Caffey, whose woodshop sat behind the Caffey-Gatlin Academy. Or a member of her brother Tennessee's construction crew, who was converting the academy property's original barn into living quarters for Angelo and Luna, his wife.

But neither was who came to a stop beside her.

"Can I help you with something?" the man asked, smelling earthy, spicy. Privileged.

"No. I'm fine," she said without looking over. She knew who he was, but doubted he remembered their paths crossing last week.

"Are you a friend of Hiram's?"

"I am, yes. Why?"

"Because friends of Hiram know he's not one for trespassing." He nodded across the street toward her Camaro where it hugged the rough ground. "He says it's bad for the bees. Strangers disturb them."

No doubt he knew as well as she that Hiram had moved before the property sold. And that the bees deterred most strangers who ventured near. Yet she'd parked in what had been Hiram's driveway. As bold as she pleased. "And you are?"

"Not a stranger," he said, that silver-spoon privilege again.

"Then that makes two of us."

He waited a moment, his weight shifting from one hip to the other. "Does he know you're here?"

Ah, this one is clever. "Hard for him to know when he moved to Boerne to be near his son."

He smiled. She felt it in the way he relaxed his stance, in the pull drawing her to face him. It was hard to resist, that pull, because she knew what she would see. But it was so, *so* easy for the same reason. Looking up at his face gave her a very great and particular sort of enjoyment. He was an incredibly handsome man.

"Have we met?" she asked, as conscious as he that, formally, they hadn't.

He was shaking his head when he said, "I was about to ask you the same."

She held out her hand. "Indiana Keller."

"Keller," he repeated, taking it, holding it, his shake firm and lasting. "As in Tennessee? Though if you're Indiana, that's a really dumb question to ask, the state thing and all."

She thought of Dakota, her oldest brother, leaving prison and walking out of her life, and her smile faltered. "And you are?" she repeated, even though she knew.

"Oliver Gatlin."

"As in the Caffey-Gatlin Academy? Though since you're standing on the center's property . . ."

"Sounds like we're both full of dumb today," he said, his self-deprecation taking her aback. It was unexpected. And terribly cute.

"It's nice to meet you, Oliver." Officially.

"And you, Indiana," he said, then released her. "Though . . . weren't you at Luna and Angelo's wedding reception?"

Oh, the games we play. "I was," she said, inordinately pleased that she hadn't been invisible after all. She never knew, actually, if what little effort she took with her appearance made her stand out, or blend in, or any difference. "And you were, too."

His expression darkened, but in a searching, curious way. It was nothing nefarious. Nothing strange. Nothing to make her uneasy. "You should've said hello."

"Then?" She shook her head. "You were too busy with Angelo."

"I'm never too busy to meet a new friend."

Friends. Was that what they were going to be? Because what she was feeling . . .

She pulled in a deep breath, blew out flutters of anticipation, and wondered about fate and possibilities. About right places and right times.

11

"It's always nice to be friends with the people you see regularly."

"Will we? See each other regularly?" he asked, and this time the look in his eyes did give her pause.

It was an interesting look, one that had her pulse blipping a bit, her anxiety rising in a very nice way as she made him wait. "Once in a while, at least, since I bought Hiram's place."

"Ah," he said, nodding. "So not a trespasser after all."

She looked over her shoulder at the buildings—the academy, the woodshop, the barn—where they sat on the five acres belonging to Luna Meadows Caffey, then down at the driveway before lifting her gaze to his. "Not on Hiram's property anyway."

"And not here," he said, returning her smile, his simply devastating, with dimples and deep lines like starbursts at the corners of his eyes.

That was good to know, though her friendship with Luna kept that from being a worry. But Oliver extending such an invitation, when they had no history and had only just met, tickled her. Warmly. "Are you working with the center now?"

While she waited for him to answer, a truck slowed in front of them on Three Wishes Road before turning to park behind her car in the driveway Hiram had rarely used. The tire tracks were more ruts than anything, and visible, though the strip between was green with weeds gone wild.

It was just like Will Bowman, however, not to care about the state of things beneath his pickup's wheels. Like Indiana, he let very little get in the way of what he wanted. And that had her wondering about Oliver Gatlin. Did he share the same trait?

Running into him at the Caffeys' reception had been a fluke encounter. They belonged to completely different worlds—his served up with a silver spoon, hers with a shovel or a spade. That juxtaposition left her uncertain as to how she felt about their being in contact. Especially with the way the buzz he'd brought with him was still stinging along her skin.

When he spoke, it wasn't in response to her question. "I'd ask if you had a trespasser, but since there's a Keller Construction sign on the side of that truck, I guess he's expected."

Will Bowman was never expected. A strange thought, but there it was. "Yes. I was early to meet him, so thought I'd enjoy the view from here."

He was quiet for a long moment, finally shoving his hands in his pockets and saying, "Then I'll leave you to it."

And that was it. He turned with only the slightest nod and walked back into the academy, vanishing as if the last few minutes had been conjured by her imagination. Such a dismissive departure was probably the norm for Oliver Gatlin, but she knew so little about men, and even less about his silver-spoon variety.

That lack of knowledge was likely the culprit behind the difficulty in her closing the gap time had left between her and Tennessee. Oh, but she was trying. For six months now, she'd been trying, putting herself in Hope Springs, in her brother's path, hoping to get back what she could of all they'd lost the year she'd been fifteen.

Tennessee just seemed . . . unreachable, as if keeping her at arm's length was the best he could do. As if he wasn't ready for anything more, fearing their closeness would cause more hurt. As if his guilt over the tragedy they shared was a burden as heavy as hers. It shouldn't have been, not when she was the one at fault.

"Too bad for you, big brother," she muttered, taking a deep breath before heading back across Three Wishes Road.

Because if all went according to plan, she was not the only family member who'd be coming back into his life, and hopefully to stay.

Leaning against his truck's rear bumper, Will Bowman watched Indy Keller walk toward him, the skirt of her sundress fluttering above her knees, her cowboy boots long past worn. It was clear that Oliver Gatlin had wanted to keep her where she'd been. Will got that. It was rare he had Indy to himself for any length of time, and that was a shame.

She made him think of a butterfly, or a hummingbird, maybe even one of her bees, but not because she was flighty so much as she was always busy. Here and there and everywhere. Never lighting in one spot for long. As if she'd used up whatever sustenance she'd stopped for and needed to refuel.

"Wasn't sure you were going to be able to tear yourself away from Gatlin over there," he said, pushing to stand at her approach.

He met her at the overgrown edge of the crushed-shell drive more suited to an ATV than even his truck. Before she could power her muscle car any farther onto the property, a heavy-duty grading was in order. Then again, every inch of this place was going to need the same or her greenhouses would topple sideways.

The look she gave him said she had business on her mind and was not in the mood for the banter they were so very good at. The banter that lifted his spirits in ways little else did. He carried on, because he knew her well enough not to take her silence personally. "And I don't think he was ready to let you go."

That had her stopping, cocking her head, crossing her arms. "Are you here to consult with a client, or are you here to poke your big nose in my personal life?"

He rubbed his hand over the end of it, frowning. "Oliver Gatlin is your personal life?"

"Oliver Gatlin is a friend," she said, adding, "Just like you," before taking off down what he supposed was a path that led to the box of a house where Hiram Glass had lived for sixty years. And giving him no chance to tell her that there was nothing about him that was *just like* Oliver Gatlin.

He walked behind her, watching her hips swing, her cloud of hair bounce. He hadn't enjoyed a woman's intimate company for a very long time. The way Indy moved reminded him of that when he'd thought he was doing a good job of forgetting. It had been easier while in prison. No women to look at meant relying on memory. And he liked his memories a whole lot more than magazines.

But forgetting didn't come as easy in Hope Springs. Kaylie Flynn. Luna Caffey, née Meadows. Indiana Keller. Gorgeous women all, and they brought to mind the time he'd done and how long he'd been alone. But he'd paid his debt, three years of his life given to the state; honestly, he would've sentenced himself to a whole lot more.

"Don't do that." Indy's words returned him to the present.

"Don't do what?"

"Swat at the bees."

Huh. "You'd rather I get stung?"

16

"They're my bees, and I said no swatting."

"It was just one bee—"

She spun, advanced, poked a finger into the center of his chest. "It was *my* one bee, and I don't want *any* of my bees disturbed. Hiram made doubly sure I understood that."

"I don't think Hiram meant—"

"Do not swat at the bees." And then she spun again and continued toward the house, brushing aside waist-high sunflowers and talking as she went. "Do you know what's going on with honeybees today? How they're dying? The decline in colonies and what it means?"

He didn't, but assumed she was going to let him in on her research.

"They're battling disease, parasites, bad nutrition, and exposure to pesticides. Heavily developed agricultural regions have stolen away their safe foraging zones." She stopped as she reached the front walk of the house. "Hiram trusts me to be caretaker here. So no swatting."

Having finished her speech that sounded as canned as green beans, she climbed the three steps onto the covered porch barely big enough for two. And because he couldn't help himself, he reached out and swatted her on the behind.

She stiffened, stood perfectly still, then turned around. He was two steps below, putting her at eye level, and what he saw there, the arched brow, the color on her cheekbones, the tightly pressed pout, looked as much like an invitation as it did a reprimand.

He wasn't sure which to respond to, so he shrugged, and said, "Had to get it out of my system. The swatting."

"Make sure you don't let it back in," she said, and pulled open the screen door.

He hesitated outside as she vanished, the house's stuffy interior sucking her up like the breath of fresh air that she was. Breezing into her brother's life, and by association into his. Blowing around her perennial good mood. Like fertilizer.

That was probably what he needed to be focusing on: how her reunion with her brother had brought her into Tennessee's circle, where her love for life had touched everyone, rather than wondering if her buying the property on Three Wishes Road meant Oliver Gatlin was going to get in the way of his plans.

Oliver walked back into the academy building to the sound of Tennessee Keller's measuring tape retracting. "I just saw your sister."

The cabinets Angelo Caffey had built to replace the rotted ones in what had once been the living room of the Caffey family home were some of the best work Oliver had ever seen. Ten was in the process of installing them, the living room now serving as the reception area for the Caffey-Gatlin Academy.

The arts center was Angelo's wife Luna's pet project. Luna had established the nonprofit in honor of Sierra Caffey, Angelo's sister and Luna's best friend, who'd died days into her senior year of high school, and in honor of Oliver's brother, Oscar, who'd spent the last decade unresponsive at the Hope Springs Rehab Institute. Sierra had been the passenger in the car Oscar had been driving when he'd lost control and the car had plunged down a ravine.

The couple had been accomplished cellists, both studying at St. Thomas Prep, Sierra on a scholarship to the elite private school. Luna's goal was to give more children than those who could afford the St. Thomas tuition the same opportunity to study music and art. Oliver had originally mocked the idea. He'd mocked a lot of things in the ten years before learning the truth of the accident. Now he served on the academy's board, though he wasn't sure his involvement wasn't too little too late.

"Saw her where?" Tennessee asked.

"Here." Oliver returned to the present and gestured over his shoulder toward the door. "Out front."

"Was she looking for me?" Ten's gaze moved beyond Oliver as if he expected to see Indiana enter the room.

Interesting that Ten hadn't made the connection between his sister, Hiram Glass, and the big "For

Sale by Owner" sign she hadn't yet removed from the property's edge. Which meant he had no idea she'd taken the house and land off Hiram's hands. "She was looking at the acreage across the street."

Frowning, Ten tossed the tape measure into his toolbox, then set his hands at his hips. "Hiram's place?"

"It was." Ten's frown deepened as Oliver crossed the newly sanded hardwood floor and headed for the adjoining kitchen. "It's her place now."

Ten followed, the thud of his work boots echoing through the rooms. "What are you talking about?"

"Then you didn't know," Oliver said, finding a clean latte mug in the dishwasher and turning on the espresso machine.

Ten braced a hand on the kitchen counter. "I knew the property was for sale. I didn't know Indiana bought it. If that's what you're saying."

Oliver nodded, popped a coffee capsule into its slot, and hit the start button. The machine steamed and groaned as it forced water through the tightly packed grind. "It is."

"That doesn't even make sense." Ten crossed his arms, leaning back, his frown now trained in the direction of the front door. "Her farm is in Buda. She lives in Buda. Why would she buy that much land in Hope Springs?"

"I can tell you what she told me. Or you could walk across the street and ask her yourself." Oliver knew which Ten would choose. Though he'd reconciled with his sister after what Oliver understood to be a lot of years, Ten had yet to give up his loner mentality. Even his relationship with Kaylie Flynn hadn't quite socialized him. Probably why he and Oliver got along so well. Their conversations required no more than a verbal shorthand, and each knew to respect the other man's space.

"Unless it's something I should hear from the horse's mouth, why don't you run it down?" Ten's response was exactly as predicted. "I'll walk over when I break in a few for lunch."

Oliver returned to the table, his tablet PC, and the financial software he was using to keep track of the arts center's expenses. He snapped the removable keyboard into place and sat, pulling the sheaf of receipts to be recorded in front of him. "She told me she was a friend of Hiram's, and that she'd bought the place. She also remembered seeing me at Luna and Angelo's reception."

"And?"

"That was it." Oliver brought his mug to his mouth to sip, and used it to hide the smirk he couldn't quite help. Ten always took himself so seriously, but then Oliver was no better at lightening up.

"That doesn't answer my question."

"I never said I could answer your question."

Ten muttered several choice words that turned Oliver's smirk into a smile, then returned to the cabinets in the living room, leaving Oliver alone with his coffee and his spreadsheets and his musings about Indiana Keller.

The first time he'd seen her had been at the Caffeys' reception. They hadn't spoken. They hadn't been introduced. He may have said "Excuse me" as he walked by her, but even that memory wasn't clear.

The one that was came from later that night. She'd been across the room talking to Luna. He'd been talking to Angelo and Luna's father, Harry, about the loft Luna had purchased in the converted textile warehouse—the original brick, the original windows, the investment versus resale value.

But his eyes had been on Indiana the entire time. At least until Will Bowman had walked into the picture, his face, as he'd accompanied her to the kitchen for a bottle of wine, close to hers in a way that said they were more than friends. That was when Oliver had looked away. He didn't intrude on another man's interest, though his conversation with Indiana this morning left him wondering whether he'd been mistaken about that.

She hadn't seemed in a hurry to cross the street to Bowman. And what the other man was doing over there instead of working over here with Ten left Oliver frowning. But how Ten chose to run his business was none of Oliver's, so he let it go. He'd learned early to observe without interfering; doing so had served him well.

At least, most of the time it had served him well.

He preferred not to think about the one time he didn't step in when he should have. What it had cost him. What it had cost his family.

The price his brother had paid.

Chapter Two

In a comparison that seemed strangely apropos, the wild mess of her new acreage reminded Indiana of her personal life. Maybe not the first fifteen years, though certainly a hefty portion of the decade that followed. But this last? She'd done a good job of hiding the turmoil, staying as busy as her bees to keep it at bay, but it was there, the roots deep and holding fast.

The yard around Hiram's cottage, now her cottage, had been busy, too, and seemingly for almost as long. The weeds were out of control, growing where flowers should have been, where grass once had been; the paths Hiram had once carefully cleared were just gone. She, at least, did a decent job of controlling her internal chaos. The property defined chaos, and not a bit of it controlled.

Trash cluttered the yard, blown there or thrown there; she had no way of knowing. It made what would otherwise have been a case of nature gone wild an eyesore. An overgrown plot, perfect in its own right, but flawed as a manageable lawn. Damaged. That might never again be as good as it once was. Too many seeds that didn't belong had found their way to the ground, sprouting where they weren't wanted, stealing resources, demanding rights.

The back of the lot that separated the cottage from the bees was a jungle of more than plants. There were insects and reptiles and amphibians. Squirrels and rabbits and what she was certain was a feral cat who shared his or her hunting grounds with any number of birds of prey. The cat won on that score; Indiana had seen freshly scattered feathers and savaged carcasses more than once as she'd walked the grounds.

She'd thought for years now that she had a handle on how best to nurture the parts of her that had been broken all those years ago. With her degree and her business, she'd thought she'd built a quite solid foundation. She'd thought that missteps might shake her, but never cause her to fall. That whatever garbage still clung would dry up and flutter away. That she could manage the mayhem. That she was fine.

She'd learned plenty of coping skills after her assault, and really, she had no right to be weak.

So many other women had gone through so much worse and survived, though she imagined the number who'd lost touch with both of their brothers in the process was small. That's why the sound of Tennessee's voice last spring, the first time she'd heard it in *years,* had been like a plow, digging beneath the surface she showed the world to the truth of all that festered. Months later, and she'd yet to smooth out what had been disturbed.

Having lost Will somewhere on their tour around the cottage, she pushed aside a tall bunch of weeds and stepped into the clearing where he'd parked, only to find Tennessee standing there instead. "Hey, you," she said, feeling her smile to her toes. "What're you doing over here?"

"Looking for you," he said, nodding beyond her shoulder toward Will, who was just emerging from the jungle that had been Hiram's backyard. "And him."

"How did you know where I was?" Indiana ducked away from a bee buzzing her face, then answered her own question. "Oliver told you he saw me, didn't he?"

Tennessee pulled his gaze from Will, who'd said nothing as he'd stopped at her side, and frowned down at her. "Yeah, and I'm glad he did or I wouldn't have known you'd bought the place."

"I had every intention of telling you." She'd missed her brother so much during their estrangement, though he was the one who'd removed himself from her life. But this Tennessee, stiff and severe and ready to pass judgment, was not exactly her favorite person. "I wanted to wait until everything was settled. I wanted it to be a surprise."

He didn't even give that time to sink in, but said, "You didn't want me talking you out of it, you mean?"

That was when Will stepped forward. "Why would you want to talk her out of it?"

Her brother bristled. "Your business is across the street, Will. Not here."

Really? Did they have to do this today? Indiana reached up to push her hair from her face. "Actually, he has business here, too. I asked him to stop by this morning." Though only if he had time—an instruction he'd obviously ignored.

"To do what?"

It was tell-all time, whether she was ready or not. "I wanted Will to walk the property with me, and to look at Hiram's cottage. I'm going to set up a greenhouse annex here, with Keller Construction's help, I hope. I'll grow heirloom vegetables to sell at local farmers markets, along with the honey from the bees."

"What happened to IJK Gardens?" Tennessee asked, crossing his arms and leaning against the rear quarter panel of Will's truck. "You get tired of selling produce to local grocers?"

"No. I didn't get tired of selling produce to

local grocers. That's my bread and butter." She didn't need to be defensive. She'd done nothing wrong; in fact, she was finally doing everything right, involving Tennessee in her life, insisting he allow her into his. "If you'd like to hear about my plans, I'm happy to take you and Kaylie to dinner and share."

"And Will?" Will asked.

"You just heard most of my plans," she said, brushing him off to get back to Tennessee.

But her brother didn't miss a beat. "So you told him before you told me."

"Uh-uh. Don't even . . ." Head canted, she jammed her hands at her hips and considered the man and his attitude. "Dinner or not?"

"Sure. When?"

"What's good for you and Kaylie?"

"Tonight?"

Did that mean he was anxious to hear her out, or that he wanted to shoot her down as soon as he could? And why did she automatically jump to such an uncharitable conclusion where Tennessee was involved?

She hated feeling as if she needed to defend her life—or her actions—to her brother. Because that's what this was: Tennessee trying to keep her safe, if even from herself, while she proved to him she didn't need a keeper. It wasn't rocket science, figuring this out, what with the history they shared.

"Tonight then," she told him, which earned her

a nod. "Malina's? Or one of the places out on the freeway?"

He cocked his head while considering his options, a gesture so similar to hers that emotion choked her. "There's a new steak house just south of the Hope Springs exit. I've been wanting to give that a try. If that works for you."

"Perfect," she said, clearing her throat. "Eight thirty okay? I've got a lot on my plate today, and I'll need to run home and clean up—"

"If tonight's not convenient—"

"Tonight's just fine," she cut him off to say. Whatever was bugging him—and she was certain it was more than her expanding her business into Hope Springs—the sooner they worked it out the better.

She'd been without her brother, her *brothers,* for almost half her life. She would not lose another minute to something as inconsequential as a supposed inconvenience. "I'll meet you there."

He nodded, rubbed a hand over the back of his neck, then gave a jerk of his chin toward the cottage. "You want to show me around your place?"

And that made her smile.

"Knock, knock?" Indiana called later that morning, having pulled open her soon-to-be sister-in-law's kitchen door. Tennessee lived in the three-story Victorian, too, but the house had *Kaylie* written all over it, as if Tennessee were still trying to fit in.

She supposed in a sense he was. Before Kaylie, he'd been alone a long time, living at the end of Grath Avenue, working insane hours. Rebuffing the family he still had in the area. Including her.

Why he thought keeping his distance would prevent further hurt . . .

Shaking her head at her brother's idea of penance, she took a deep breath, and swore she smelled warm brownies. She let the screen slam behind her and glanced at the countertops, but she was too early. The goodies were giving off their killer aroma from the oven as they baked.

She was studying the timer when Kaylie walked in. "What're you doing here?"

"Deciding if I can stay till these are done. It looks like . . . eight more minutes?"

Kaylie laughed. "Eight to finish baking, then thirty, at least, to cool before cutting. That's the secret, you know. Letting them set."

Indiana considered her must-dos for the rest of the day, and decided everything could wait. "I think I can spare thirty-eight minutes for my favorite sister-in-law-to-be."

Another laugh, bubbly and infectious and true. "For your favorite sister-in-law-to-be's new brownie recipe, you mean?"

New ones. Ooh. "I make an awesome taste-tester."

Kaylie grinned at that. "Ah, so you and your brother share that trait."

That she wouldn't know. Their mother hadn't been much of a baker. Or much of a mother, for that matter. "Did he call you about dinner tonight?"

"About dinner." Kaylie's ponytail swung when she nodded. "And about you buying Hiram Glass's property."

Of course he would've already told her. They shared everything in a way few couples did. "I was going to surprise you both with that, but made the mistake of talking to Oliver Gatlin."

Kaylie reached for a toothpick and a long oven mitt. "What does Oliver have to do with anything? Where did you see him?"

"At the arts center." Indiana turned to open the screen door, having heard Magoo whimper. Kaylie's dog came into the kitchen and nuzzled Indiana's hand, sniffed the air, then trotted back to the mudroom and his water bowl. "I was waiting for Will, so I walked across to the school's driveway to look at the lot from there. He came out when he saw me."

Having donned the mitt, Kaylie pulled open the oven door to check the brownies' doneness. "And you were waiting for Will why? I thought he was working at the school with Ten?"

"He is." Though not to Tennessee's standards, judging by her brother's annoyance with his employee. "I'd asked him to walk the property with me. His ideas for the school were absolutely spot-on. And have you seen what he's done so far with Luna and Angelo's barn? I wanted to get his impression of the cottage, and what I might do with it."

"And? What did he think?"

"Actually," she said, laughing to herself at the realization, "we never talked about it. We looked around, and when we were done, Tennessee was there, so Will headed across the street to work. Tennessee was not exactly thrilled that I had hijacked his workforce."

Kaylie was shaking her head as she closed the oven door. "I would say I don't know why he puts up with Will, but the truth is, Will's brilliant, and Ten can't afford to lose him. Not with his current workload. Besides Will, he's only got three men on the payroll. Too many of the regular applicants want more than he can pay, or don't have the right experience."

Regular applicants. Meaning they weren't ex-cons. "Manny hasn't been sending him anyone else to help out?"

"It's been a few weeks," Kaylie said, resetting the oven timer for two minutes. "I guess none of Manny's new parolees fit Ten's criteria."

Tennessee's agreement with Dakota's former parole officer, who was Will's parole officer now, was that he'd give a leg up to men who, like

Dakota, and obviously like Will, had done the wrong thing but for the right reason and served their time. "I'm not sure if that's a good thing or a bad thing."

"It's not good for Ten, that's for sure," Kaylie said as she set about brewing a pot of coffee. "He needs the manpower desperately. I can't help thinking how different things would be for him if he and Dakota had gone into business together as planned."

Indiana had entertained similar thoughts about what life would've been like had her oldest brother stayed close. Which brought her back to why she was here. "I really did stop for a reason other than your brownies."

"And a reason other than seeing me?"

Guilty as charged, she mused, boosting up onto a stool at the kitchen island. "Tell me about the investigator you hired to find your mother. Was he affordable? Efficient? Is he still working for you? You haven't said anything about his finding her . . ." Indiana let the sentence trail, because Kaylie had yet to respond, and her expression was as pained as her face was pale, which hadn't been Indiana's intent at all. "I'm sorry. I shouldn't have brought it up—"

"No, it's fine," Kaylie said, her hand pressed to her stomach as she shook off whatever cloud had leeched away her light. "I'm happy to tell you everything, but first can I ask why you want to know?" She poured her coffee, offered the pot to Indiana, but she declined. "Is this about Dakota?"

"I want to know he's okay," Indiana said with a nod. Having Tennessee back in her life had her missing Dakota desperately. "I don't want to intrude in his business, or beg him to come back, or berate him for not being in touch. I want to know that he's living well somewhere. That he's not hurting. Maybe that he doesn't hate us . . . me . . ." She left the thought to live or die on its own, and shrugged. "I just need this. For me."

Kaylie took her time climbing onto the stool opposite Indiana's. "Are you going to tell Ten?"

Ah, the question of the hour. She loved her brother dearly, but . . . "So he can try to talk me out of it? So he can tell me that if Dakota wanted me to know where he was, he'd reach out?" She shook her head. "This is for me. Not for Tennessee. Not even for Dakota. I just . . . It's my fault he's gone—"

"Uh-uh," Kaylie said, reaching across the island to squeeze Indiana's wrist. "None of what happened is your fault. Dakota did what he did out of his love for you. Going after the boy who attacked you?" Kaylie shook her head. "He knew what he was doing, and he knew he'd have to pay the price."

"Is that how Tennessee tells it?" Because she couldn't imagine she was the only one blaming herself.

"No." Sitting back, Kaylie brought her mug to her mouth and held it there with both hands but didn't sip. "That's how I tell it after listening to Ten. He blames himself for Dakota's absence."

"I don't know why." Indiana dropped her gaze to the granite island, ran a thumb over the surface, wishing for a similar smoothness to replace the sensation of having swallowed a load of gravel. "We haven't talked about it, you know. He and I. Since he finally contacted me." Even though he'd done so because of Kaylie's garden, and not because Indiana was family. "I thought we would. I thought it would be the first thing we settled. That night. Dakota leaving the house to find Robby and beating him half to death. Then refusing to come home after his release from prison. But it's still there. A big brick wall that's too tall for me to climb without his help."

The timer buzzed, and Kaylie set down her mug to check the brownies again, pulling them from the oven and placing them on the counter to cool. When she returned to the island, she did so with a knowing look, her fingers knitted loosely together as she rested her hands. "You think finding Dakota will help Ten get over the past?"

The reasons she'd given Kaylie were true. But she couldn't deny wanting more, wanting both of her brothers close. Wanting the three of them to salvage what they hadn't lost, or maybe find some of what they had.

If anything remained. "Will any of us ever get over the past?"

Kaylie let that sink in, toying with the handle on her mug. Her gaze was downcast when she finally spoke. "You haven't talked much about what happened either, you know. The assault."

For more reasons than Indiana cared to admit. "It's not exactly a topic I like to bring up."

"Have you discussed it with anyone? Ever?"

"A therapist, you mean? A counselor?"

"Or a friend."

She thought back to the girls she'd counted as friends while in high school. She hadn't stayed in touch with any of them, and hadn't made many in college. She didn't have many now, her best being employees. None she would've encumbered with the story of her past. It was bad enough that Kaylie, a woman she loved dearly, now knew.

"Logically, I know Dakota left for reasons of his own." She didn't need a therapist or counselor to tell her that. "That doesn't mean I don't blame myself."

"Something tells me you've been doing a very good job of that for a lot of years," Kaylie said, again lifting her mug.

As right as her favorite sister-in-law-to-be was, Indiana wasn't ready to talk to Kaylie about the burden she carried. "So we're on for tonight then? Dinner?"

"Definitely. I don't care where we eat as long as

it's not here and I'm not the one doing the cooking or the cleaning." Kaylie crossed to a drawer and tugged it open, coming up with a long, serrated knife. "Brownie?"

Indiana looked at the watch she wasn't wearing. "I don't think it's been thirty minutes."

"Desperate times call for desperate measures, and I think we're looking down the barrel of both."

Chapter Three

As close as Hope Springs was to Austin, Indiana was always taken aback by how few options for dining the town offered. She shouldn't be, she supposed. She lived in Buda and had equally few choices, but Hope Springs seemed incredibly . . . vibrant, or culturally progressive, for appearing so externally quaint.

Then again, she spent her days at IJK Gardens: in the office, on a tractor, up to her wrists in dirt. It didn't take a fancy restaurant for her to feel as if she were out for a night on the town. Chili's, Applebee's, Macaroni Grill. She was the cheapest date she knew. Even if her brother *was* the one paying, and *date* was a nice way to describe being raked over the coals while she ate.

Still, it took a lot to ruin her enjoyment of mashed potatoes and chicken-fried steak. Even

Tennessee's intimidating, big-brother glare fell short.

"You know I've been on my own for ten years, right?" she told him. "That I worked my way through college? That I used the money from Grandpa Keller to buy the farm that's now IJK Gardens? And that I did it all without your permission? Or even your input?"

"I'm not saying you need my permission," Tennessee finally said, glancing at Kaylie, then back. "Or my input. And actually, no. I didn't know any of that. At least not at the time. I didn't stay in touch, remember?"

"I'd ask whose fault that is"—because it was just as much hers for not touching base to tell him—"but I'm pretty sure the hard heads in the family went to the boys." Indiana smiled as Tennessee snorted and Kaylie chuckled, then added, "But you did know where to find me. So that's something, I guess. You keeping me on your radar."

Tennessee laid down his fork, rested both wrists against the table's edge, and leaned forward. His eyes were bright with emotion both solemn and intense. "You were never off it. Not for a minute. I need you to know that." Unlike their brother, whom they'd both lost track of, though that was on Dakota. He obviously didn't want to be found, giving Tennessee the leg up in that argument.

"And here I thought out of sight, out of mind meant just that."

"Indy—"

"It's okay." She hadn't wanted this evening to turn maudlin. "I didn't have to wait for you to call. It's not like I didn't know where you were, too."

He huffed at that, and went back to his food. "That's different. I made it clear when I left home that I needed the distance."

He had, and she'd done her best to honor his eighteen-year-old self's desire to be a solitary man. But he'd been on her radar as well, which made them two of the stubbornest people she knew. "And now? Are you still needing the distance?"

He looked up, but instead of meeting her gaze, his attention was all for Kaylie. If Indiana hadn't been aware of the connection the two shared, she might've felt dismissed. As it was, what she felt was envy. To share what Kaylie and Tennessee shared . . . To be so sure, so much a part of another person, so comfortable with publicly displaying that level of emotional intensity . . .

She thought of Will Bowman. Then she thought of Oliver Gatlin. Then she thought of the mess she'd made of both her brothers' lives, and her mood deflated. How could she ever trust herself not to ruin things with those she let close, when that was exactly what she'd done to two of the most important men in her life?

"No," her brother finally said, his gaze seeking

out hers. "But that doesn't mean you need to take on whatever this new gardening project of yours is just to stay close. I'm not going anywhere."

Arrogant man, thinking her greenhouse annex had anything to do with him. Even if it did, that was her business, her prerogative. Her albatross to deal with.

"This new project of mine," she said, mimicking his words, "is something I've been thinking about for a while, and the timing was finally right. I've got the money. I've got a business plan. The property has tons of potential, and was exactly what I was hoping to find. The fact that it's in Hope Springs, and close to you and Kaylie, is an added bonus. As are the bees."

"And what about the cottage?" he asked, getting back to his meat, glasses and silverware clinking around them, soft conversations and softer laughter and lights almost too soft to see by setting a deceptively tranquil mood.

Inside, she was an emotionally agitated mess. "What about it?" She forked up a bite of her potatoes, then dragged it through her gravy. "I've been living in a rental for a long time. It's not exactly the best use of my money."

"And making Hiram's place livable is?"

"I have to side with Ten on this one, Indy," Kaylie said. "From what I've seen, and the talk I've heard, Hiram really let the cottage go after Dorie died."

"Will said the structure is sound." Though what he'd said was that he'd have to dig deeper to know whether that was enough to make it worth saving.

"So you've got a good shell. What about the wiring? The plumbing? You'll have to paint," Tennessee said. "Replace the kitchen cabinets and probably the entire bathroom. You'll need a new roof." He reached for his beer. "I don't get why you'd want to live in Hope Springs anyway when your primary business is in Buda."

The cottage wasn't big enough that a new roof would break her. And she'd known the place was going to need a lot of work. But she didn't like having her choices criticized. Or feeling ganged up on, because that was exactly what seemed to be happening here. "It's not that far, Tennessee. And I do have a car. You don't do all your work where you live."

"Apples to oranges. Being a contractor means going where the job is."

The man defined aggravation. "And how many professionals living on the east side of Hope Springs commute to Austin?" She glanced toward her brother's fiancée. "Help me out here, Kaylie."

"Well, it is at least a thirty-minute drive, meaning an hour's bite out of your day. But," she added, turning to Ten, "she is right about Hope Springs being a bedroom community."

Tennessee huffed and dug back into his food.

Indiana did the same, minus the huff, plus a hidden roll of her eyes. Her life. Her business. What about that did her brother have such a hard time with? Then again, she wasn't the best example of having let go of the past. And Tennessee was obviously still thinking of her as that fifteen-year-old girl he'd found cowering in the kitchen following Robby's attack.

Yet here she was, a grown woman, looking for the brother who'd dropped out of her life—who'd made no attempt at communication, who most likely didn't want to be found—while moving nearer to the one she was finally back in touch with, no matter the inconvenience of having her business split between two locations, and her home, once she moved into the cottage, a fair distance from one.

He was right that making the cottage livable was a ridiculous idea when there were so many places better suited, both in Buda and in Hope Springs. But she couldn't let the cottage go, and hanging on to it made no sense. It had been Hiram's home, not hers, and any emotional attachment his.

She didn't know why she found herself drawn to the tiny little house, considering its value, or lack thereof, and the cost of renovations. It would work for one person. And obviously the Glasses had made it work with two for a very long time. They'd even raised their son there, so were she to ever start a family . . .

She laid her fork on the side of her plate, thrown by the sudden shift in her train of thought. Her farm was her baby. Her employees her family. Tennessee and Kaylie, obviously, and Dakota. The occasional postcard her parents sent letting her know they hadn't fallen off the face of the earth reminded her they were family, too.

But a husband? A child? Children? Why was she even thinking such a thing when the debt she owed her brothers for the rift she'd caused had to be paid before she could think of a future for herself? And if she couldn't find Dakota . . .

"Excuse me for a minute," she said, gesturing in the direction of the ladies' room, then leaving the table before either of her dinner companions could say another word.

This was just crazy, she mused, pushing open the door, then closing herself in a stall. Reuniting with Tennessee, seeing him standing there as she'd rounded the side of Kaylie's big blue Victorian, his smile broad, his arms welcoming, his voice croaking with the same emotion tangled up in her throat . . .

It had been one of the best days she could remember living. Yet here she now was, feeling at times as if she and her brother were still estranged, and wondering if finding Dakota would make any difference in any of their lives. Or as if she were wishing on a star that didn't even exist.

She exited the stall just as Kaylie walked into

the room, and she stood washing her hands silently, waiting for the other woman to say what she'd come to say. A couple of minutes later, Kaylie joined her at the sink, her expression drawn, as if she feared taking the wrong step.

Indiana met Kaylie's gaze in the mirror as she dried her hands, and broke the ice. "It's okay. Just tell me."

Kaylie's expression softened. "You know he's eaten up with guilt, don't you? That his interference is nothing but the manifestation of that."

It wasn't a hard leap to make. Indiana had done so within days of reconnecting with her brother last spring. For some reason she'd assumed his reaching out after a decade apart meant he'd worked through it.

Stupid, really, since she hadn't taken but baby steps into the overgrown jungle of her own. "You haven't said anything to him about my looking for Dakota, have you?"

"I told you I wouldn't," Kaylie said, tossing her towels into the bin. "But I think you should."

"I will once things are set in motion. Not that he could stop me . . ."

"You just don't want to take the chance."

That had a smile pulling at Indiana's mouth. "I may have lived with him the first sixteen years of my life, but something tells me you know him a lot better than I ever did."

Kaylie leaned closer to the mirror and blotted

away a smear of mascara from beneath one eye. "Maybe not better. Just a different part of him."

"Or a different him, period. He's . . ." Indiana paused, her hands on the vanity as she pulled in a deep breath. "He's not the brother I remember. Or the brother I knew."

"He's thirty years old, Indiana. He left home when he was eighteen and you were sixteen."

A year after Robby Hunt had tried to rape her.

A year after Dakota had gone to prison for stopping him.

Kaylie went on. "You can't expect him to be who he was then. *You're* not who you were then."

"I get that." Really, truly she did. "I knew when I heard his voice, that message he left on my answering machine wanting my advice on your garden, that he wasn't the Tennessee I'd grown up with. But he is an adult, and I'm an adult, and all I want is for him to respect that. To allow me to make my own decisions, my own mistakes. Not to treat me as if I'm still fifteen and making questionable choices."

"Which is why you have to tell him about looking for Dakota. And appreciate that he's going to try to stop you. You said yourself he believes Dakota doesn't want to be found. Allow him to be who he is, Indy. To be wrong at times. To disagree with you because he believes he's doing what he has to do as your brother."

Kaylie was right. Indiana was asking him to respect her need to look for Dakota while she was unable to respect his need to stop her from making a mistake. She wasn't sure whether to laugh or to cry. Whether to keep her plans from Tennessee or share them. Whether to move to Hope Springs, or stay in her Buda rental, or find a suitable house in one city or the other to buy, then use the property on Three Wishes Road for her bees and her heirloom garden.

The property across the street from the Caffey-Gatlin Academy.

Where she was likely to run into Oliver Gatlin.

She shook off the thought. Oliver Gatlin did not play into any of her plans. Neither did Will Bowman. Tennessee and Dakota were the only men who did. And if she found Dakota, and he didn't want to come back to Texas, much less settle in Hope Springs . . .

Because that's what she was hoping would happen, wasn't it? That she and her brothers would each live their own lives but share the same happily ever after.

"We should probably get back—"

"I will tell him. I promise," Indiana said, not wanting Kaylie to question her choices, too. "I just need time to figure out what to say."

"I don't think you need time for that."

"Yeah, well, it feels like I do. He's not the easiest brother to talk to."

"And you're the only sister he has," Kaylie said, pulling open the door and waiting.

Indiana took a step closer, then a step through. "I guess one of these days we'll both get our acts together."

The grin that broke over Kaylie's mouth spoke of her hope, and her doubt. "I, for one, can't wait."

Since joining the board of the Caffey-Gatlin Academy last month, Oliver had dropped by the center once a week. Doing so was more about staying in touch with those working to bring Luna Caffey's dream to fruition than his duties as a director. He didn't need to be on-site; he could manage the school's money from his office at home, or the one he kept in the River Bend Building in downtown Hope Springs.

But he was back this morning for only one reason, and her name was Indiana Keller. Stupid, really, because he couldn't imagine her visiting her property again today with the ground not yet broken and nothing going on. It had been pure luck he'd been at the school to approve outstanding invoices yesterday. Instead of hoping for another chance encounter, he should've asked for her number then.

He could get it from her brother, but after having the other man grill him earlier about why he was back for the second day in a row, that wasn't going to happen. Oliver had a feeling any interest he showed in Ten's sister would go over like the proverbial lead balloon. He didn't like having to explain himself. The Gatlin name meant he rarely had to, and he was used to having his way.

He carried his coffee to the center's main room, stopping in front of the big picture window. Stopping, too, with his mug halfway to his mouth. The very woman he'd been thinking about was standing in the very spot where he'd last seen her. He held his coffee still, the steam from the mug rising in front of his face.

Like yesterday, she had on worn cowboy boots and a sundress that hit just above her knees. Her hair was pulled back from her face in some kind of barrette or clip, and hung free between her shoulder blades like a coffee-colored cloud.

He wondered what she wore when she worked at her farm. If she got down in the dirt on her knees and dug in the ground. If she was the hands-on type, or if she delegated. If she was better with people than he was. If like him, she found it easier to stay buried in her work.

"Go on. Talk to her."

Oliver huffed. He hadn't heard Angelo Caffey come into the room, and gave him a quick glance before looking back. "She's here about her property. Not to talk to me."

"Yeah, I heard she bought Hiram's place," Angelo said, gesturing in that direction with his own coffee mug. "That man's something else.

47

And his wife was crazy about him. Just crazy."

"That's right," Oliver said. "I keep forgetting this was your family's home."

"And we always had Hiram's honey on the table at breakfast. Sometimes at supper, too." Angelo paused as if reliving a memory, then added, "I wonder if she's keeping the bees. Indiana."

"I have no idea."

"You could ask her, you know. When you go talk to her." And then he gave a slap to Oliver's shoulder and disappeared to wherever he'd come from.

Oliver considered the inevitable another ten seconds, then left his mug on the windowsill and headed out the front door. He stopped beside her where she stood on the driveway, much as he'd done when they'd been here before.

"I'm surprised to see you back here so soon," he said, then realized he had no reason to be; it was her property she was looking at, after all. "In this driveway, anyway."

She glanced over, then back at her place. "Good surprised, or bad surprised?"

He hadn't really assigned an adjective to the emotion. "Just . . . surprised."

"I'm rather surprised myself," she admitted, rubbing her hands up and down her bare arms as if cold.

He would've offered her his jacket if he'd been wearing one, but didn't think the issue was temperature as much as hesitation. Or indecision. Or nervousness.

He didn't like thinking he made her nervous. "You didn't find what you came for yesterday?"

She screwed up her nose, shaking her head before answering. "It's not that so much as I wanted to get another perspective after sleeping on all the input I did get."

"From Will?" He hated bringing up the other man's name. Not really knowing why he hated it. Lying to himself about that because he wasn't a stupid man. He just wasn't . . . ready for what that meant.

"Less Will. More Tennessee," she said. "Brothers. You know how it is."

"I used to," he said, before he could stop himself from making the mistake.

It took her a moment to react, and the ten years of anger he'd only just begun to deal with turned over in his gut, a motor trying to catch, a storm brewing, a pain sharp and intense. Undeniable.

He fisted both hands, shoving them in his pockets, refusing to give in, pushing down the guilt and sadness that for a decade had manifested destructively. Cruelly. He had the truth he'd been looking for. And he had to accept the choice his brother had made when he'd gotten behind the wheel of his car.

"Oh, Oliver. Sheesh." Indiana reached over and squeezed his biceps, lingering a moment before letting him go. "I'm sorry. Me and my big mouth. That was so thoughtless."

"No, I shouldn't have said anything." And actually, he was touched by her response. She didn't live in Hope Springs, though ten years was plenty of time for news of his brother's accident to filter outward. And it was common knowledge that the second name on the Caffey-Gatlin Academy was not in deference to him.

"Of course you should have. I was being terribly self-centered. As if my sibling issues are of any comparison. Please forgive me."

"Nothing to forgive," he said, adding, "but okay," to keep her from insisting, and curious about the issues she had. He lived with what had happened to Oscar in the accident. It was his burden, and never far from his mind. But he didn't expect others to consider his situation when they spoke. They would first have to stop and remember, while he would never forget.

"Thank you," she said, taking a deep breath and pushing her hair from her face. He'd noticed her doing it before, a habit, he guessed, even though she'd pulled it back, getting things out of the way.

It had him wondering . . . "You've got more on your mind than the property."

A smile broke at the corner of her mouth. "How did you know?"

"Because you're standing here, looking across

the street, but I don't really think you're seeing much of anything."

Her sigh was weighty, proving him right. "I'm thinking of hiring a private investigator."

Huh. That wasn't what he'd expected. "Do you need a recommendation?"

"I got one from Kaylie."

Another surprise. "Would you like me to vet him for you?"

She turned to face him, to consider him, a slight frown having replaced her smile. "Because, of course, you have all the connections."

He supposed that had sounded presumptuous; she wasn't a business associate, or a social contemporary, though now he just sounded like an ass. "Did he work out for Kaylie?"

She shrugged. "It's no secret she's trying to find her mother."

It wasn't, no. Neither was the fact that she'd yet to be successful, though that didn't necessarily speak to the investigator's efforts. "And you want to hire the man she's been using."

"I'm thinking about it."

Because Kaylie trusted him? Because Indiana didn't have the resources Oliver did? "Do you mind if I ask why you need a PI?"

Another long moment passed before she answered. A moment during which she pushed her hair back again, warmed her arms with her palms again.

Her voice, when she made her decision, was soft. "To find my brother."

Her brother. Hmm. As curious as he was, he remained silent. He liked Indiana Keller. He didn't want to pry, and she'd rebuffed his offers to vet her man or recommend another. Was she waiting for him to repeat them? To ask for details? To tell her he'd be happy to find her brother for her? Because he would . . .

"Please don't say anything to Tennessee," she said suddenly, spinning to face him as if regretting the admission, her skirt twirling, her hair moving, too. "I haven't told him yet, and he's going to try to talk me out of it."

A truck rumbled by on Three Wishes Road, washing them in the smell of diesel, the noise giving him time to gather his thoughts. "Wouldn't this be his brother, too?"

"Yes, but Tennessee likes things done a certain way, and he likes to be the one to make them happen. And that only after he's analyzed every possible plan of attack, dismissing most as wrong. Or ridiculous." She laughed softly to herself. "At least, that's how it used to be with him. I don't know him well enough anymore to say it's still the same."

"I imagine that'll take time. Getting to know him again," he said, the platitude sounding weak; what, other than its existence, did he know about the siblings' previous estrangement?

"I imagine it will. But I'm not going to put off looking for Dakota until I've worked things out with Tennessee. I've wasted too much time already," she said, shaking her head as she added, "I've wasted so much time."

He understood the sentiment. "Dakota, huh? I might've thought, well, I guess Dakota would have to be it. For a sister, I'd have guessed Georgia. Or Carolina. Virginia, maybe. Not sure I would've ever picked Indiana."

Her chuckle was cute. "I can't even tell you all the *Dr. Jones* jokes I've been the brunt of."

"It's a good franchise. The first three, anyway." So they'd moved from talking about Dakota Keller to Indiana Jones? "Your brother," he began, diving in without thinking better of it, which wasn't like him at all. "Is he missing? Or do you just not know where he is?"

She considered him curiously. "Aren't those the same thing?"

"Not really. No. Though I suppose they can be." Rambling. Very impressive. He shrugged before trying to explain. "It's a viewpoint thing. But since I don't know Dakota's story . . ."

"Do you want to?"

One heartbeat, two, a third, and then he said, "Only if you want to share it."

She turned to look at her property again, scraped back her hair again, causing him to wonder again what it was she was trying to get out of the way.

"Have you had breakfast?" was what she finally asked him, as if a clear line of sight had helped her make her decision.

He thought about the coffee he'd left inside. About the work he'd supposedly come to do. About the appointments he had before he could even think about lunch.

Then he thought about his brother, unresponsive in the same bed for ten years. "I haven't, no. Would you like to grab a bite before Malina's closes?"

"Do the Gatlins eat at Malina's?" she asked him, her tone teasing and making him wonder what she'd think if he told her the truth.

He couldn't remember having eaten there since high school. Instead, he reached into his pocket for his keys and gestured toward his car. "It's Hope Springs. Doesn't everyone?"

Chapter Four

On the ride to Malina's, Indiana kept asking herself whether she'd returned to Three Wishes Road this morning not to consider the things Tennessee and Kaylie had said over dinner last night while viewing the place with fresh eyes, but hoping to see Oliver Gatlin again. She didn't think so.

At least, she hadn't consciously put the two together as any sort of plan. But there was something about the way he paid attention, really paid attention, that she liked. He'd suggested Malina's, rather than waiting for her to do so. He'd offered his services in regards to her hiring a PI. He understood the challenges she faced with her brothers because of all he'd been through with Oscar.

On the shallow side of the spectrum, she also liked his car, a lot, and the way he drove, a whole lot. It wasn't but a five-mile trip from the arts center to the diner, but while the same five miles didn't allow for much in the way of deep conversation, she had no trouble using the time to appreciate his hands on the wheel, the cushy leather of the seats, his shifting gears.

Strange how much she enjoyed watching him when he was doing something so simple: clutching and braking, accelerating into a turn, steering the BMW effortlessly. He seemed to be one of those men for whom things just worked. She doubted he was often disappointed. Or stood up. Or put off. And it wasn't just about his name, though she wondered if growing up Gatlin had instilled this level of confidence, or if he'd been born with the trait.

She wondered, too, if Oscar Gatlin had been equally sure of himself. Then she wondered what, besides her assault and the aftermath, she and her brothers might still have in common. They'd all three been athletic—volleyball, baseball—and they'd all been big fans of the food groups their parents abhorred: pizza, ice cream, sodas, burgers, and fries. They'd all been good students, her grades coming easier than Dakota's, his easier than Tennessee's. And they'd loved their pets. That was one thing she couldn't fault her parents for; they'd had big hearts when it came to rescuing and fostering both dogs and cats.

"Still hungry?" Oliver asked, and she blinked, realizing he'd parked, and was waiting for her to respond before he got out.

"Oh, yes. Sorry," she said, and stayed where she was while he exited the car and circled to open her door. She wasn't used to chivalry, or gallantry, or being the passenger in a car, for that matter. She drove herself everywhere. But sitting and watching him, in his navy Dockers and a yellow crew-neck sweater she was certain was cashmere —she couldn't imagine him wearing anything else—was a rather elegant sort of pleasure.

And when he reached her door and pulled it open, she wished she were wearing something a little less humdrum than her worn cowboy boots and faded dress and comfy cotton underwear that left her feeling anything but elegant. She, who had cared very little about her appearance for the whole of her adult life, was suddenly caring very much.

"Great," she found herself mumbling, Oliver asking, "Excuse me?" in response. She shook her head. "Nothing. Talking to myself. Ignore me."

He laughed at that, a deep husky sound she wasn't certain she'd been meant to hear, but one that had her wishing again for silk and lace close to her skin. Skimpy pieces of both. Solely for her own benefit. She didn't need Oliver to know, or to see, but if he laughed like that again, oh, she wouldn't mind hearing that at all.

He held the diner's door and waited for her to step inside, his hand finding its way to the small of her back, and she wanted to wiggle against it, to squirm as he settled it more heavily. But her inelegant underthings had her stepping away, and leading him through Malina's long, rectangular dining room to a window booth. The high back offered more privacy than a table in the open, and even if that was an illusion, it was one Indiana seized.

Moments after they were seated, their waitress arrived bearing two glasses of water. "Morning, folks," she said, placing the drinks on coasters and giving them both knives, forks, and spoons wrapped in double paper napkins. "Can I get you some coffee? Juice? Tea?"

"Do you have Earl Grey?" Oliver asked.

"Sure do, sweetie," she said, turning to Indiana and smoothing the back of her upswept hair. "How 'bout you, sugar?"

Sweetie. Sugar. Indiana didn't think she heard the words anywhere but Malina's. "I'll have the same, thanks."

"Be right back with both cups. Menus are right there," the woman said, nodding toward the laminated place mats tucked between the condiment caddy and napkin dispenser.

Oliver reached for two, handed one to Indiana. "I can't decide if I'm in the mood for pancakes, or biscuits and gravy."

That made her smile. "Somehow I can't picture you eating biscuits and gravy."

"Oh, well," he said with a shrug. "I do it from a silver spoon."

Touché. "I'm being a snob, aren't I?" she asked, her smile as genuine as it was self-deprecating. Sometimes it really was better not to speak her mind.

"I don't know," he said, his gaze on the clip-art menu. "You tell me."

"Okay. I am. Or I was, and I apologize. I just—" she said, and stopped, because what was she going to say? She didn't know why he was here with someone like her. And what did that even mean? That she didn't think herself good enough for him? Really?

He waved off her apology, and thankfully didn't press for her to finish what she'd been going to say. "It comes with the name. I get that. My mother uses it to her advantage. But I'm not my mother. Or my father. And there are times I'd just as soon not be a Gatlin."

What an interesting thing for him to say. "You want to know how the other half lives?"

"Something like that," he said, then went silent as their waitress delivered two cups of steaming water and two tea bags in paper packets before stepping away. Oliver tore his open, dropped the bag into the mug, and draped the string and tab over the edge.

Indiana did the same, breathing deeply of the fragrant bergamot as she smiled. "This is one of my favorite smells in the world. Bergamot. And mandarin and tangerine and, well, lemon meringue and key lime pie, and fresh-squeezed Ruby Red grapefruit."

His smile was indulgent. And curious. "Do you have citrus trees? On your farm?"

She shook her head. "I can't compete with the growers in the Rio Grande Valley. And my operation is fairly small. I stick to greens and gourds and peppers and corn. Tomatoes. Watermelon. Cantaloupe. Okra. Sometimes strawberries, but not often."

"You sell at farmers markets?"

She nodded, stirring sugar into her tea. "I supply a few local grocers, too, and have contracts with a couple of larger chains for their stores in the area."

"That doesn't sound small," he said, and she

wanted to say he was right. It wasn't small at all.

In fact, it was huge. Not the farm, but the fact that she'd made it herself. Her degree. The business loan. The equipment and the buildings and the people she employed, whose labor and advice she depended on.

But she was saved from bragging by the return of their waitress, and was glad. The success of IJK Gardens, the ups and the downs and the hard, hard work—all of it was worth bragging about, but not to this man. He'd been born into privilege; how could he possibly understand?

And, wow. What was up with her and snobbery today?

"All righty, then. Y'all ready to order?"

Oliver didn't hesitate, saying, "I'll have biscuits and gravy with a side of sausage and two scrambled eggs," holding Indiana's gaze as he did.

An unexpected blip in her pulse had her swallowing, then telling their waitress, "I'll have what he's having." Once the woman left, promising to be back in five minutes with their food, she said, "You're welcome to tour the farm anytime."

"I'd like that," he said, wrapping his cup in both of his hands, a small vee appearing between his brows as he asked, "Why expand into Hope Springs instead of building your annex in Buda?"

She brought her cup to her mouth, wondering whether his question was a simple query, or as loaded as it seemed. Because wasn't that subtext, real or imagined, the very reason they were here?

"Because of Dakota," she said before she sipped, setting her cup back in its saucer. "Well, Dakota and Tennessee. Tennessee's business is based here. Kaylie is here. If I find Dakota, I'm hoping he'll come back, maybe settle here, too, and make my dream of a big happy family come true."

Oliver studied her over the rim of his cup as he drank, obviously gathering his thoughts. She'd noticed that about him. How he didn't blurt or blab the way she seemed unable to stop herself from doing. She should probably take a lesson and think.

"Is that your dream?" he finally asked. "Having a big happy family?"

"It's complicated," she said, taking her own advice and weighing responses ranging from the full truth to just pieces. "My parents are still in the area, though they're gone a lot. We grew up in Round Rock. So I do have a family, though it's not particularly big. And I'm not sure where we would fall on the happy scale."

"You're not close?"

"We're not even in touch, really. They stay busy with whatever current cause demands their time. They always did. Never was much left for them to, you know, parent," she said, trying to be flip, but the words tasting bitter and raw. "But I guess it was easier that way."

Oliver toyed with his cup, his gaze cast down, and asked, "How so?"

She sipped again, then shrugged, then sipped once more as if doing so would keep her from saying things she shouldn't and sounding resentful. It didn't. "Baby seals didn't talk back. Melting glaciers just went away and left them alone. Climate change affects billions, while the changes in their daughter's attitude were simply phases to get through. Mine. Not theirs."

She cut herself off before she ended up going to that place she refused to visit, much less while in the company of a man who had her thinking there might be something missing in her life. Something she'd diligently prevented herself from considering before.

Something she wasn't sure she could ever trust.

"I can't tell if that's resentment or sarcasm."

"I'm over the resentment. But I'll never get over being sarcastic," she said, though her reach for levity wasn't quite long enough, and the joke fell flat.

"Tell me Dakota's story," he said, sitting back as their food was set in front of them.

She'd brought him here for this—not the biscuits and gravy and sausage and eggs that smelled like all the best bad-for-her things about food, but to tell him why finding her brother mattered so much. And as the thought crossed her mind, she wondered if Dakota, more than Robby, was the reason she'd chosen to live her life alone.

Or if it was, as she'd thought all this time, her own actions and considerable regrets.

There was something she didn't want to tell him, or something she didn't want him to know, and that made Oliver more curious than he would've been otherwise. He wasn't one to push, but Indiana had talked around the subject of her brother all morning. And that after asking if he wanted to know why she was eager to find the man.

Oliver had lived in Hope Springs long enough to have heard rumors of the Keller brother who'd spent time in the Huntsville state prison. Assault with a deadly weapon. He'd learned at some point the weapon had been a baseball bat, and Dakota Keller eighteen at the time.

Dakota had also been his baseball team's star slugger. Added to the fact that he premeditatedly went after the boy he'd beaten, well, he'd been lucky to have served just three years. Those things were easily discovered with a Google search of news articles from a decade ago. He'd done that late last night when he couldn't sleep and she'd been on his mind.

What Oliver couldn't discover were the things Indiana was keeping secret, had no doubt been keeping secret for years. And her skating around the reason for this meal left him wondering if someone else might be better equipped to handle her confession. Someone like a therapist. Or a priest.

"You probably know, or maybe you don't, that Dakota spent time in prison," she finally said, unwrapping her silverware and picking up her fork. "I think that's as much common knowledge as Tennessee hiring parolees *because* of our brother's prison time."

Having worked with Ten Keller at the Caffey-Gatlin Academy, Oliver had learned about the other man's hiring practices. And about Will Bowman spending time behind bars.

"I did," he said, cutting into his biscuit with the side of his fork, and waiting for her to go on. His opinion of Will didn't matter, though why he had an opinion at all . . .

"Dakota went to prison because of me."

At that, Oliver's head came up, his fork stilled, and he frowned. He knew what he'd heard. She'd been very clear: her words, her tone, her expression as her gaze held his. She'd said what she'd said expecting a reaction. He'd yet to give her much of one, and she was still waiting.

He had a feeling she hadn't made that statement to many other people, and he forked up the bite of biscuit, saying, "That can't be all there is."

She heaved out a sigh, shoved her eggs around on her plate. "In a nutshell."

"So crack it open. Pull it apart. Show me what's inside." When she filled her mouth with eggs instead of answering, he pressed. "Or were you hoping to scare me off with that declaration?"

Of course, the idea that she was hoping to scare him off came with all sorts of implications he hadn't meant to make, but rather than retract his question, he let her stew. And finished off his biscuit while she finished off her eggs.

Once she'd swallowed the rest of her tea, she rushed forward. "When I was fifteen, a friend of Dakota's and Tennessee's attacked me," she said, then added, "assaulted me," then finally told him the truth. "He tried to rape me."

That didn't scare him off, but he was horrified. No fifteen-year-old girl should have that experience. No girl of any age. No woman ever. "I'm sorry. That had to have been terrifying."

A curious look passed over her face, as if she'd never had anyone ask about her fear. "It was, but I played volleyball and probably had more upper-body strength than he did. And I had my brothers. He wasn't a very big guy."

She'd fought off the bastard. Good for her. "Apparently he thought so."

"What he thought . . ." She shook her head, and when she reached for her empty tea, her hand was shaking, too. "We had a bit of a history. Nothing too carnal, but enough of one that it wasn't hard for him to assume his attention was invited."

Without thinking, Oliver covered her hand with his own, feeling the ice of her fingers as he gestured to their waitress for two more cups of tea. When he looked back, Indiana's face had paled to the color of her bloodless fingertips, and it was all he could do not to move beside her and offer her his warmth.

Instead, he released her, and after a moment she put both her hands in her lap, waiting silently for their drink refills. Once they arrived, and as he dunked his tea bag into his water, he said, "Sex isn't about assumptions. It's about the mutual decision to share that particular pleasure. Whatever had happened between you and this boy prior to the assault is moot."

For a strangely long moment, she held his gaze, studying his eyes as if surprised he would make such an observation. He couldn't imagine why she would be; it was an obvious one to make. But then she finally said, "Thank you," and he wondered if no one else had ever put the same two and two together, letting her off the hook for a wrongly placed self-blame.

Then, because he knew enough of the history, he prodded her on by asking, "I'm assuming your brother went after him?"

"He did," she said, adding sugar to her tea. "With a baseball bat. And after Robby had already left the house."

Making Dakota's actions premeditated, and the bat a deadly weapon. "Was there a trial?"

"There was supposed to be, but his lawyer

made a deal because it's what Dakota wanted."

Huh. "And Robby got off with nothing?"

Nodding, she brought her cup to her mouth, holding it with hands that had steadied. "Dakota didn't want to put me through testifying. I told him I would. His lawyer told him my doing so would most likely help reduce his sentence. But he said no."

"So the deal was Dakota's call."

She sipped, swallowed, then held his gaze as she said, "He didn't want me to have to spend two more years in school as the girl Robby Hunt had tried to rape."

And to make sure it didn't happen, her brother had chosen to do three years in the state pen. This part Oliver hadn't known. This part had him wondering about Dakota Keller, the man he was now, and why, after the sacrifice he'd made for his sister, he'd disappeared from her life.

"When's the last time you saw him?"

"I saw him the day of his release, except I didn't know it was him." She set down her cup and returned to her breakfast. "He'd changed so much. He'd gone in at eighteen, and was almost twenty-two when he came out. He wasn't any taller, but he'd filled out so much that it seemed like he was. Tennessee and I were waiting for him, and he got into a cab before we knew he was the man with the crew cut and big buff body. I'm pretty sure he knew we were there. I'd written him that we would be. But I guess he'd already decided to take off on his own."

Interesting. "Did you visit him? While he was incarcerated?"

Another nod. "Not as often as I wanted to. Huntsville's a bit of a drive, and the first year, Tennessee and I were both in school. Weekends were the only times we could get away, and sometimes we had tournaments or games."

"And your parents?"

"Honestly, I don't know," she said, her voice tinged with what he wanted to call contempt. "They were out of town so often. I'm sure they visited when they could."

Or when it wasn't inconvenient, Oliver mused, never having met the Kellers but having no trouble drawing a mental picture based on what he'd learned. "Did he write back?"

"He did."

"But no clue that he wasn't coming home?"

"Not a one. He and Tennessee had planned to go into business together once they were both out of school."

"Construction," he said, though he knew.

"It's nothing I would've expected from either of them; they were both such jocks. Managing a sports bar, or a gym, yeah. But Tennessee loves it." Her fork stilled, and she smiled softly. "I like to think Dakota found a way to do what he wanted to do, too."

Oliver spent a moment with his food, wondering if Indiana was prepared should this search not go her way. "If he came back, do you think he'd go into business with Ten?"

Her smile faded. "I don't even know who he is now, or what he might like. It's been ten years. He could've gone back to school, become a doctor, left the states to work in Darfur."

"Do you ever wonder if that's on purpose? That he doesn't want you to know where he is, what he's doing, rather than just having moved on?"

"I wonder about it all the time, but I don't care. I need to know for me. And I need to apologize."

That had Oliver frowning. "I don't think he'd want an apology."

"Why do you say that?" she asked, frowning, too, and wary.

"What do you have to apologize for?"

"The assault—"

"The assault wasn't your fault."

"I know, but—"

"I don't think you do know. You want to take blame for what this friend of your brothers' did. To apologize for being a part of it." And listen to him, talking about blame, and brothers. As if he weren't weighed down with the same. "But you were a victim. And I'm sure Dakota knows that. Apologizing . . . It might be a better idea to thank him instead. Make sure he knows how much you appreciate what he did. Especially with what it cost him."

"That's assuming I'm able to find him," she said, when he'd feared she would tell him to stop butting in. "And that Tennessee and I don't have a big falling out over the whole thing."

"I'm going to guess Ten's lack of support isn't just about his doing things his way. That maybe he's got more than a little bit of guilt of his own."

"Kaylie told me that he regretted letting Dakota go after Robby. That he didn't do it himself. He was younger, and Dakota was known for his swing . . ."

"Under the circumstances, the premeditation, Ten could easily have been tried as an adult."

She nodded. "He's got a lot of resentment toward our parents, too. They were taken in by Robby's tales of a hard home life."

"He didn't have one?"

"He had parents who disciplined him, who set curfews and rules. Who expected him to do chores. Our parents didn't do any of the above. And he liked that. A lot."

That, as well as access to a young girl with, no doubt, a healthy curiosity. And with that thought it was time to change the subject. He sliced up his sausage, then asked, "What's next with the house? And the property?"

"I don't even know anymore. Tennessee thinks it's ridiculous for me to consider moving to

Hope Springs when my farm is in Buda. Even though, how many people drive from here into Austin every day? That's another fifteen miles. And since I'll be busy getting the annex up and running, I might only need to make the trip three times a week."

Sounded reasonable. "Did you tell him that?"

"Not yet, but I will. And I've promised Kaylie I'll tell him about hiring the PI." She placed her used napkin in the center of her plate. "I was just thinking. Life wasn't so complicated before Kaylie moved back to Hope Springs."

"How's that?"

"She hired Tennessee to do the renovations to the house and the conversion for the café. And when she decided to put in a garden, Tennessee called me." She reached for her wallet and began sorting through bills. "That's what brought him back into my life. And I don't think a day's gone by since then that we haven't argued about something, most of it stupid."

Life might not've been so complicated, he mused, pulling cash from his pocket to cover both of their meals and the tip, shaking his head when she offered to pay her share, but he was quite sure the real truth was that she wouldn't change a thing.

This he knew because he'd gladly give a limb to have Oscar whole again.

Chapter Five

"You want to gut the whole thing?"

Three days after his initial visit to Indy's new digs, Will was standing beside her in the tiny front room of the cottage that, even empty, smelled of the man who'd lived here at least a half century: mothballs, of course, because Hiram Glass had been of the age where chemical pesticides were all the rage.

But the sickly sweet scent of naphthalene hung beneath others: cigar smoke, strong coffee, licorice, Old Spice. Musty books bound in aging leather. Onions and grease from ground beef. Bourbon. Beer. The twenty-pound tomcat who'd sprawled at the end of the driveway and twitched his tail at passersby, though he had spent enough time inside to leave his mark.

Funny to think of a man being defined by his odors, which had Will wanting to lift an arm to sniff his pit.

Indy caught him with his elbow up and frowned. "Can you give me one good reason not to?"

Since he'd already been thinking about handing her a match . . . He shoved both hands in his pockets, his shoulders hunched. "Depends what your plans are for the building. Storage? Office space? A caretaker's cottage? A rental for

72

income? Unless you're going to be the one living here."

"Maybe," she said, her mouth pursed sideways. "Eventually."

Women and their prerogative. "What does that mean?" he asked, and she gave him a withering look.

"It means maybe. Eventually."

Right. How like him to miss the obvious. "You're thinking of moving to Hope Springs?"

Rather than answer, she went on walking through the rooms. Kitchen to bathroom to bedrooms, and then again in reverse. He stayed near the front door because the layout of the house kept her in his sight.

He supposed he could see her living here; she was just one person, and didn't seem the type to need a lot of room for a lot of things. He liked that about her. It rather reminded him of himself. Doing away with all but the necessities. Knowing the differences between need and want. Getting by simply, austerely, free of clutter and other burdens.

Didn't remind him at all of the woman who'd put his life in storage while he was on hold behind bars. The woman he'd thought for a while he'd like to spend the rest of his years with.

Until he hadn't.

"Why would you move?" he asked, because it was a lot easier to talk about Indiana's screwed-up life than to think about his own. "To be closer to Kaylie and Ten?"

She was back in the living room now, casing the perimeter and measuring it with boot-heel-to-boot-toe steps. One wall, another, a third, the fourth, and she was at the door. "I like it here. I like the community. The location. The people."

Except she still hadn't answered his question about being near her brother. "All the people?"

"All that I've met, yes." She pushed aside the yellowed lace curtain and peered through the door's driveway-facing window. "I'm sure there are others I won't like as much, but that's not a reflection on Hope Springs."

"You know I don't plan to stay here," he said, crossing his arms and leaning a shoulder against the wall.

"Did I say anything about moving here for you?"

"I'm people."

"I suppose you are."

"You're being all cryptic again."

Brow arched, she glanced over. "I'm pretty sure it was Luna who told me you said you'd been raised by wolves."

He gave a snort, amused. To this day he had no idea where that had come from, but yeah. He'd popped off with the explanation to keep from talking to Luna about who he was, where he'd been.

He didn't want to talk to anyone about where he'd been.

And that included Indy Keller. "Raised by. I'm not actually an animal."

"I guess that depends on how you define animal," she said and straightened, letting the curtain fall.

The words hung between them, tense and still, the air humming as if she'd loosed a hive of bees inside the tiny enclosure. He hadn't intended his use of the word *animal* as a come-on. He hadn't been trying to flirt.

But the implication was there, in her comment as well as in his, so he seized the moment and said, "Would you like to go to Austin? Get dinner? Go to a club? See a show?"

Her frown was playful, as was the curious cock of her head. But the way she crossed her arms told the truth of things. She wasn't quite sure what he was getting at—or what she was getting into. "Will Bowman. Are you asking me out on a date?"

He didn't know if he could give her an answer. He hadn't been thinking that far ahead. "I've got tickets to see the Decemberists. I'm asking if you'd like to grab a bite to eat and go with me."

"When?"

"Tonight, actually."

"I don't know—"

"Don't know if it's a good idea? Because it's

probably not. It's short notice. It's late in the day. Your brother wouldn't approve," he said, unsure which of them he was trying to talk out of it. He should've kept his mouth shut.

She sputtered as if she found *his* objections to *his* invitation ridiculous. "I hardly need Tennessee's permission for what I do. I have a mind of my own."

All right, then. "Show's at ten," he said, shoving his hands in his pockets again, his shoulders hunched again, this time against what he feared was a very bad idea. "We'll need to leave at seven to eat. I have reservations at Qui."

Her expression was a curious mix of excitement and apprehension. "You have reservations, but you're just now asking me to go?"

It wasn't that complicated. "I was going to eat alone if you didn't. Or . . . whoever didn't."

"Okay . . ." She drew out the word as if using the time to weigh the possibility of his having ulterior motives. "But I need to know if we're two friends getting away from the everyday grind, or if it's a date."

"What does it matter?" It was all the same to him.

But apparently not to her. She rocked from the toes of her boots to the heels as she considered him. "A date means different hair and makeup. Different clothes. Different . . . expectations."

His gut tightened. "You don't want to date me, Indiana."

She stopped rocking. "And you don't want to forget that mind-of-my-own thing, Will."

"Fine, but don't say I didn't warn you," he said, and watched her bristle.

"What exactly are you warning me about?" she asked, her chin coming up. "That you're not a nice man? That I'm going to regret saying yes?"

"That's what you got out of what I said?" Though he couldn't blame her. He wasn't so good with words—choosing them, using them, even if he'd get some argument about that from people he'd known in the past.

She reached up to clear her flyaway hair from her face, exasperated, or confused, or maybe just tired of dealing with his brand of crap. "If you want me to get something else, you'll need to spell it out."

He went for straightforward. "You know where I spent the last three years. I'm not up on social niceties."

The look she gave him seemed nothing but a stand-in for rolling her eyes. "I'm pretty sure social niceties are the same now as they were before you went to prison."

"I'm out of practice, then," he said, and shrugged.

"Practice on me. Tonight."

Oh, he wished she hadn't said that. He wasn't ready to hear any woman say that. "Meet me at my place. We can take your car."

"We can?"

"Unless you want to take my Keller Construction truck."

"That's the only vehicle you have?"

He had another. In storage. One day he'd get it out. Start it up. Hit the road and vanish. "I like your Camaro."

"Fine," she said, and he swore she barely stopped herself from grumbling the words. "I'll see you then."

She'd said yes to Will because of how much she'd enjoyed Oliver's company, yet Oliver hadn't asked her out and Will had. It was logic that made no sense in any world but hers, where this absolutely ridiculous need she had to be wanted continued to rear its ugly head.

Then again, she couldn't help but wonder if, away from Hope Springs and their shared social circle and their client/contractor relationship, she and Will might find there was more to their friendship than either had realized. That, and not the illogical rest, was what she'd told herself to keep in mind; for most of the evening, she had.

Except going out with Will had her feeling disloyal to Oliver, even though Oliver hadn't indicated any interest in seeing her again. He'd fallen silent while driving away from Malina's, and when she'd exited his car on Three Wishes

Road, their good-bye had been awkward, both lost in thought.

That left her curious to know if he'd come with her to breakfast because he'd been unable to find a way out, her invitation being so sudden, and him being too polite to lie his way out of accepting. Of course, all of that was her projecting. He might very well have wanted to come. And then regretted it.

Look at their conversation. When she'd asked him if he wanted to hear about Dakota, he hadn't exactly jumped for joy. "Only if you want to share it." Even she knew that wasn't a yes. And her assault? Really? What man would want to hear such a thing on a first date? Except breakfast had not been a date. And Dakota would have no story—no incarceration, no life spent as a convicted felon—if the assault had not happened.

In fact, Indiana's expansion into Hope Springs, Tennessee's *Keller Construction* lacking the word *brothers,* and Dakota's ongoing absence were all tied to that night in the kitchen with Robby Hunt. Except those events had been set in motion long before. And she'd been the one to do the setting.

She and Oliver had been two friends sharing a meal. It was that simple. She'd needed to get the weight of the last few days off her chest. Her missing Dakota had been worse than usual since her decision to hire Kaylie's PI and her acceptance that there were no guarantees of success. She'd wanted a willing, impartial ear. For some reason, Oliver had offered one, and all she'd been able to think about since was telling him more.

And not even things about her brother, but her life, and his. Movies and books and TV and food. Travel. Her greenhouse annex. Her Buda farm. She'd wanted to ask what he did for the Caffey-Gatlin Academy. What he did, period, because she had no idea how he spent his time, made his money. If he even needed to make money, being a Gatlin and all.

And then it hit her. Before tonight's date with Will, and as well as she'd thought she'd known him—they'd been friends for months, after all—she'd only scratched his surface, too. Which had her wondering what exactly she'd been feeling about him before now. She enjoyed his company, of course, and he wasn't the least bit hard on the eyes, all lanky and gaunt and haunted. He was quick-witted and clever, too clever at times, fox-like clever, and a complete pro at deflecting her questions. But none of that had given her the insight she'd gained over the hours they'd spent at dinner.

There was something about him, sitting beside her now as they drove through the wee hours into a very quiet Hope Springs, that had her thinking back to Dakota and his last girlfriend, Thea Clark. The clandestine nature of their relationship. The secrets. *Forbidden* was the word that came to mind, though why her spending a night out in Austin with Will should fall into that category . . .

They'd talked nonstop, their food growing cold, their drinks, too. They'd talked so long, in fact, that they never made it to the Decemberists' show. Indiana didn't mind; Will fascinated her with the things he knew, obscure things, things she wouldn't have thought worth knowing until hearing him go on in such depth. Literature. Science. The economy. Pop culture. He knew as much about *Assassin's Creed* as he did Vladimir Bartol's *Alamut*. As much about Sheldon Cooper as Niels Bohr.

They'd talked about her cottage, her property, her bees, Will always asking questions, learning more about her than she had about him. Still, she'd learned enough to make her more curious than ever about who he was and where he'd come from, why he'd settled in Hope Springs after being released from prison.

Why he'd gone to prison in the first place . . .

And then, after chatting themselves silly, they'd made the drive home from Austin in silence, save for "Calamity Song," "This Is Why We Fight," and the rest of the Decemberists' *The King Is Dead* album, making good use of her car's sound system. Yet rather than being awkward, the calm of the trip lulled her into feeling comfortably numb. She was tired from talking, from listening, from absorbing, and imagined Will was, too.

But a part of her was simply exhausted from his intensity. He'd been on all night, the air around him buzzing. Energy had poured off him, and been so bright, she'd felt as if she could reach out and grab it, could harness it and use it for fuel.

It was the first time she'd ever seen him so animated, and she wondered if he'd been putting on a show, or reacting to being with her, or if he'd simply been having fun. But she also wondered if the spirited conversationalist was the man he'd been before prison, and the sulky emo mask he usually wore some kind of self-defense.

She pulled to a stop at his curb, his building in the town's historic warehouse district looming with dark disapproval as if the strict mores of the past still lingered and judged. They needn't worry. She wasn't going inside. That much she'd determined before they'd set off for home. As much as she liked him, there was something about him that was off, or wasn't quite right, while still incredibly compelling. And as interested in him as she was, as curious to know him, as charmed, it was too soon to be alone with him and tempted.

"I'm not coming up," she finally told him, when he hadn't moved to get out. When he hadn't said a word in the two or three minutes since she'd parked. When he'd done nothing but look through the windshield where the street lamps caught every hint of moisture on the pavement and sparkled.

"I didn't ask you to," he said at last, still facing forward, hunched a bit, his busy hands pressed between his knees. That left her a bit uneasy. His nervousness. How antsy he was. How out of sorts.

"Then . . . good night, Will. Thank you for the evening—"

"What do you want from me, Indiana?" he asked, his head turning slowly until the look in his eyes, so bottomless and dark as they stared into hers, had her heart rising to pound at the base of her throat.

"I don't want anything. Well, except for what I've hired you to do. With the cottage," she said, her pulse making itself known throughout her body. "I mean, at the very least I'd like your friendship, but if for some reason we can't be friends—"

It was all she got out before his hand was in her hair, bringing her face to his, her mouth to his, her lips and tongue to his in such an act of desperation, she couldn't find the strength to back away, or to say no, or to do anything but share in the devastatingly draining emotion.

What was this man's damage? What was he looking to her to fix or to make whole, or just to soothe because he couldn't do it alone?

He kissed her as if he were on fire, as if she

could douse whatever it was burning him up. His hand at the back of her head was hot. The fingertips of the other, where they brushed her jaw, were sure to leave blisters on her skin. An obvious exaggeration, but oh, everything about this moment felt that way.

She didn't know what to do with her hands. Should she touch him? Should she leave them where they were, wrapped tightly around the wheel? Should she tuck them between her knees to keep from reaching for him? What was she supposed to do? She didn't know what she was supposed to do because she didn't know if this, from Will, was what she wanted.

But she wasn't unmoved, so she kissed him back, finally reaching up to grip his wrist, a grounding, an anchor, a solid reminder of where she was, because everything around her seemed too ethereal to grasp, and all she knew was Will. He smelled like rain on a dark night, rich and electric, a dangerous storm set to strike.

He tasted like the wine he'd had with dinner, the bourbon he'd had after, the coffee he'd had with dessert. The barest hint of the cigarette he'd smoked while waiting for the valet to bring her car. It was the first time she'd ever seen him indulge, and the lingering hint of tobacco wasn't unpleasant.

His tongue made hers tingle, and the pressure of his lips, soft yet slightly chapped, started a sweet, exquisite tension building in her body. Oh, this was so unexpected, so beautifully, frightfully out of the blue. She didn't know whether to revel in the sensation, or run far, far away.

Before she had a chance to decide, and almost as quickly as he'd started, he stopped, releasing her mouth, then pulling his wrist from her grip. His hand in her hair was the last to let go, and she fought against feeling bereft. Surely she wasn't that hungry for human contact, that desperate to be wanted?

His door opening had her searching out his darting gaze; he was leaving just like that? Yes, she'd told him, and herself, that she wasn't coming up to his loft. But she needed to figure out this push-pull thing between them, and she couldn't if he was going to walk away. "Will?"

"Thanks for driving," he said, adding, "friend," as he stepped out of the car. Then he leaned back in, one hand on the roof, one hand on the door, his eyes, wicked and bright, reflecting the glow of the street lamps through the windshield. "Be safe. And don't be sorry. Don't ever be sorry."

Then he slammed the door and turned for the sidewalk, leaving her staring after him without a clue as to what they'd just done. Or what he'd meant by his parting remark.

Chapter Six

Rather than driving back to Buda after leaving Will at his loft, Indiana spent the night in her empty cottage, roughing it with the two furniture pads she kept in her Camaro's trunk. The water was on. The power was on. And the pads, which she used when she found herself needing to transport starter plants or bags of soil, smelled like the life she loved. The life she thought perfect. The life well suited for living alone.

After breakfast with Oliver and dinner with Will, she had to remind herself of that. Oliver and his silver spoon were out of her league, and Will . . . Will, too, was off-limits. He had to be. *Both* had to be. A relationship done right required nurturing, and she had too much on her plate to be anything but selfish with her time.

Besides, she knew nothing about being part of a couple. Her parents had been partners in their crusades, and obviously lovers at some point to have produced three children. But their inter-action reminded her of coworkers. There had been no public displays of affection, no terms of endearment, no gazes colliding across crowded rooms.

Then there was Kaylie and Tennessee, as well as Luna and Angelo. The latter were newlyweds,

Kaylie and Tennessee engaged. And boy, was the difference between those couples and Indiana's parents obvious. Gazes collided constantly, heated and longing-filled. Affection was as automatic as breathing, endearments spoken in lieu of names as if the most natural thing in the world.

But what struck her hardest wasn't the chemistry, or the physicality of what the couples shared. It was the respect, the friendship, how Kaylie anticipated Tennessee's moods, or Tennessee Kaylie's needs. They were that tuned in to each other. As if they didn't need words to communicate. As if love had given them super-powers.

It was a nice reality to strive for. If one hadn't already screwed up two of the most important relationships in one's life. But Indiana had. And until she fixed those, she would never trust herself with such a bond. Or at least with being able to make it right should she make more bad choices and break it.

Anyway, she had an established business to run, a new business to launch, a brother she couldn't quite figure out, and another brother to find. She couldn't afford the distraction of a relationship. And it seemed even simple meals with interesting men were destined to cause her grief. She would eat alone. She would live alone. She would probably die alone.

But, she mused, stepping onto the porch, she

did need coffee. And she'd have to shower and change clothes before heading to the farm. Seeing Kaylie's Jeep turn into the arts center's driveway and head toward Luna's barn, and seeing no sign of Oliver's BMW, Indiana ditched the idea of making the trip home decaffeinated, and instead hurried across the street.

She caught up to Kaylie just as she and Magoo reached Luna's front door. Well, Kaylie reached the door. Magoo ran off with Luna's dog, Francisco, who was a quarter his size and obviously in charge. Indiana would've enjoyed watching the mismatched two rough-and-tumble across the yard, but she was too focused on the Butters Bakery box in Kaylie's hand. "I hope you have an extra muffin in there. I'm starving."

Kaylie laughed, then as Indiana came closer, frowned. Luna opened the door just as Kaylie asked of Indiana, "Are you okay?"

"I'm fine, why?"

"Well, not to be rude, but your hair is a bit wilder than usual. You obviously slept in more makeup than I think I've ever seen you wear." Kaylie paused to continue her once-over. "I'm going to guess you also slept in the clothes you have on, clothes, by the way, which I have never seen on you before."

"Those are date clothes," Luna said, causing Indiana to look down at her skinny black pants and frothy white swing top, at the ruby stilettos on her feet that had her missing her boots. "And that's what's left of a date face."

Then it was back to Kaylie. "Which brings us to the question of *where* you went to bed, and if you went there alone."

Indiana started to ask herself if caffeine was worth this grilling. Then she stopped. "I slept on the floor of the cottage between two furniture pads." Truth *was* stranger than fiction.

"Because . . ." Kaylie let the sentence trail.

That one was easy. "I got back late from Austin and didn't want to drive home."

But Kaylie wasn't appeased. "Buda's between Austin and Hope Springs. That doesn't make sense."

"It does if she had to come back here because she wasn't alone," Luna said, still standing in the barn's doorway.

These two women gave better third degree than Tennessee. "I wasn't alone in Austin. I was alone in my cottage. And I think I may have a problem."

"You think?" Luna asked on top of Kaylie's "You don't know?"

"I'm kinda in over my head here," Indiana said in answer to both.

"There's only one thing it can be." This from Kaylie.

"A man." This from Luna.

"Yes. And no." Indiana looked from one woman to the other. "More like two men."

Kaylie glanced down at the box she held. "I'm not sure we have enough muffins for this story."

It wasn't the muffins Indiana was worried about. "There won't be any story if I don't get coffee ASAP."

"Coffee I can do," Luna said, urging both Kaylie and Indiana through the door, then through what had once been a barn, but had since been converted, and into a kitchen Indiana could see herself never leaving.

She, who grew vegetables for a living but wasn't much of a foodie, not to mention a terrible cook. "Luna. This is amazing."

Spice racks and suspended copper pots and bakeware glazed in delicious shades of olive and aubergine. The walls were exposed brick and what looked like original wood weathered to gray, the floor a variegated travertine to match. The small appliances were the same stainless steel as the large ones, all of it brought together by a center island with barstools along two sides.

"It is, and it's more deserving of someone who actually has time to enjoy it." Luna turned on the espresso maker, and filled the milk-foaming attachment before snapping it into place. Then she pulled three latte mugs from the cupboard. "Angelo and I end up eating out way too often, though it turns out when he has the time, he can put together Tex-Mex to die for."

"In this kitchen?" Indiana wondered if she

could replicate this design on a smaller scale in her cottage. "Even I could put together Tex-Mex to die for."

"Which reminds me," Luna said, as she switched out a full mug for an empty and ran the machine through its cycle again. "You're coming to our Halloween party next week, yes? Mitch and Dolly are doing a huge taco spread, and we'll have tons of goodies."

"Of course, though I have no idea what I'm going to do about a costume." Indiana accepted the mug and sugar bowl Luna handed her, stirring in a spoonful while she added, "But I do know what goodies I'm going to bring."

"The goodies can wait," Kaylie said, setting out muffins on the three plates that matched the mugs, and matched the linen napkins bearing the same exclusive Patchwork Moon label found on the scarves Luna wove. "It's time to hear about the men. Both of them."

"And," Luna said as Indiana swallowed her first mouthful of coffee, "I'm going to guess their names are Will and Oliver."

Indiana nodded, but before she could reply, Kaylie did. "Wow. I think I see your problem. I can't imagine picking between two more different men."

"I didn't exactly pick them," Indiana said, breaking open a glazed lemon-blueberry muffin, her stomach growling in anticipation. "They just happened. Kinda like Francisco just happened to Luna, showing up when she wasn't looking for a dog. I mean, I wasn't looking for a relationship, and it's not like I have a relationship—"

"Two," Luna said, holding up her fingers in a victory vee. "Two relationships."

"Two friendships," Indiana said, making the state of things perfectly clear. Then, feeling a remembered rush of the heat Will Bowman had generated, hovering when they'd kissed, she admitted, "Though I'm not sure using one's tongue is the best way to kiss a friend good night."

"Who was it?" Kaylie asked as Indiana reached for another bite of muffin, only to have her very impatient sister-in-law-to-be nearly slap it out of her hand. "Enough with the torture already. Luna and I are very happily paired off, and must now get our thrills vicariously."

"I don't know about you," Luna put in, "but my thrills are very much the real thing."

"Well, sure," Kaylie said, pulling the paper from her muffin. "Mine are, too. But there's just something so exciting about new love—"

Okay. Time to rein in the runaways. "No one said anything about love. And it was Will," she said, and when she got nothing but silence, added, "Bowman. Will Bowman. Will is the one I went out with last night. The one I kissed. The one who kissed me."

"Huh," Luna said, frowning. "I would've sworn

you were going to say Oliver. Angelo told me . . ."

And now Indiana was the one to frown. "Angelo told you what?"

Lifting her mug, Luna shrugged. "Nothing, really."

"If it was nothing, you wouldn't have mentioned it. Now spill."

Another shrug, then, "He walked into the living room at the arts center the other morning, and saw Oliver watching you."

"Watching me?" Indiana asked, wondering if she had Oliver's interest all wrong. Wondering, too, what she'd been doing, what she'd been wearing, though it had to have been her boots and a sundress. One of these days she really should try a little harder . . .

"It wasn't anything pervy," Luna was quick to assure her. "You were standing in the driveway staring across the street. He was drinking his coffee."

That must've been the morning they went to breakfast. "And looking at me."

"Unless he was looking at some other scenery," Luna said, fighting the twist of a smile.

"Oh, so now I'm scenery."

"To Oliver, I'll bet you were," Kaylie said, adding, "Or are. To Will, too."

Luna huffed. "Every woman is scenery to Will."

It was hard to argue with that, Indiana mused, having seen Will's gaze wander more than a few times when they'd been in the same room. But it hadn't wandered once last night. He'd talked to her. He'd paid attention to her. He'd looked only at her. He'd needed her.

And then Luna went on to say, "Though I suppose, considering his situation, that's not surprising."

"I know it's none of my business," Indiana said, having finished off her latte and nodding when Luna offered a second, "but has he ever said anything to either of you about why he went to prison?"

Both women shook their heads; then Kaylie said, "I don't even think Ten knows."

"And he hired him anyway?" Luna asked.

Kaylie handed over her mug for a refill, too. "Manny knows Ten's requirements for the parolees he takes on. He doesn't send him violent offenders, or sexual offenders, or repeat offenders."

Giving them the second chance he hadn't been able to give his own brother. Indiana knew what drove Tennessee to do what he did, and that made her more curious than ever about Will's crime.

"It does make it hard not to wonder what he did. And why," Luna said, giving Indiana back her mug. "But mostly I want to know which one of you asked the other one out."

"We were looking through the cottage, and out of the blue he asks if I'd like to have dinner and see a show," Indiana said. "I was so surprised I almost blurted out yes, not even thinking, but I kept my wits long enough to make him tell me if we were friends having dinner, or if it was a date."

"And?"

The word came in stereo, and Indiana smiled. "All he said was that I didn't want to date him."

"Do you?" Luna asked before Kaylie could free her mouth of muffin.

"I don't know."

This time Kaylie was ready. "Because things didn't go well? Which is hard to believe, looking at you the morning after. Or because of Oliver?"

"I don't know," she said again, until both women gave her a look letting her know that answer didn't cut it. "Okay. Okay. It's not about Oliver, and it's not even about Will, and things did go well, thank you. It's about me, and needing to fix things with my brothers."

Luna glanced at Kaylie. "Did she say brothers?"

Kaylie glanced at Indiana, as if to ask permission before giving Luna an answer. Indiana nodded, and Kaylie said, "Brothers plural, yes. She's hired my investigator to find Dakota."

"Oh. I had no idea you were going to look for him."

"No one knew but Kaylie. I haven't even told Tennessee yet."

"Why wouldn't you tell Ten?"

She thought back to the explanation she'd

given Oliver. "Tennessee doesn't like it when he's not the one putting things in motion. If I tell him now, before I have something, anything, to report, he'll want to put the kibosh on the whole thing until he can be the one to make the arrangements."

"That doesn't make sense," Luna said. "Dakota's his brother, too. Why wouldn't he be just as anxious to find him as you are?"

"He'll say that if Dakota wanted to be found, he'd let us know where he was. Except I don't believe that." Indiana wrapped her hands around her near-empty mug and stared down, focusing on the one thing that mattered. "I need to hear Dakota tell me that himself."

"And if he does?"

Luna's question was one Indiana had forced herself to consider, and it broke her heart to respond. "Then I'll leave him alone."

"In the meantime," Kaylie said, "you never know where things might go with Oliver or Will. And I can't imagine Dakota being happy about you putting your life on hold for him, because that's what it sounds like you're doing."

No. That wasn't it. That wasn't it at all. "It's moot anyway. With the annex going in, I can't afford the distraction of a relationship."

"You know," Luna began, picking at her muffin as she weighed her words, "it almost sounds like the annex, and even the search for Dakota, are the distractions."

96

"How so?"

"If you stay busy enough, you won't have to make a choice."

"I don't know if I *can* make a choice," Indiana admitted. "They're such completely different personalities. Both are so smart, and so . . . compelling, I guess is a good word. Oliver seems to have everything going for him, though he has so much tragedy in his family. Will just seems lost, yet has absolutely no fear. He asks what he wants to know; he does what he wants to do. It's like consequences don't exist for him. Oliver is much more reserved, but so aware and deliberate at the same time."

"You've gone out with Oliver, too?" Kaylie asked.

Indiana nodded. "I had breakfast with Oliver Friday morning, then dinner with Will last night. And I've spent time with both when I've been here to check on the property. Really. I'm not dating either. I just don't get why, after all these years of drought, I have two men in my life at the same time."

"I get that it's frustrating," Luna said, "but it's not a bad problem to have."

"Can you roll with it?" Kaylie asked. "Don't think about it so much? Don't worry about it? Just see what happens?"

"If I want to stay sane," Indiana said, thinking it was probably too late, "I don't have much choice."

Chapter Seven

Halloween night, Indiana arrived at Luna and Angelo's barn bearing chocolate cupcakes frosted with chocolate buttercream, and orange marmalade cookies with an icing of orange zest. The chocolate wasn't exactly black, but close enough to serve as one of Halloween's traditional colors. The orange spoke for itself.

It was a strange holiday this year, not being home to give out candy to costumed kids, but she liked this new circle of friends she found herself a part of. All because seven months ago Kaylie had wanted a garden, and Tennessee had wanted to give Kaylie everything. That it had taken her brother's love for a woman to get him to reach out to her might have given Indiana pause if she, too, didn't find Kaylie irresistible.

Through Kaylie, she'd met Luna; her husband, Angelo; and Kaylie's father, Mitch Pepper. Mitch had been a constant around Kaylie's house as she prepared again—second time being a charm, the first delayed by a fire—to open Two Owls Café. Kaylie baked most of her own brownies, but Mitch, along with his new wife, Dolly (they'd surprised everyone by getting married last Saturday), would be responsible for the daily buffet of casserole, salad, and the best hot rolls

Indiana had ever eaten in her life, the recipe handed down to Kaylie by the foster mother with whom she'd lived in the very house she now owned.

Then there was Will. And Oliver. She doubted Oliver had ever worked a day in his life. Nice gig for those who could get it, or those born into that world. Will was more of an enigma. He did construction work for her brother, but she couldn't imagine him using what Tennessee paid him for more than pocket change; after all, he'd bought a loft in the same building as the one where Luna now did her weaving and would've needed a substantial chunk for that.

Like Oliver, Will appeared to be financially independent, though the source of his wealth wasn't as obvious. If he came from a well-to-do family, he'd never let on. In fact, he hadn't said much to anyone about his past, except to tell Luna he'd been raised by wolves. Sometimes, Indiana believed that he had been. He had a certain look, predatory, she supposed, though Oliver often gave off the same vibe.

Oh, what did she know about men? Her brothers had vanished from her life when she was only sixteen. She'd never told her parents what had happened with Robby Hunt, and doubted Robby had spoken of it to anyone; why would he? A would-be rapist confessing his crime willingly to explain why he'd been beaten with a baseball bat by his victim's brother?

No, he'd stayed just as silent as Indiana had, letting Dakota take the fall. Growing up with that on her plate had made dating less than palatable. She was a smart woman. She'd been a smart teen. She knew what had happened had not been her fault, no matter her history with Robby. That didn't make it any easier to deal with. She'd been plagued for years with *if onlys . . .*

If only her parents hadn't gone out that night. If only Robby's parents had insisted he go with them on his family's spring-break vacation rather than allowing him to spend the week with Dakota and Tennessee.

If only Tennessee had been the one to come down and check on the frozen pizza. If only Dakota hadn't been playing his stereo loud enough to drown out the scuffle, though since most of that had been outside . . .

Funny how her *if only*s weren't anything she could've controlled or done differently—though *if only* she'd stayed in her bedroom with the door locked all night had crossed her mind more than once.

"Look at you!" Luna said, breaking into Indiana's musings while giving her costume a once-over. "Turn around. Do you have a stinger?"

Indiana turned, wiggling her backside. The padded cone fixed between the black and yellow tiers of her bumblebee skirt wiggled, too.

"Absolutely adorable. Also, the corset is a very nice touch."

"That's all the costume company's doing," she said, tugging up on the asset-revealing bodice that was making it hard to breathe. "I don't have that much imagination, but you certainly do," she said, taking in Luna's halo and wings and the rest of her sexy-angel getup—the sheer white stockings, the white minidress with a bustier top, and the very high and sparkly heels with white feathered cuffs.

"With all the remodeling going on, I was lucky to manage this, though Angelo made it a lot easier when he decided to dress like the devil." Luna cast a glance toward the new river-rock fireplace where her husband stood with friends. He was dressed all in black, a collared, red cape over his shoulders, horns on either side of his head. "Which, I must say, suits his new look, all that slicked-back long hair."

"The goatee doesn't hurt, either," Indiana said, looking from Angelo back to the treats she'd brought. "Where should I put this?"

"Did you bake these?" Luna took the platter of cookies off the top of the bakery box Indiana still held, revealing the logo when she did. "Ah, Butters Bakery. I think we should probably just put these away in the kitchen until everyone else is gone."

"My first choice was to put them away in

my kitchen, but yours will work just as well."

Indiana followed a laughing Luna through the great room, where tables bearing goodies sat beside tables bearing drinks, and a long buffet-style setup of every taco fixing known to man butted up against a margarita machine. The smells of chili powder and cumin and onions and warm corn tortilla shells had her staying to fill her plate.

While there, she was swept into conversation with Luna's mother about the impending arrival of her second child twenty-eight years after her first, then with Luna's father about sheep farming and providing the wool Luna used in her Patchwork Moon scarves.

Mitch Pepper joined them shortly, and Dolly showed up soon after. She shooed Indiana along, insisting she spend time with those her own age and not waste it on her elders. That had the other three loudly objecting, and Indiana laughing as she walked away.

She spoke to people she had come to know well and to those with whom she'd only just become acquainted. She ate too many cookies on top of too many tacos and begged off a second dance after Morris Dexter, an old classmate of Kaylie's, talked her into a first.

Before she circled back to the margarita machine, Angelo stopped her and introduced her to one of the board members who served the Caffey-Gatlin Academy with Luna and Oliver.

Still drinkless, she talked with Manny Balleza, Dakota's former parole officer, and met the most recent parolee he'd sent to work for Tennessee.

Kaylie, ignoring Indiana's playful insistence that she needed alcohol, showed her off as family to a young woman who'd lived in the big blue Victorian three of the years Kaylie was there in foster care, but she'd done so too quickly for Indiana to catch her name. Cindy maybe? Then she turned and found herself facing Will.

He was wearing the same uniform of skinny black jeans and long-sleeved black tee he always did, though instead of work boots he wore slip-on Vans sporting glow-in-the-dark bones. His concession to the holiday, she supposed, though the fact that he owned said shoes . . .

She thought back to the last time she'd seen him, the kiss that preceded what had seemed like a regretful good-bye, his telling her to be safe as she drove, but to never be sorry. She was still working out what he'd meant by that, because he couldn't know the things she was sorry for, her regret over ruining her brothers' lives . . . Could he?

"So tell me," she said, after tucking away her past to give him a thorough appraisal. "What does it say about a man that he wears a costume every day?"

"Indiana," he said, ignoring her heavily loaded question. "Long time no see. Long time no talk to." He leaned down, his lips just brushing her ear. "Long time no kiss."

"Shh." Wolves. He'd definitely been raised by wolves. She took a step back. His cheek trailed along hers as he straightened, and she shivered from the feel of his whiskers on her skin. "It hasn't been that long."

"It's been three days."

"It's barely been two and a half," she said, stepping closer to give another couple room to pass. He smelled like autumn, woodsy and spiced. "It was well into Tuesday morning when we got back to Hope Springs."

"Feels like three years to me, and I know what three years feels like."

If she hadn't known him as well as she did, she might've fallen for his sympathy bid. "Yes, but time also drags when you're not staying busy."

He frowned as he looked away. "How would you know how busy I am?"

She reached up and, holding his chin, turned him back to face her. "I haven't heard a word from you about the cottage. Is that because you haven't thought more about it? Or because you forgot to charge your phone?"

"Ouch," he said, as she let him go. "That's some sting you've got there."

He was right. This was a party. Wrong time and place to talk business. "It's extra sharp because it hasn't yet been dulled by a margarita."

"Would you like me to get you one?"

"The biggest one you can find," she said, and watched him go. Once he was lost to the crowd, she took a deep breath, then took in the party-goers, the conversation, the laughter, the music, the overwhelming joy filtering through the room.

Rather than wander and visit, she stayed where she was and waited for Will, speaking when spoken to, waving back when someone across the room caught her eye. Sharing quick hugs with the more demonstrative of her friends and soaking in all the fun. And it was fun.

There was no second-guessing the plans she'd set in motion for the cottage, no wondering if ordering larger greenhouses for the annex would've been the way to go. No worrying about either of her brothers, though the second the thought crossed her mind, she started, because it had been that way with her ever since Tennessee had reached out in March.

He was here; they'd touched base briefly before Kaylie had called him away, but Indiana couldn't help thinking about Dakota and dropping the man he'd be now into the holiday season. Had he married? Did he have children? Was he out with them tonight trick-or-treating? Had he dressed up, too, because it made them laugh?

Ugh. She was so angry with herself for causing this rift. She needed to set it right. To somehow make up for all the missed Halloweens before the next one rolled around. A year away, but it would be here all too soon. Thankfully, before she grew completely maudlin, Will returned, a margarita in one hand, a beer in the other.

"What did you mean when you told me not to ever be sorry?" she asked, as she took her drink.

"Just that," he said, holding her gaze as he lifted the longneck to his mouth. "Do what you do, and don't regret it."

She considered him over the rim of the glass as she sipped. "You weren't referring to a particular event in my past?"

"Do I know the events of your past?"

Not from her, but that didn't mean he hadn't put Google to use and gone looking. Days into knowing him, and curious as to what had brought him to work with her brother, she'd googled him. She hadn't found a single news article. Her past, on the other hand, at least the part Dakota had played, was easily searchable.

"Do you?" she asked.

He shrugged, stepped out of the way and closer to her when Mitch walked through with another brazier of refried beans. "Only what you've told me and what Ten has let slip."

"Tennessee would never let anything slip," Indiana said.

"Then obviously I know nothing," he said, but she swore this time when he lifted his beer, his

106

hand trembled. Because of what he did know? Because of past events of his own?

Because he was hiding the truth? "So telling me not to be sorry . . ."

"How about this," he said, spinning to back her into the nearest wall and blocking the room from her sight. "Regrets aren't worth wasting time on, because no amount of wishing away what's happened is going to change a thing."

Her heart slamming hard enough to choke her, she asked, "Are you talking about me now, or about you?"

"Who cares who I'm talking about." He was breathing hard, his eyes wide, his nostrils close to flaring. "You. Me. It's all the same."

"Will . . ."

Surely her curiosity hadn't set him off. And it wasn't that he frightened her; even with all she didn't know about him, she knew him well enough not to be afraid. But this way he had of flipping switches, hot to cold, black to white . . . She couldn't help but wonder if this was his natural intensity, or if this was due to his time served.

Saying nothing more, she let the moment pass. His breathing leveled, and he stepped back, giving her room to move, bowing his head and softly saying, "I'm sorry."

"I shouldn't have brought it up. Not here. Not tonight."

"It doesn't matter," he said, the fight gone out

of him, his whole frame going limp as he leaned against the wall. "Not when. Not where. Not anything."

She didn't know what to say. She hadn't meant to ruin his evening, though had a feeling anything she'd brought up in conversation would've produced the same result. This was who Will was, and whether prison's doing or that of his DNA, she couldn't imagine he'd ever change. And that was something it was best she come to realize now rather than later.

"I think I'm going to head home." He drained the bottle in his hand as he pushed to stand straight. "You need another drink before I go?"

"I'm good, thanks," she said, though after their encounter, she was just about ready for a second. "But if you feel like stopping by the cottage tomorrow, I'll be there."

His grin, as he walked away, was equal parts apology and touché. Watching him go, and suddenly exhausted, she did her best to put their confrontation out of her mind, then made her way upstairs. She walked through the media room, then onto the balcony, finding it empty, which pleased her to no end. Seeing couples and friends and family members enjoying the evening had her missing Dakota fiercely.

There was so much time between them, time and distance and words needing to be said. It was her need, and it was desperate, and she had to accept that it might not be his. That Tennessee might be right: Dakota didn't want to be found. Dealing with that, accepting that . . .

She didn't know if she could do either. And she didn't know why all of these feelings—the loneliness, the guilt, the regret she promised herself she'd never mention to Will—were suddenly coming to a head.

She'd been fine on her own all this time. Or as fine as anyone who'd sent their brother to prison could be. She thought she was living with the separation. Waves of anger and sadness came and went, but until Tennessee had reached out, nothing had stayed.

The things she was feeling now . . . They had taken root, and they lived with her, growing inside of her, squeezing when she least expected to feel so choked. It floored her every time, leaving her dizzy and weak and forgetful. And she knew this wasn't a healthy way to live.

Then there was the fact that both of the men she was interested in were here. And, yes. She was interested. No matter what she'd said to Kaylie and Luna about having no time for a relationship. That much was true, but it didn't keep her from wanting to explore the difference a man might make.

Uh-huh. Wasn't that what had gotten her into trouble all those years ago? Hadn't her curiosity about a man, a boy, been the very reason Dakota had ended up behind bars? Hadn't she learned her lesson? Getting involved with a man, with two men, with three or ten . . . The number wasn't the issue.

She had no filter when it came to letting things go too far. Except she didn't believe that. Maybe as a teen, growing up in a home where parenting had not been a priority . . . But even in those days she'd known right from wrong, though it hadn't exactly done her—or Dakota—any good, had it?

"It looked like you might be having a party for one. I didn't want to interrupt."

"A *pity* party for one," she said, her pulse quickening, hating that anyone had seen her, but more so that it had been Oliver to catch her nursing this mood she was having more and more trouble sloughing off.

He leaned his elbows on the railing beside her, then narrowed his gaze and stared across the street in the same direction she'd been staring. "Are you not happy with the progress on the annex? I saw the heavy equipment—clearing the space for the greenhouses, I guess?"

"I am." Though she wouldn't be completely happy until it was done.

"And the cottage?"

"That's going more slowly, but well enough, too."

"Did you miss out on a cupcake?"

"No," she said, and found a smile lightly teasing her mouth. "I'm just not happy about the lack of progress with other things."

"Anything I can help with?"

She shook her head. "Can you make time move faster?"

He was silent for a long moment, weighing what she'd said. She was struck with the sense that he wanted to fix what she couldn't, but all he said was, "I don't mean to pry."

"I don't mind. It's the thing with my brother, Dakota."

"Right. You were going to hire Kaylie's investigator."

"We're meeting next week." She shrugged, stared into her drink. "He's in demand. It's the holidays. I need to ask Santa to stuff my stocking with patience."

Oliver was silent for a moment, his margarita glass empty. When Angelo popped out with a tray asking if they'd like another, Indiana shook her head, no longer feeling the need, but Oliver switched his empty for a full.

"I always get oranges in mine," he said after Angelo was gone.

"Oranges?" she asked, having to backtrack to their conversation. His stocking, yes. Not his margarita.

He laughed, thumbing at the salt on the rim of his glass. The gesture had Indiana swallowing, even when she knew he was unaware of the sensual motion. "Not valley oranges. Or navels or Valencias. Blood oranges. Imported from Italy or Spain."

"Fancy schmancy," she said, teasing him. She couldn't imagine growing up living the life he had.

"Half the time they weren't even any good. I'd much rather have had a Ruby Red grapefruit, but our parents, our mother really, wanted us to broaden our horizons. Texas fruit wasn't good enough."

Strangely, having never met Merrilee Gatlin, Indiana had heard enough rumors that she wasn't surprised by Oliver's tale. "Sometimes it's not," she said. "I've bought plenty of boxes of valley oranges from FFA fund-raisers, only to use most in the garbage disposal as air fresheners."

He grinned at that, the quirky little lift of his lips that showed off his dimples. "I suppose you're right. Oscar never wanted . . ."

The grin faded. His hand tightened on the glass he then brought to his mouth and halfway drained. The pain he lived with . . . At least her brother wasn't trapped in his body, confined to bed, fed through tubes, unaware. She reached over and took hold of Oliver's free hand, laced their fingers together, and squeezed.

After a moment he squeezed back, and then they stood there, unspeaking, listening to the music and the chatter and the laughter swirling through the room behind them. She wasn't sure what to think, sharing this intimacy, even a fairly simple one, with a man like Oliver Gatlin. Especially with the moment that had just passed between them not being simple at all.

Strange that of all things they were both dealing with brothers. Not that her problems held a candle to his, but it was nice to be able to offer him a shoulder. Doing so left her feeling not quite so sorry for herself. She needed that. A lot. Especially now, after Will's strange behavior that had her—unironically—ignoring his admonition and regretting how they'd left things.

God, she was tired.

"It's late," she finally said when it became clear Oliver was done talking, and freed her hand from his. "I should get going."

"Let me drive you home."

She shook her head. "You're very sweet, but I've got my things in my car. I'm staying over at Kaylie's and—"

"Then let me drive you there. We'll get your things, and Ten can bring you back for your car in the morning."

"If you're sure," she finally said, and when he nodded, she realized she wasn't ready for her time with him to end.

They said their good-byes separately, though she couldn't imagine their leaving at the same time wasn't obvious to everyone—not just to her brother, who scowled, or to Kaylie and Luna, who both grinned like fools. Indiana thought back to the advice her two friends had given her to see what the days ahead would bring from her admirers. Admirers. Ha. Was that what Will and Oliver were?

She did feel rather like the heroine in a Jane Austen novel, caught between two heroes equal parts brooding and enigmatic and handsome . . .

Less than fifteen minutes later, Oliver pulled to a stop in Kaylie's driveway behind her red Jeep. The house was dark, save for a light in the third-floor turret, though no doubt Magoo was waiting in the kitchen to see who had arrived.

"Do you have a dog?" Indiana asked, because she wasn't ready to go in.

"Actually, I do. She was, or is, my mother's dog, but she seems to prefer my company."

Funny. "What's her name? Your dog?"

"Susan," he said, and Indiana started to laugh, only to have Oliver lean close and stop her.

His kiss was nothing like Will's, and that was the only thought she spared for the man who'd kissed her first. Oliver swept her away until she forgot where they were, why they were here, everything but his mouth pressed softly to hers, coaxing and gentle and so very insistent. Yet his urging never had her feeling uneasy at all.

What she felt was cherished, treasured, and

hungry for more than the front seat of his car allowed. Which meant it was a very good thing she hadn't invited him in for a nightcap. *O, that way madness lies*. And madness she did not need; her life had known plenty.

But something told her this rush of fluttering wings tickling her skin was a different sort of insanity. One she didn't want to miss when it might never come again. And so she pulled him closer, and breathed him in, stunned by the desire rising so fiercely between them.

This was a complication, this physical attraction to a man she'd already determined was out of her league. But he was here, and he wanted her. *He wanted her*. And his want was so controlled she couldn't stand it. She ached to find a loose thread in his façade and pull until he unraveled, to see him come undone. To be there when he could no longer hold back and let go.

Madness, she thought again, because she'd been here before, and his wanting her meant nothing, yet believing that diminished everything about this moment. And she wouldn't allow herself to conflate the present with the past. She would enjoy this, every moment, every touch of his fingertips, his whiskered cheek, his tongue.

His breath against her cheek was labored. His heart pushed into her palm, where it lay against his chest, with each beat. He was not unaffected. Of that she was sure. Yet he seemed more intent on the things going on with her: the rapid rise and fall of her breasts against the squared neck of her costume, the sounds she couldn't keep in the back of her throat no matter how hard she tried.

"Let's go inside," she said.

"I'll walk you to the door, but then I need to go."

Wait a minute. "So . . . You don't want to . . ."

He laughed, a deep, throaty sound that answered her better than words. "Of course I want to, but my car being here and me being with you behind closed doors . . ." He shook his head, regretful. "I don't think your brother finding us together is a good idea."

That, she couldn't argue with. But still . . . She was going to go into the house, and he was going to . . . just leave? "I can't decide if you're looking out for me, or looking out for yourself."

His grin widened. "Let's call it a little bit of both."

Because all is fair in love and war?

They sat there for a moment after that, neither one moving, neither one speaking, his gaze holding hers, or vice versa, yet neither one able to let go. It was a strange sort of tension, full of unfinished business and this fragile intimacy and questions waiting unanswered in the wings.

And still they sat there, breathing, the motor humming, Indiana flexing the fingers of one hand in the square-dance tiers of her skirt, Oliver flexing his around the steering wheel, until she couldn't take it anymore.

She beat him to the punch by exiting the car first, but he grabbed her bag from the backseat before she could reach for it. They walked to the house, Indiana pulling open the screen when they arrived and listening to Magoo snuffle on the other side.

"Thanks for seeing me home. And for . . ." She left the sentence dangling, closing her hand around the overnighter's handles.

He held tight for a moment, then let go. "You don't have to thank me for that."

She shrugged, doing her best to appear nonchalant when she thought she might be embarrassed. "Seems like the thing to do."

"I'll see you again soon?"

I certainly hope so was what she wanted to say, but keeping up the ruse told him, "I imagine so. I'll be at the annex a lot over the next few weeks."

His crooked smile made clear that wasn't what he'd meant, but he didn't say anything more. All he did was touch his hand to her cheek, then turn for his car, waiting at his door until she opened hers and went inside.

Only after she'd closed it behind her did she hear him leave, his headlights cutting across the kitchen as he backed out of the drive; then the room went silent and dark.

INDIANA

Growing up with two older brothers was a blessing as much as a curse, though Tennessee and Dakota did most of the cursing, and I blessed my lucky stars I never had to take out the trash.

Something about all my girlfriends thinking our house was the best one for sleepovers and pool parties got on my brothers' nerves. Like having dozens of girls throwing their bikini-clad selves in front of them was such a hardship. They had the pick of the crop.

If anyone suffered a hardship growing up, I did. A girl has two brothers with heartthrob faces and hard bodies, and it's nearly impossible to tell true friends from fair-weather. Girls would drop by to study. Girls would drop by to borrow my Incubus CDs.

Girls would drop by to see who else might've dropped by, because someone always had. As much as Tennessee and Dakota drew females like flies, our home was like a watering hole for both sexes. Predators as well as prey.

See, we had the "cool" parents. Parents who didn't set curfews, who enforced only what rules fit conveniently into *their* schedules. Ours were the parents all of our friends—mine and my brothers', true and fair-weather—wanted for their own.

That's because they didn't know what it was like growing up being *air quotes* RAISED *air quotes* by Drew and Tiffany Keller. I often thought harpy-eagle parents did better jobs caring for their chicks, plucking monkeys from the jungle canopy to feed their young.

Rather than killing for sustenance, our parents liked to save things. To fix things. To support causes. The ones they most enjoyed backing were those guaranteeing photo ops and sound bites—even if they came across as crunchy airheads, which I'm certain they did, and they no doubt had the organizations they championed cringing every time they opened their mouths. They were as oblivious as they were uninformed, though they swore otherwise on the recycled soles of their vegan shoes.

Don't get me wrong. From a kid's point of view, my brothers and I had a wonderful childhood. We were spoiled within an inch of our teeth. It was all about our self-esteem, our parents told us. No child should be made to feel lesser. No child should go without a trophy, and no trophy should be bigger than any other. Every child should receive encouragement and praise, even if said child, as a five-year-old, scored the winning soccer goal for the opposing team because she knew nothing of the rules.

It was the effort that counted, right? The

camaraderie and the teamwork and most of all, the having fun.

Right.

That makes me sound ungrateful, or disrespectful maybe, but mostly I just wanted life to be like Fox News: "Fair and Balanced." Ha. When has life ever been fair? Or Fox News . . . never mind.

Though I would never have admitted it to any of the trues or fair-weathers, I wanted a curfew. I wanted my TV watching restricted, my homework checked. I wanted someone to tell me I could not buy that CD with the explicit lyrics if I could not defend their purpose. Someone to ask to speak to the parents hosting the end-of-school pool party rather than taking my word it would be chaperoned. Someone to care.

I did not like being given so many choices. I wanted a compass.

I wanted to be parented. And, well, to be loved; weren't they one and the same?

I can't say either of my brothers shared my viewpoint; they tried everything and got away with everything, which made them try to get away with even more. Testing limits has always been part of being a teen, but Tennessee and Dakota's concept of doing so went too far. I knew it. They knew it. And yet . . .

Was it because they were boys? And boys would be boys, as it were? Or was it a deeper need to challenge our parents? Some sort of test I didn't understand? Whether or not they planned their escapades, or discussed their pranks, they never shared any of their shenanigans with me.

Then again, I was two years younger than Tennessee, female, the source of the constant stream of girls who got on their nerves as well as the ones who climbed into their beds. And the ones who caused trouble. For Tennessee, that had been Shelley James.

For Dakota, Thea Clark.

Thea made no bones about why she picked me to hang out with. She played at being my friend so she could get to Dakota. And she happened to be one of the ones he let close. Closer than a fourteen-year-old girl needed to be to a sixteen-year-old boy, but what happens in a teen boy's bedroom, stays in a teen boy's bedroom. Right?

Oh, wait. It doesn't. Everybody knows.

Thea was a year ahead of me and three inches taller than me, but my seventh grade volleyball team often practiced with her eighth. My brothers were both in high school by then, and both on their way to being big baseball stars. I don't think our parents knew what to do, having three athletes instead of three civics enthusiasts and tree huggers. The fact that we sold candy to raise money nearly sent their green hearts into cardiac arrest.

Why weren't we selling seedlings to replenish

trees lost to thoughtless development? Or dishes made of biodegradable sugarcane, or plant-based household cleaners?

Why weren't we collecting donations for Mercy Ships, or some other charitable organization, contributing the bulk and setting aside a small percentage for whatever our sports programs thought was more important than improving the quality of life for thousands of children in third-world countries?

They loved Thea, though. They really loved Thea, and it wasn't hard to see why. She was a master manipulator and gorgeous to boot. I'd inherited my mother's freckles and dark cloud of coarse hair. Tennessee and Dakota pulled their genes from our father's side, as if Ian Somerhalder and Matt Bomer had had kids.

Thea looked more like Dakota's sister than I did, but their relationship wasn't familial at all. She used him; this much I knew to be true, because she made no effort to hide it. And I'm certain, because he was a sixteen-year-old male, he used her as often as she let him. Considering *they* disappeared into *his* room almost as soon as *she* came to see *me,* it wasn't hard to imagine the using going on.

Except, being a brand-new teen, I wanted to be like Thea. I wanted her confidence, her attitude; at the time, it never occurred to me that her behavior was all for show. A bid for the attention she didn't get at home. A plea for someone to save her. Unfortunately, Dakota wasn't even capable of saving himself, much less Thea. None of us were. We hadn't been given but life's most basic, and perfectly clichéd, instructions.

Wash your hands. Brush your teeth. Get a good night's sleep and good grades. Do unto others as you would have them do unto you. Most of all, be kind to your winged, webfooted, finned, and furred friends.

When it came to making any sort of meaningful decisions, we were on our own. Our parents did nothing but look the other way. Or so it seemed at the time. Especially the last week of school before semester break the year I was in seventh grade. The year Tennessee and Dakota, with Thea's help, got it into their heads to tip the outcome of the high school's football play-off game our way.

It was a simple plan, really, with a part Thea was born to play: seductress. All she had to do was tempt the opposing team's quarterback into the right car after the pep rally for a little pregame warm-up courtesy of her mouth. If he'd been older, or wiser, or less of a slave to what Thea could do with her tongue, things would've turned out differently.

As it was, two well-to-do twin brothers, seniors and delinquents both, whom Dakota had no trouble convincing to help, were waiting. They drove the kid, bound and gagged, to Clovis, New

Mexico, and stranded him there—no car, no money, no mobile phone, no pants, no shoes, no ID. Then they, having worn masks the whole time, continued on to Colorado for a ski vacation with their family, who was already there.

It was a near-perfect crime, and could've been a lot worse. The boy wasn't hurt, or left tied up, and only had to travel five miles for help. A high school senior, an athlete, a humiliated and pissed-off teen, he got to a phone in under an hour, but he missed the game, not to mention the win.

If Thea hadn't been wearing Dakota's sophomore letterman's jacket, he would never have been suspected of being involved. There wasn't proof he had been, and even Thea denied knowing anything about the boys who'd pulled her out of the car and driven the quarterback away.

But having their son questioned by the police was too much for our parents. They were nervous wrecks for days after, and blamed Dakota for putting the family through the stressful ordeal, without considering—or caring about—his guilt or his innocence or even his reputation, only their inconvenience, their time wasted with something so trivial when they had petition drives to organize, protests to attend.

And instead of administering some sort of appropriate discipline, they gave Dakota (and by proximity, me and Tennessee, too) the silent treatment. And they frowned a lot. As if they were the teenagers, their sulking intended as some kind of punishment. The reality was a different color. All three of us loved it when we didn't have to hear them talk.

They did very little talking the two weeks we were out of school on Christmas break that year. What Thea and Dakota had done was Big Bad. They couldn't process it. They couldn't deal. They went about their merry way, saving growing things and living things and frozen water—basically, anything and everything that didn't have an opinion, a mind of its own, that couldn't inconvenience or embarrass them.

I also can't help but wonder: If our parents hadn't failed in the biblical admonition to spare not the rod for fear of spoiling the child, would things have worked out differently for Tennessee, Dakota, and me? Because seeing Thea Clark with Dakota is why I did what I did with Robby Hunt.

I never thought twice about it. I'd never been given a reason why I should. Yet my decision, the poorest, most ill informed I ever made in my life, changed everything for all of us. Our futures, our relationships, nothing that mattered was left untouched.

Thanks to me.

Chapter Eight

"Thanks, Derek. Call me as soon as you come up with anything, no matter how small."

"Will do, Ollie. Take care."

Oliver swiped the "End Call" command on his phone's screen, then tapped the device to his chin a couple of times before laying it on his desk. It had been a while since he'd spent any time in this room, preferring of late to work in the arts center kitchen.

His mother had set up his home office when he'd come home from Rice, decorating it to match the rest of the house rather than his personality. The desk was an antique, too large for his needs and too dark for his taste and too heavy to move without help. Anyway, doing so would've had his mother fearing she hadn't pleased him.

That had been two years after Oscar's accident, and Oliver hadn't been able to tell his mother no, or criticize her efforts, or bring in a decorator to replace the drapes and the art, the furniture and the rug. A decorator who understood space, symmetry, lighting. Color. He hadn't planned to use the room, so he let it go. And when it became obvious he had no clue what to do with his degree—or his life—having it had come in handy.

It was also handy for making phone calls

without being overheard. Especially with the likelihood of Tennessee Keller working today at the Caffey-Gatlin Academy. This thing with Indiana wanting to find her brother . . .

It wasn't his business, Oliver mused, crossing his hands behind his head and leaning back in his chair. She'd turned down his offer to help. But after last night in his car, he was hard-pressed not to want to see things go her way, and Derek could make that happen.

Oliver didn't know what he'd been thinking, taking their kiss where he had, seeking an intimacy he doubted their relationship was ready for. He wasn't even sure this thing between them had been destined to be more than a friendship, and now one he may have screwed up because . . .

Why? He was curious? Impatient? He had no self-control? He hadn't had sex in months? He swiveled his chair side to side, lost for an answer. He had no idea what he'd been thinking, and no explanation for his behavior other than the obvious: there was an undeniable chemistry between them.

He found Indiana unconventionally attractive. Most of the women he dated, and he used the term in the most casual way, were ones he knew from his mother's social circle. He didn't have much of a circle of his own. He worked for himself, keeping only the hours he wanted to, and spent a whole lot of time alone.

He went to the gym alone, though he had buddies he met there for racquetball. He dined alone, though those same buddies were forever trying to talk him into joining them. Occasionally, he did, and there was usually an unattached woman in the group intended to round out the number. Intended, too, to rouse his interest.

It had been a long time since his interest had been roused beyond the superficial. He wasn't celibate, but the women he took to bed knew the score. He wasn't looking for anything long-term, and he hated the idea that he'd ruined things with Indiana.

Yes, she'd let him touch her, and he would never have done so if she'd given him the slightest hint of being uncomfortable. Honestly, her receptiveness had surprised him. Especially with her history. He was quite certain she'd surprised herself, too. And that was the thing, that connection. It didn't happen often. At least not for him.

So pursue it or let it go? He didn't want to risk their friendship when he had his physical needs covered, though he had to admit he was less interested these days in sex for the sake of sex. Funny thing that, when he still wasn't ready to commit to something more.

His calling his family's investigator . . . He didn't want to think of it as a thank-you for Indiana allowing him so close. And he certainly didn't want her to think he was paying her for said privilege.

In fact, he couldn't think of a way to explain his interference without it coming across as an insult. Which meant he'd have to keep his involvement to himself, then later, if things went as he expected them to, share the good news.

Except that didn't really sit well, either—

"Were you talking to Derek Wilborn?"

"I was," he said, standing as his mother entered the room and interrupted his unproductive musings. It was a habit instilled early, his standing, that show of respect and good manners. Over time, the respect had lessened, he hated to say, though the habit and manners remained.

"Whatever for?" she asked, fiddling with a paperweight, then his fountain pen, before arranging her slim skirt and sitting in one of the room's two leather wingback chairs.

His parents had turned to Derek dozens of times over the years—usually in situations they could have taken care of themselves, or that were none of their business, or didn't matter: Who was buying the house at the end of the street? Where did they come by their money? Who were their friends? Where did they send their children to school? What charities did they donate to? How did they vote? What church did they attend?

His father couldn't be pulled from his art to dig for the info himself, though Oliver was certain that his father wasn't the one to care. And his mother didn't want to get her hands dirty with things that truly mattered, much less the mundane. She had people for that. She had people for everything. He couldn't remember a time when she hadn't, and his memory went way back.

"A friend of mine isn't having much luck with the investigator she hired," he said, returning to his chair. "I thought Derek might do a better job for her."

"This friend is a her?"

"Yes, Mother. I do have female friends."

She looked at him askance, her lips pursed. "Female opportunists, you mean."

In some cases, he'd have to agree. But not this time. "Trust me. She's not the least bit interested in the Gatlin name or the Gatlin money."

"Oh, none of them are." His mother fluttered a hand, the one where she wore only her wedding band and a silver cuff bracelet, a birthday gift Oscar had given her the last week he'd been truly alive. "Until they realize what you're actually worth."

Huh. Turned out he was not in the mood for this. "Indiana has no interest in me at all." Though what they'd done in his car begged to differ.

"Indiana? What kind of name is Indiana? Do I know her? Who are her parents?"

Her parents were Drew and Tiffany Keller. They lived in Round Rock. They spent their time and money on creatures who swam in the deep, on melting ice, on beetles, now homeless, who'd lived in trees felled for expansion.

He'd discovered those things on his own, after learning what Indiana wanted him to know.

And now, whether or not she'd realized the truth, she was following in their footsteps, saving one brother from himself, another from his vagabond life, herself from being alone, and her bees.

"You wouldn't know them. Or her," he said, picking up his phone and clipping it to his belt. "Though maybe you've heard of her brother. He's been a general contractor in Hope Springs for ten years. Tennessee Keller."

"Oh, Ollie," she said, crossing her legs. "What business would I have with a general contractor? Tod takes care of whatever the house might need."

Ah, yes. Her people. "Hmm. Since most of his crew is made up of ex-cons, I thought he might be worthy of some gossip."

"Ex-cons?" she asked, having recovered from her gasp. "And you're expecting Derek Wilborn to help these people?"

Did she really think Derek didn't get his hands dirty working for her? "Not the ex-cons, Mother. The sister of the contractor who hires them."

"I don't like it." She shook her head, not a silver hair out of place. "I don't like it at all."

"You don't have to. This isn't any of your business."

131

"If you took Derek off something he's doing for me, it certainly is," she said, her lips mewed in distaste.

"Was there anything else?" He was done discussing Indiana with his mother.

"Yes." Hands laced in her lap, she sat forward as if finally interested in the conversation. "I wanted to see if you would be bringing a plus-one to Thanksgiving this year."

Might as well get the bad news out of the way. "Actually, I won't be home for Thanksgiving this year."

"Oh." She paused, taken aback. "I wasn't aware you were traveling."

"I'm not," he said, and crossed his legs, bracing himself for the inevitable battle. "I've been invited to dinner at Two Owls."

"Two Owls?" she asked, and almost looked like an owl herself when she blinked. "What in the world is Two Owls?"

Had she always sounded this condescending, and he just hadn't noticed? "The café on the corner of Second and Chances. The big blue Victorian."

She let that sink in, considering him as she did, her wide eyes narrowing, her blinks slowing. "You're going to eat Thanksgiving dinner at a café?"

The look on her face would've had him laughing had she not been his mother. For all her faults, which seemed strangely conspicuous today, he did love her, and hurting her was not something he enjoyed. "Kaylie is serving early afternoon, so I should be able to get back here for at least part of the evening."

"Oliver. How could you?" She collapsed back into the chair. "You know what Thanksgiving means to me."

He did, but it didn't mean the same to him. The holiday had been Oscar's favorite, not his. It had been years since he'd actually looked forward to the day. Spending it with Indiana Keller and all of her friends . . . Yeah, he was looking forward to that.

"I do," he said. "But I'm not seeing anyone, so I'd be an extra with no plus-one, and would have very little in common with anyone on your guest list."

"That is not true. Gordon Harvey and Barry Cohen both work in finance."

Gordon Harvey and Barry Cohen were bankers long past their prime, with no interest in updating their antiquated ways, or in anything but padding their pockets. "They work with money, not in finance. And I'm down to a single, nonpaying client now." Though he kept the fact that it was the Caffey-Gatlin Academy to himself.

"Nonpaying? Oliver, you're a financial adviser. How is it going to look to future clients when you can no longer provide current references?"

He was only a financial adviser because at eighteen he'd been the oldest son bearing the weight of family expectations. And because two years later, his brother's BMW had tumbled down a ravine. "Finance was your idea, Mother. Not mine."

She was out of her chair and pacing now, her impatient gestures punctuating her words. "It was also what your counselor recommended based on the proficiency you showed in your aptitude tests. You, more than most, knew that a career in art was no guarantee of a stable living."

The irony was, he didn't need to make a living. He never had, and his mother knew it, too. But then none of this was about what he did with his life. She'd lost one son to his art; Oscar had used the excuse of a music workshop to run off with his cellist lover. She didn't want to lose another. "I'm not Dad. And I'm not Oscar—"

"Oliver!"

"I've given a decade of my life to a field that doesn't interest me in the least," he said as he got to his feet. It was time she knew the decision he'd come to earlier this month, having learned the truth about Oscar and Sierra and the accident. "I'm not sure what I'm going to do next, but I'm leaving my options open."

"Is this the influence of your new friends and their . . . arts center?"

"Mother, I'm thirty-two years old. I'm past

being influenced by peer pressure, or being pressured by my peers at all." But he wasn't past being able to see how happy Tennessee and Kaylie were, working at what they loved. Luna and Angelo, too. And how happy Indiana was, expanding her business, even if it meant catching Tennessee's grief.

Oliver wanted a piece of that. The happiness as much as the friends who were as close as family. He'd been the dutiful son when his mother had most needed him to be. But he'd put his own life on hold to do so.

No, he wasn't lying in a bed in a rehab facility where he would never in a million years be rehabilitated in any significant way. But he was wasting away as surely as his brother, and it was time he put such foolishness to a stop.

And then it hit him. Indiana Keller was the first person he'd ever wanted to talk to about what had happened with Oscar. About how he'd failed to protect his brother. About how those failures had cost his brother his life.

Chapter Nine

Early November kept Indiana as busy as the rest of the year, and for the first time in memory she wished her schedule allowed for more downtime. Or really for any downtime at all. She found herself in the fields as often as in the green-houses, and in the office more often than she liked.

All of that made it tough getting to the annex in Hope Springs, which meant she couldn't oversee the daily changes being made to her cottage. She trusted Keller Construction, and Will Bowman specifically, and both he and her brother most likely appreciated her not being around to nitpick their work to death.

And she did miss seeing Will, though in a completely different way than she missed seeing Oliver. Over the last few months, Will had become someone she could trust to give her straight answers, though as with his comment about being safe but never sorry, she was often left having to parse out what he'd meant.

Then there was Oliver, and thinking about him, about Halloween, about the very fortuitous choice she'd made to wear thigh-highs as part of her costume . . . Except doing so reduced what she felt for him to so much less than he deserved. He, too, was honest with her, never soft-pedaling his replies.

They'd talked a couple of times since that night in his car, their schedules conflicting any time one suggested dinner or drinks, and neither had managed to be at their respective places on Three Wishes Road at the same time as the other. But that was okay. In Oliver's case, absence did make the heart grow fonder, and their conversations allowed her to get to know him better without their physical attraction getting in the way.

But most of all she missed the days when she didn't have men on her mind. The worrying, the wondering, the what-ifs, the daydreams and imaginings, the fantasies, the recollections. The regrets. It had been that way for weeks now, for months, really, ever since she'd reconnected with Tennessee. Having done so meant she couldn't stop thinking about the reasons they'd lost touch in the first place. Reason, really, and his name was Robby Hunt.

Thoughts of Robby were the most unpleasant. She'd done a fairly good job over the years of keeping his memory at bay, but lately, as she worked to put her family back together, it wasn't as easy. And then, connected to Robby and Tennessee was Dakota, and her frustration over not knowing his whereabouts was all tangled up with her guilt and the self-hatred she doubted she'd ever be able to shed. Doing so would mean forgiving herself, and she was a long way from being able to do that.

On top of her issues with her brothers and her past was the kiss she'd shared with Will, and the intimacy she'd shared with Oliver, and what was she supposed to do when a relationship was the last thing she had time for? The last thing she wanted? How could she live in the moment when her choices, her history, the mistakes she'd made lived there, too, and took up so much room? Ha. Those who advocated being aware of the present hadn't accounted for overcrowding, had they?

Maybe she was just overthinking things. Maybe Luna and Kaylie were right and her past had her hesitant to take risks of a romantic nature, which made perfect sense. Could she really "roll with it" and "see what happens"? When both men made her think about life, and what she wanted, as much as what she didn't? She loved Will's bad-boy spontaneity. And she loved that upstanding Oliver Gatlin had his own bad-boy side.

With her background, it might seem strange she would find the trait attractive. Except for the fact that the boy who'd attempted to sexually assault her had been bad in the most unattractive of ways. And she hated thinking she might be looking at Will and Oliver as men worth knowing better simply because they were nothing like Robby Hunt.

One thing was certain, she mused, stepping from the cottage's hallway into the small eating nook. It was time to come clean with Tennessee about her search for Dakota, and not just because she'd promised Kaylie she would, but because he deserved to know.

And since Tennessee, not Will, was the one working in her kitchen today . . . *No time like the present.*

She took a deep breath and spilled. "I need to tell you something."

First he grunted. Then he asked, "Something I'm not going to like?"

Really? They were going to start this conversation on the wrong foot? "Why do you assume it's going to be something you don't like?"

Leaning over her sink, he shrugged. "Why else announce something instead of just saying it?"

"Fine. Whatever." She crossed her arms, stood her ground. "I'm going to find Dakota."

He swiveled slowly, but only his head, his hands holding the wrench he'd just fastened to the ancient faucet. A deep vee marred his forehead between his narrowed eyes. "Come again?"

"I've hired a private investigator to find Dakota."

"You hired a PI. Behind my back." They weren't even questions, but accusations.

Indiana did her best not to bristle—he was her brother, after all—but failed. "I hired a PI," she said, thinking it time to lay things on the line because, estrangement or not, they couldn't go on like this, his finding fault, her defending her life. "Did I tell you about it? No. I didn't tell you I bought Hiram's place either. Or that I used my part of Grandpa Keller's inheritance to start IJK Gardens. Again. My life. My decisions. My money. As happy as I am that we're here, together, this isn't about you."

Propping the wrench on the hot-water handle, Tennessee straightened, rubbing a frustrated hand over his jaw. "That came out wrong. I wasn't accusing you of hiding it."

"That's what it sounded like," she said, surprised when she shoved her hands in her skirt pockets to find them shaking. She had been hiding it, but she did not want to argue with her brother. She loved him, and she'd lost so much time with him, and she didn't want to ever lose any more.

"You should've told me."

"Why? So you could've talked me out of it?" A guilty tic popped in his temple, and it made her sad. "That's what you would've done, isn't it? Or at least tried to do." Because she wouldn't have let him. She'd meant what she said. This was what she had to do.

"I don't know—"

"I do. I'm not you, Tennessee, though really," she added with a sigh, accepting her share of the blame, "I'm just as bad, aren't I? I didn't come to see you. I didn't call you. I didn't reach out—"

"Yeah, you did." He smiled, but it took the coaxing of his memories. "When I came to your high school graduation."

She'd forgotten about that, Tennessee being the only one there for her, Dakota in prison, their parents who knew where. After the ceremony, he'd taken her out to dinner. A small group of her classmates had begged her to go with them. It

140

was party time. They were free. The beach and the booze were calling.

She would've had a whole lot of fun, but she'd had more spending the evening with her brother. It was one of the last times they'd talked before drifting so far apart. "Do you realize how long ago that was? I barely remember that girl."

"I remember everything about her," he said, turning to lean against the counter's edge, his ankles crossed, his arms crossed, too. "Especially how much lasagna and garlic bread she put away."

"Are you kidding?" Stepping forward, she punched him playfully in the arm. "It had meat in it. And real cheese. And I was starving."

"I noticed that," he said, and before she could tease back, he added, "I don't think I'd ever seen you so thin."

She'd been thin?

"I didn't know if Mom and Dad weren't feeding you," he went on to say, and shrugged. "Or if maybe you were in a bad place over Robby."

"It wasn't an eating disorder," she assured him. "Just senior year. And my bad place wasn't about Robby. It was about Dakota." Though the two would always be connected in her mind.

"Yeah. I wasn't exactly in a good place myself."

"I hate that we weren't able to see him more often," she said, walking to the refrigerator and pulling it open just to have something to do. "And then to have him disappear like he did." She

141

closed her eyes, closed the door, leaned her forehead against it, then turned to face her brother again. "I hope I didn't wait too long to start looking, and that he hasn't covered his tracks. I just expected him to show back up, you know?"

Tennessee nodded. Then kept nodding as if it helped him think, or jarred loose the things he wanted to say. "I wish there was another way to do this. I can't stand the idea of you getting hurt all over again."

There was no *all over again*. She hadn't stopped being hurt. "If I can't find him, you mean?"

"Or if what you find, what *we* find, isn't good."

She liked hearing him say *we*. She liked it a lot. "I have to know. One way or the other. If things aren't great, I'll deal. But if he's okay, I need him to know how sorry I am. That I love him for what he did, and hate that he felt he had to do it."

Tennessee pushed away from the counter and walked to the back door. It was open, the screen letting the autumn breeze through, and he turned his head to look at her, his expression sadly resigned. "If he hadn't, I would have, you know. He just got there first. And he had a better swing."

She wanted to laugh. She wanted to smile. Instead, tears welled and she had a hard time holding them back as she stepped forward and wrapped him in her arms. "If I recall correctly, you weren't too shabby yourself."

"Shabby enough that these days I'm swinging a hammer instead of a bat," he said, hugging her tightly.

She leaned back far enough to meet his gaze. "You do a whole lot more than swing a hammer."

"It's not the same," he said, heading back to the sink, all business again. "He was supposed to be here. Keller Brothers Construction. We talked about it forever. And now . . . I'm just a man with a wrench."

They both went silent after that, Tennessee breaking the faucet's seal and removing it, tossing the aged and useless parts in a barrel he'd brought in for trash. That done, he wedged himself under the cabinet to disconnect whatever it was keeping the sink in place.

There was something about watching him work that set her at ease. He knew what he was doing. Not a move he made was hesitant, or wasted. As if being "just a man with a wrench" was the lid on a bottomless well of knowledge and experience, all the things he'd done for himself that he'd wanted to do with Dakota. And she couldn't help but wonder how much of who he was now was Kaylie's influence, or if this was who he'd become on his own.

"So you're not going to fight me on this?" She needed to get back to Buda, but she wasn't leaving until she was sure this was settled.

"Why would I fight you?" he asked, tossing out

clips and old rubber washer things and nuts and bolts and pipes. "He's my brother, too. I should've gone looking for him a long time before now. I shouldn't have left it up to you."

"Because I'm not capable?" she asked, frowning.

His snort echoed from beneath the sink. "No, silly. Because I owe him a huge apology."

"It can't be as big as the one I owe him."

Scooting out from the cabinet, he stopped what he was doing and glanced over. "So we're going to compare our failings now? Because I'd really rather not."

If he only knew . . . "No. But maybe we can work together? I'd like that a lot better than you thinking you need to run the show."

"When have I ever . . . Never mind," he said as he started gathering up the detritus. "Just tell me what you need from me. And keep me in the loop. Oh, and I will be paying my half of the investigator's bill."

Her heart swelled. This is what she'd wanted. The two of them on the same page. "Are you sure?"

"It won't be a problem." He grabbed a red shop rag from the counter and wiped it over a wet spot on the floor. "I'll just allocate what I'm not paying Will."

That didn't sound good. "Why aren't you paying Will?"

He held out his arms as if asking her to look

around her. "Do you see him here? He doesn't work, he doesn't get paid."

Come to think of it, there hadn't been much going on at her cottage since their dinner date in Austin. And that had been before Halloween. "Have you talked to him?"

Her brother gave her another look. "Does he answer his phone?"

That didn't surprise her. "What about calling Manny?"

But Tennessee shook his head. "I'm not ready to go there."

"This may be a crazy question," she said, tendrils of something bothersome and anxious twining tightly along her limbs, "but have you gone by his loft to check on him? Could be he's sick?"

"I don't think it's that. Luna and Oliver saw him yesterday when they were at the warehouse. He seemed to be okay then."

"Wait." Had she heard that right? "Luna was there with Oliver? Why?"

"He's renting out part of her loft for something. You'll have to ask one of them."

Luna, maybe. She wasn't quite ready to see Oliver. Which was ridiculous after how close they'd been, the way he'd touched her, how much she'd enjoyed making out in his car. If what they'd done was even called making out . . .

"Are you blushing?"

"Of course not," she said, gathering her hair away from her face and moving into the breeze from the back door. "It's just warm in here."

Tennessee grunted at that. "It'll be a whole lot warmer come summer, and you'll do a whole lot better cooling the place with a small central unit. That thing in the living room window isn't even safe for rats to nest in."

A change of subject. Thank goodness. "Believe it or not, I don't have rats, and I'm guessing that's because I seem to have a cat."

"Not Hiram's old orange tabby."

She pictured the cat's black-and-white markings, the tiny feet that looked like they had on socks, and wondered how feral was feral. "No, this one's a little bowlegged tuxedo. Looks like he, or she, could beat the crap out of an elephant."

"Then you'll want to keep her around," Tennessee said. "Rats are as fond of honey as the next guy."

Great. That was exactly what she needed to hear.

"Why aren't you at work?"

"Hello to you, too, Ms. Keller," Will said, leaning against the loft's elevator frame as Indiana tugged open the recalcitrant accordion gate.

He was up and dressed, save for his steel-toed boots. He'd had coffee for breakfast and again for lunch. But he hadn't gone looking for his truck keys, which he'd need in order to leave, and wasn't sure he had looking—or leaving—in him today.

Ennui, he supposed it was, though he'd be more inclined to call it self-indulgence, perhaps even self-pity. Except he wasn't really feeling sorry for himself. He wasn't feeling much of anything at all.

That was the problem with closing off one's emotions in order to survive. Because now that he was a free man, he felt just as imprisoned as he had behind bars. And he wasn't quite sure how to fix that. Or if he wanted to.

He'd been thinking a lot about leaving town, but there was the issue of his parole. He could talk to Manny, see what—if anything—could be worked out to keep him on the straight and narrow elsewhere, because he was just this close to being done with, well, giving a crap about getting back to real life.

He worked for a company based here. He owned property in a building that had been here longer than he'd been alive. He got along with the circle of people in Hope Springs he called friends. Whether they really were . . . What did he know about friends? What did he know about anything anymore?

Did he keep working for Ten at a job he did well? Did he return to school to finish his master's? Did he get his car out of storage where it had been for three years, now almost four, and go some place else? Anyplace else? Anywhere at all?

The woman standing in front of him would be the only one he would miss. He couldn't tell her how much. Neither could he tell her that he hadn't meant to kiss her. Or that he was sorry for letting his own regrets muck up Halloween.

He had meant to kiss her. He'd meant to for days, for weeks, for months. Since the first day they'd met. And he wasn't sorry about Halloween. Only that no matter what move he made, his king was going to get checkmated by Oliver Gatlin.

He'd have to chalk up whatever wasn't going to happen between them to bad timing: his finally getting out of prison, her finally reconnecting with Ten, Oliver Gatlin growing out of his years as a dick. Finally.

"Come in," he said, pushing himself out of the way as he realized she was standing there waiting.

She did, crossing the threshold of his very large and largely unfurnished loft for the very first time. "Why aren't you at work?" she repeated, hands at her hips as she turned to face him, frowning. "And why don't you have any furniture?"

"I have furniture." He walked past her into the center of the space, gestured grandly toward the

148

bar stools, the futon, the side table, and the lamp. "Please. Take a seat. Can I get you something to drink?"

Shaking her head as if dodging one of the bees she valued so much, she held up a hand, putting a stop to the mundanities. "I don't want to sit. And, thank you, but I don't want anything to drink. I want to know why you aren't at work."

He didn't have an answer for that. Unless he wanted to voice a repeat of his recent thoughts. "At work for Ten? Or at work for you?"

"At work. Period." Her frown deepened. "Are you not feeling well? Because you look terrible."

That made him smile. "I feel fine. The terrible just comes with the territory."

"And what territory is that?" she asked, crossing to his long wall of windows, then turning. "Are you going to start playing the part of woe-is-me ex-con?"

This was what he liked most about Indiana Keller. There was no using past crimes as excuses for present ones. Whatever she'd been through to cause her longtime estrangement from Ten, she didn't stand on it like a platform, and she didn't put up with anyone else trying it with their sins.

"I'm just tired," he said, plopping down on the futon and squaring one leg over the other.

Again with the shake of her head. Again with the hands at her hips. "Tired of what? Working for a living?"

That was something he didn't have to do, but she didn't know that. No one in Hope Springs knew that. He shrugged. "Bored, then. I'm just bored."

This time she swung her arms wide to the side. "With what? Work? Life? Not having furniture? Shopping for furniture? Because your history with prison aside, you've got one of the cushiest lives of anyone I know."

Cushy. Was that what this was? "Did Ten send you after me?"

"Tennessee would come after you himself if he was that worried," she said, looking out the window again.

That was probably true. "Then why are you asking me about work?"

"Because Tennessee needs to be spending his time at the arts center, and my cottage isn't going to remodel itself. Plus, I'd really like the annex finished so I can start planning for next year's schedule."

"I thought that was the point of a greenhouse," he said, stretching his arms along the futon's cushion. "No need for a schedule. Year-round temperature control."

"Not the growing schedule. *My* schedule." She came back to where he was sitting and perched her hip on the futon's corner, not too close, but not too far away. "Why are you being so . . . I don't know, contrary? After dinner the other night, I thought—"

150

"That I would be at your constant beck and call?" Because he needed to rid that idea from both their minds. His especially.

"No. Good grief. Why would you say that?" She held his gaze, a long moment of frowning, then looked down at her hands where her fingers were twined in her lap. "I don't understand you, is all. I thought after dinner I might. I mean, we talked for hours, and yet everything about you is still . . ."

"Still what?" he asked, when she dropped the sentence.

She took her time responding, as if weighing what she wanted to say, what would be safe to say, what he probably most needed to hear. In the end, she simply told him, "You, Will Bowman, are a mystery."

It really was a shame the chemistry between them was so one-sided. He was going to miss her when he was gone. "You didn't need to make a special trip to tell me that."

"I didn't," she said, bopping him on the knee. "I came to ask you about work. But if something's going on . . . Or if you need to talk . . ."

He didn't, he never would, but he still hated how perceptive she was. During dinner, he'd done such a good job keeping the conversation impersonal. He'd gone down his list: pop culture, politics, science and money and art.

Yet somehow his carefully manufactured coping

mechanism had gone awry. And he wasn't sure he'd got it all put back together again, à la Humpty Dumpty.

He reached over and chucked her on the chin. "Let's talk about what's going on in your life. Something besides the annex and the cottage, which, yeah . . . I need to get back to work on."

"Ah, you're assuming that like you, I have all the time in the world to chat. I do not," she said, and got to her feet, seeming to bounce with excitement. "But I do have a bit of exciting news."

"Hit me," he said, as he stood.

"I've hired a PI. Well, Tennessee and I have hired a PI. We want to see if we can find Dakota."

"Dakota. He's the other brother. The one who was in prison."

She nodded as she headed for the door. "We haven't seen him or heard from him since he got out, and now that I've reconnected with Tennessee . . ." Her hand on the elevator grate, she turned, smiled softly, shrugged. "I shouldn't have waited so long to look. He's family."

Yeah, well, that didn't necessarily mean anything, though he wasn't going to be the one to burst her bubble. Best if her brother was the one to do that. Meaning Dakota Keller would need to be found.

If nothing else, that was one thing Will could do.

Chapter Ten

A week later, having seen Will once at the cottage, and having talked briefly to Oliver in the middle of Three Wishes Road, both in their cars heading in opposite directions, Indiana was standing behind her desk in her IJK Gardens office, frowning down at a vendor invoice, when she realized she wasn't alone. She looked up, expecting one of her employees, or a fertilizer sales rep, or another vendor with an invoice that didn't look quite right.

Instead, the woman waiting just over the threshold . . . Well, she didn't belong on a farm. It was the first thing that came to mind. IJK Gardens was no place for pearls. Or pumps. Or a handbag with a designer label even Indiana recognized.

The whole package hit her like a punch to the gut. Something had to be wrong. She set down the invoice, reaching for her stapler to use as a paperweight, and asked, "May I help you?"

"I'm looking for an Indiana Keller."

An Indiana Keller? This was either going to be very good, or very, *very* bad. "I'm Indiana Keller. What can I do for you, Mrs. . . ."

"Gatlin." It was all she said. It was enough.

And it was bad. Definitely bad. Indiana stopped herself from reaching for the invoice again to have something to do with her hands. "You must be Oliver's mother."

"I am," the woman said, walking several steps into the room, looking around the office, disapproving of the mess. And of everything.

Indiana disapproved, too. She just never had time to straighten or clean or replace the broken guest chairs. Either one of them. "Well, then. I can't imagine you're here about anything to do with gardening. So this must be something about Oliver."

"What exactly are you doing with my son?" Merrilee Gatlin asked, her chin high, her nose higher, turning to look down at Indiana as if from a physical throne instead of the one in her mind.

"Doing with him? I'm not sure what you mean. We're friends. That's all." No need to explain about the kiss, or the bond over lost siblings they had in common that seemed to be drawing them close.

Oliver's mother took her in as if examining polygraph results. "You're saying you didn't ask him to hire a private investigator on your behalf?"

Indiana heard the words, but they took several long seconds to register. She had hired her own PI. Oliver knew that. Knew, too, that she'd turned down his offer to help her with her search for Dakota. Had he gone behind her back? Really?

Chest tight, she released the breath she'd been holding, filled her lungs with another, and said, "I did not, and if he did, this is the first I'm hearing of it."

But of course Merrilee couldn't take Indiana at her word and leave. Her handbag hung from her elbow and bounced against her hip as she crossed to the office's windows. They looked out at the farm's equipment-repair shop and warehouse storage building, at the greenhouses and small market building where she sold her extra inventory, and stocked jellies and relishes and pickled produce from local artisans.

To Indiana, the sight was the most impressive thing ever. She'd built her farm from the ground up, and her reputation had followed. The operation was small, but successful. She provided jobs, and quality organic produce, and made a comfortable enough living that she'd been able to buy the property in Hope Springs and expand.

Looking out the windows always had her saying, "I made this," but something told her Oliver's mother couldn't have cared less.

"He did. That's why I'm here. That's the *only* reason I'm here."

Of course it was. "As I said, I can't speak to what Oliver might have done—"

"There is no *might have*. I heard him speaking to our family's investigator."

Heard? Or overheard? "Then he's the one who'll

155

have to answer your questions." She could've said more, but no need to add ammunition to this woman's arsenal. And as to Oliver painting this target on her forehead . . .

What had he been thinking? She'd told him she didn't need his help, though maybe she should've used those exact words, because there had obviously been an incredible disconnect.

"How do you know Oliver?" His mother switched her handbag from one arm to the other, a silver cuff bracelet circling her wrist catching the light. "I can't imagine him coming all this way to buy produce."

Even though you came all this way to find out if he had? "I own the property across Three Wishes Road from the Caffey-Gatlin Academy. We met there one morning last month." And why in the world was she offering up so much information?

"That arts center," Merrilee began, waving her hand as if even the words were pesky flies, "is going to be the ruin of our family."

Then before she could add to the insult, Indiana interrupted to ask, "How so?"

Oliver's mother had been absently looking around the office, but her head came up sharply at that. "The very fact that you have to ask . . . He's there, even today, fiddling with their money when he should be handling the finances for one, if not several, of the companies who have courted him. He has no business wasting his time with this nonprofit. Just like you have no business keeping company with my son."

Keeping company? What? Was that like cavorting? Carousing? Canoodling? "Like I said, we're just friends."

"Were you aware that Oliver graduated cum laude from Rice University? That he was offered a position at one of Houston's most prestigious investment firms before he had his diploma in hand?"

"No. I wasn't aware." And even with what little she knew of Oliver, his credentials didn't surprise her. "But really, as impressive as those details are, they have nothing to do with me."

Merrilee pulled herself upright, her handbag close to her body, one foot turned out from the other in a stance that spoke of dance lessons and debutante balls. "Those details, as you call them, have everything to do with you."

"Mrs. Gatlin, please trust me when I say I have absolutely no designs on your son's name or his social standing or his obvious wealth. He's been spending time at the arts center, and that makes us neighbors in a way. And we're friends. We had breakfast one morning. I saw him on Halloween," she said, hoping the heat of the memory didn't show in her face. "But I saw a lot of other friends, too. Friends I've been known to share breakfast with. Friends with equally impressive credentials."

And it struck her then that Hope Springs was about friendship as much as it was about family. Her friends in Buda were for the most part connected to IJK Gardens—either employees, vendors from whom she bought supplies, or the artisans who sold their wares in her store. That didn't make her relationships with them stilted, or awkward, but it did have talk turning to business—and staying on business—almost every time.

In Hope Springs, talk of IJK Gardens, as well as that of Keller Construction and Patchwork Moon and Two Owls Café and the Caffey-Gatlin Academy, was peppered into conversations about family happenings and vacation plans and well-loved books. She liked that. No, she'd needed that. But where Oliver fit in . . .

"Then I suggest you set your sights on those friends and leave Oliver to his."

Okay. This was getting ridiculous. "Who Oliver spends his time with is really none of my business either."

"Either?" The word hung in the air, a gauntlet. "Was that directed at me?"

A worthy adversary, this one. "Oliver's thirty-two years old. I can't imagine you trying to run his life."

Merrilee gave a snorting sort of sound. "I suppose you'll be there at this café for Thanksgiving."

This really is killing her, isn't it? "I will. And

I'm very happy Oliver's decided to join us."

"Of course you are. Who cares about his abandoning years of family tradition?"

Huh. She hadn't been aware he'd had other plans. "Maybe he's decided it's time to start a tradition of his own."

"I'm sure he's decided nothing of the sort. All of this newness will wear off soon enough and he'll come back to where he belongs."

Really? Did the woman not realize her son was an adult? "Well, then. Thanks for stopping by." Merrilee stiffened at the obvious dismissal, and Indiana found herself adding, "Unless there was something else?"

"No. I've learned all that I need to," the older woman said before she turned and left. Just like that. Not another word.

And that was okay with Indiana. In fact, she'd be fine with never speaking to Merrilee Gatlin again.

"I learned something about you today," Indiana said later that afternoon, as Oliver pulled open the back door to the Caffey-Gatlin Academy at her knock.

Rather than fly down the freeway and demand he explain his interference, she'd waited a whole hour after his mother's departure before making the drive to Hope Springs. It hadn't been an easy delay to endure, but work had called, and the stay had given her time to calm down.

And boy, had she needed to calm down.

How dare the woman barge in and be so incredibly insulting? It would be one thing if they shared a history and she'd disappointed Mrs. Gatlin somehow. But they'd never even met, meaning Oliver's mother was judging her for no reason but snobbery.

Now that she was here, she didn't know if she was more angry with his mother than she was upset with him. Then there was the very real possibility her feelings had been hurt by Merrilee Gatlin's assertion that Oliver was doing no more than playing with her.

That would mean she didn't matter to him at all.

"Good afternoon, Indiana," he said, stepping back and inviting her into what she guessed was now the center's break room or staff lounge, but had once been the kitchen for the original house. "And what exactly is it you've learned?"

"You don't take no for an answer," she said, having brushed by and turned back to face him. And oh but it was good to see him, to be in the same room with him, talking to him in person rather than on the phone, and without his car door and hers keeping them apart. If she took a step toward him, they'd be close enough to touch, but she stayed where she was, her fingers tingling, her pulse racing, her chest tight.

"You'll have to be more specific," he said, gesturing for her to take a chair at the table where he'd obviously been working. Spreadsheets and financial statements and invoices littered the surface, along with a very fancy tablet PC. Nothing but the best for the Gatlins. And since, according to his mother, she wasn't the best . . .

"You asked if I wanted you to vet the investigator I hired. Or if I wanted you to recommend someone. I told you I didn't need you to do either," she said, and stopped, because he *hadn't* done either, and nowhere in that initial conversation had she asked him not to hire an investigator of his own.

"And I respected your wishes," he replied, then gave a huff, followed by a knowing scowl. "You talked to my mother."

To was the right word, because she certainly hadn't talked *with* Merrilee Gatlin. "She came to see me," Indiana said, sitting when it was obvious he wasn't going to until she did.

He stopped halfway to his chair, as if fearing it had just been pulled out from under him, then sat, and asked, "To see you? Where?"

"At my office," she said, her keys in her hands, her knees pressed close together. "In Buda."

"My mother drove to Buda?"

"Unless she has a driver, or took a cab, or has wings," she added, not sure why she was being sarcastic. Unless it was a defense to stave off a nervousness she didn't understand. He was so polite, his manners impeccable. But all she could think about was having his hand between her legs, his mouth on hers, the heat between them.

"She has a driver," was all he said, frowning, and ignoring the rest of her offered options.

And her original point. "You hired an investigator when I asked you not to."

"No," he said, crossing his legs, then picking up the mechanical pencil he'd left with a legal pad on the table. "You told me you didn't need me to vet the one you had hired. You never asked me not to hire one of my own."

She hated having her own logic, not to mention the truth, used against her. Rubbing her hands down her thighs, she asked, "Is this a spirit of the law versus the letter of the law thing?"

He shrugged, flicked his thumb over the pencil's eraser end. "I wanted to make sure you had the best possible chance at finding your brother."

Why? was what she wanted to ask, but instead she came out with, "And your investigator has resources Kaylie's does not?"

"I don't know anything about Kaylie's investigator," he said, finally looking at her, his gaze sharp and focused. "You didn't want me to look into him for you."

Oh, but his being right was frustrating. Even more so than dealing with Tennessee. "I don't appreciate having to hear about you hiring an investigator from your mother. You should've told me yourself."

"You're right, and I apologize. It's just that I've seen Derek work magic, and I thought—"

"It's not your place to think," she said, and stopped, holding up both hands. "I'm sorry. I didn't mean that. It's just . . . I need to do this myself. Finding Dakota."

He nodded, considering her closely before asking, "Do you want me to call him off?"

Oh, that's hardly fair. "If I say no, does it make me a hypocrite?"

"Not at all," he said, pushing up from his chair and walking to the counter to brew a latte. "You care about your brother. Finding him is more important than how it gets done. But I'd like to think you would've come to me eventually if you did need the help."

She looked down at her hands, at her keys, at the marks the teeth had made in her palm. "It's hard for me. To ask. I've been doing things on my own so long."

He held her gaze, the espresso machine hissing behind him, hot coffee streaming from the spout, neither one of them moving, or doing more than breathing. After a moment, he broke the strange tension, gesturing toward her with a second cup. She nodded, and he went back to the task, saying, "I get that. But that's what friends are for."

So was that what they were? Friends? Sure. She could work with that. "It's weird, but since Tennessee got in touch back in March, I've made more here in Hope Springs than I've had since college. Kaylie and Luna. Angelo. Mitch and Dolly. Will. You."

He brought both coffees to the table and sat, crossing his legs again and lifting his mug as if he had all the time in the world for this conversation. As if he was used to being on no clock but his own. As if he was, indeed, Merrilee Gatlin's son.

She thought back to the reason she was here. "Your mother basically told me to leave you to your friends and go play with my own."

"Somehow I don't see you as the type to pay a lot of attention to my mother," he said, hiding the tic in his jaw behind his mug as he drank.

He got points for not being unaffected. "Thank you. For hiring the investigator. You shouldn't have, but thank you."

He set his mug on the table, held it by the rim with one large hand, turned it in a circle as if the motion helped center his thoughts. As if his thoughts were weighing heavier than he liked. As if that heaviness wasn't easy to shake.

Then he looked up and caught her gaze. "Would you like to get dinner one night? Maybe see a show?"

His words were almost an echo of Will's, yet the tone, the intent, none of that sounded familiar.

She was glad, because she didn't want to make the mistake of conflating the two. They were not the same at all.

She would wonder later whether asking her out was what had given him pause, but at the moment, the only thing she cared about was that he had. And it was hard not to split her face grinning when she asked, "When?"

"Saturday night? If you're not busy."

"Not at all," she said. "It's a date."

Because she didn't question for a single moment that it was.

Chapter Eleven

Deciding where to take Indiana wasn't hard at all, though Oliver hadn't realized the timing was perfect until the reminder of his father's showing popped up on the calendar synced to his phone. He'd been looking forward to going, but not having to go alone was a plus. Especially since he'd get to introduce his father to Indiana, and show her off in return.

Strangely, he was anxious to do both. He wanted Indy to see that his father, though often distant and somewhat neglectful, was never purposefully rude the way his mother was. And he wanted his father to know Indiana for no reason but that she was who she was, a free spirit. There wasn't a doubt in his mind that his father would approve of her at first sight.

That sounded like he needed to have his choice of companions Gatlin rubber-stamped, but such wasn't the case at all. Indiana's personality was just impossible not to enjoy, and he wanted to spread her around—even while a part of him wanted to keep her all to himself. That part was giving him trouble tonight, because she looked like an absolute dream.

He was so used to her boots and her sundresses and her T-shirts and jeans that having her open her cottage door wearing heels and a long-sleeved, body-hugging, knee-length black dress left him speechless. Then she turned in a circle, giving him the full effect of the low-scooped back, and he thought he might've drooled. He knew he'd felt his blood stirring, and he'd had to shift his stance to keep it to himself.

"Wow." It was all he was able to get out. "You are absolutely stunning."

He thought she might've blushed when she asked, "Didn't know I had it in me, did you?"

"Honestly?"

She stepped onto the porch and laughed while pulling the door closed behind her. "I don't need that much honesty, thanks."

"I'm not even sure what I expected." Being that honest seemed safe enough. "Especially because you told me to pick you up here. I haven't kept up with your progress on the cottage. I wasn't sure if you were still roughing it."

"I've got electricity, hot and cold running water, and enough lights and mirrors to see what I'm doing," she said as she walked down the stairs.

Whatever she'd been doing, she'd done every bit of it right. He offered her his hand. She took it, then made her way gingerly across the uneven ground to his car. Getting in, she couldn't help but flash a whole lot of leg, and as he shut her door and circled to his side, he told himself to back off. This date was not about getting her out of her dress, though as he drove, and as she crossed her legs and her skirt rode high, he knew he'd be reminding himself of that several times before he brought her home.

The gallery was small, off the beaten path even for the Hope Springs warehouse district, and the last place he imagined anyone expected to see Orville Gatlin's metalwork on display. That was the thing about his father that probably irritated his mother most. She hated seeing him stoop— as she called it—to such a pedestrian level when he had the attention of critics worldwide. As if only their opinions held sway, and those of the audience who'd launched his career were now moot.

But this was Orville in his wheelhouse; he lacked every bit of pretension his wife wore like social armor. He knew himself as an artist.

He wanted his work to live in the eye of the beholder. Art was an experience, he said, and no two people would have the same.

Judging by Indiana's expression, what she was seeing was not what she'd expected. Oliver wasn't surprised. His father's pieces were not what usually came to mind when picturing metal sculptures. Most, in fact, didn't appear to be constructed out of metal at all, but flower petals, and feathers, spiderwebs, and cat whiskers, and lace.

But as fragile and ethereal as they seemed, they were unaccountably sturdy, especially for their size, and took hours of patience to solder and weld, which Oliver well knew. As a child, he'd sat and watched, falling asleep only to wake and find his father still engrossed in perfecting the same foot-long strand.

"And what about you?"

Her question rolled out of nowhere and into his musings, so he took in her unbound cloud of hair and dark shining eyes and asked, "What about me?"

She looked back at the piece in front of them, gesturing with one hand. The motion had the fabric of her dress clinging, and had Oliver appreciating that it did. "What is your artistic talent, because I can't imagine you didn't inherit some of this."

"This fascination with metal? No. And working

in 3-D isn't my thing, no matter the medium. But I do paint. Or I used to paint. I haven't in a while," he said, and left it at that. She didn't need to know why he'd stopped, when, the connection between the two.

But instead of pushing for an answer to that, she asked, "What about music?"

"Do I have any musical talent? No." Though he had enough taste to applaud the string quartet playing in the adjoining room. "But I grew up with Oscar, so I have a great respect for the art form."

Thankfully she didn't angle for any revelations about his brother, or drop into sympathy mode. She simply asked, "And your mother?"

"What about her?"

She shrugged, reached out, and tugged on his tie. "I'm just trying to decide if she really *is* your mother, or if you're only your father's son."

He laughed at that. "I can be a bit of a snob. I guess I get that from her."

"Oh, yeah?" She turned, talking as she walked away. "What are you a snob about?"

He followed, wondering where to begin. "Clothes. Cars. I like to fly first class. Food. But I fell off the truck somewhere, because I have totally lowbrow tastes in movies and TV."

She stopped and looked back. "So you're human."

"I wouldn't be half this much fun if I wasn't,"

he said, taking her arm and pulling her aside to allow another couple to pass.

She moved close, her thigh brushing his, one hand pressed to his chest. And though the contact was fleeting, he swore he felt her fingers flex before she ducked through the doorway into the next room. He touched the spot, took a deep breath, and followed.

"I'm not sure you and I have the same ideas about fun," she said, once he'd regained his mental balance and caught up with her.

That had him frowning; was she not having a good time? "We don't have to stay. But I thought you might like to meet my father."

"Are you kidding?" she asked, her expression wide-eyed and awed. "I would love to meet your father. And I am having fun. It's just . . ."

He thought about her sundresses and boots, the dirt that defined her life. "Art galleries aren't your thing."

She shrugged as she turned to take in the room over his shoulder. "Since I can't remember ever walking through one before . . ."

"Then you picked the best ever for your inaugural visit," he said, his words bringing her gaze back to his.

She studied him closely, her chest rising and falling, her teeth catching at the edge of her lower lip before she asked, "How's that?"

He reached up a hand to scratch at his temple,

because otherwise he was going to wrap his arm around her waist and pull her to him. "The owner, Phil Munro, is a friend of my father's. I went to school with his son, and he's the director now, which makes him taskmaster extraordinaire. He works as curator, he wrangles the artists, handles the art . . . Basically, he's the one who coordinates all the logistics."

"Is he here? I'd love to meet him, too."

That makes one of us, though the thought, when it came, caught Oliver off guard. He and Indiana weren't exclusive, even if his body wanted to argue about that. But Adam Munro had a reputation for seduction that had Oliver wanting to steer clear. "I imagine he is. With the work of an artist like my father on display, Adam will want to micromanage everything."

"Adam? Adam Munro?"

"You know him?" he asked, swearing he saw her cheeks color.

"Actually, I do. I can't believe I didn't make the connection. He used to bring his mother to the farm for okra. She pickled it by the bushel and said no one could beat my prices." She brushed her hair from her face, then again when it refused to stay put, and paused a moment before adding, "You know he lost her last year."

He nodded, sensing there was more to the story of Indiana's past interaction with Adam, but not wanting to press and possibly bring up old

171

memories. He didn't want anything to ruin what was so far a wonderful night.

"There's my dad," he said, gesturing ahead to where the gallery's featured artist stood talking to a couple Oliver recognized from one of his mother's recent dinners. The woman served on one or another committee, but he couldn't recall which one, or either of their names.

He started to pull Indiana aside and wait till his father was alone, but Orville caught sight of him and waved him over. "Oliver! What a surprise," he said, offering his hand, then pulling Oliver into a hug. "It's good to see you. You remember Dean and Joanne Larsen."

"Of course," he said, wondering how his father had known he needed saving. "And this is my good friend Indiana Keller."

Smiling, Indiana shook the Larsens' hands, stepping aside as the couple excused themselves to tour the rest of the gallery, then turned her full attention on his father. "I'm so happy to have the chance to meet you. I know your name, of course, but hate to admit I'm totally unfamiliar with your work."

"Oliver? Is this true?" his father asked, his gaze all for Indiana. "Do you not speak of your old man's work to your friends?"

Oliver held up both hands and laughed. "Don't look at me. I haven't even had a chance to talk to her about mine."

"And what about your passion, Indiana?" Orville offered his arm, and Indiana hooked hers through, Oliver taking up the rear as the two moved to the nearest exhibit. "Tell me what you do and how you came to know my son."

"Actually, I'm a farmer," she said, and Oliver had the time of his life watching his father's jaw fall.

"That absolutely cannot be true," Orville said, stopping in front of a sculpture Oliver didn't remember having seen before, one that had him thinking of Dickensian steampunk, with its tiny filaments and lantern windows and bits of patina-greened brass.

"If you don't believe me," she said, smiling over her shoulder at Oliver, "you can ask Adam Munro."

"You know Adam?" Orville's question had Oliver wanting to roll his eyes.

Indiana nodded. "I knew his mother, too, though I haven't had the pleasure of meeting his father."

"Then we must remedy that right away," Orville said, escorting her from one displayed piece to the next.

They walked by fragile-looking spheres and what appeared to be wings, or maybe feathered tails, unattached to any sort of being. Freestanding branches and blossoms with no stems sat on pedestals or hung suspended, and Oliver was struck, for really the first time, how many of his father's projects were parts instead of wholes.

Was there something missing in the older man's life that had him echoing the same in his art? Had this only been the case since Oscar's accident? Were the pieces designed to appear unfinished, or did he lose interest and leave them so? Was his father, as an artist, simply more interested in the bits and pieces than anything that might be complete?

And what, Oliver was left thinking, did any of those options say about the absentee parent Orville Gatlin had been? Or the husband, distant more than he was present, oblivious more than he was aware, that he was in name only?

On the way through the gallery, Orville spoke to friends and art patrons, introducing both Indiana and Oliver every time, and when at one point he was drawn into deep conversation with an entertainment editor from an Austin paper, Indiana stepped back and asked, "Where's your mother?"

Uncanny how her question came on the tail of his recent musings. "It's probably her book-club night, or she has some meeting."

"Isn't she interested in what your father does?" When he found himself frowning instead of answering, she asked another question. "Or does he not want her here?"

Where to even begin. "What they have, their marriage . . ." He held Indiana's arm and guided her away from the group where his father held court. "It's complicated, I guess. I mean, whose marriage isn't in one way or another? But my parents have never been who I'd hold up as marital role models."

"Even though they've been together all these years."

"It works for them," he said with a shrug. "I don't know why. Or how. But it does."

"Absence making the heart grow fonder maybe?"

Oh, he was pretty sure it wasn't that—

"Indiana Keller? Is that you?"

At the sound of her name, Indiana turned, while all Oliver had to do was look over her shoulder as Adam Munro approached. "Adam. Hello," she said, allowing the other man's quick embrace and kiss to her cheek before turning to include Oliver. "You know Oliver Gatlin."

"I do." Adam stepped forward to shake Oliver's hand. "Though what you're doing here with the likes of him . . ."

Yeah, yeah. "Good to see you, Munro. Nice turnout."

"Hardly a surprise," Munro said. "We're showing the work of Orville Gatlin. You may have heard of him?" Grabbing three flutes of champagne from a passing server, Munro led them into a small alcove out of the meandering flow of traffic. "It really is nice to see you, Indy.

And you, Ollie. Wow. It's been a long time. I know since before Mother passed."

"I was so sorry to hear that," Indiana said. "And I've missed seeing you. Orville was on the way to introduce me to your father. The one member of the family I haven't yet met," she said, giving Oliver a smile he would be a long time forgetting.

"I think Dad stepped out." It was all Munro said in answer before moving on. "And I'll have to get back to work here, but fill me in. What's going on with the two of you?"

They spent the next ten minutes talking about IJK Gardens and the Caffey-Gatlin Academy and Munro's work with the gallery. And they compared notes on Orville's pieces, Indiana loving the same steampunk sculpture that had caught Oliver's attention earlier, Munro favoring the bigger, bolder ones because of how they defied all scientific principles that would have them bending and breaking and crashing to the ground.

Oliver didn't mention his parts-versus-the-whole observation, still brooding over what, if anything, it might mean. And when Munro regretfully took his leave and returned to his duties, Oliver found himself guiding Indiana toward the door. "We should probably go."

"Do you want to say good-bye to your father?"

Orville was standing in the center of at least a

dozen admirers, gesturing with both arms as he held his audience captive. "No need," he said, knowing his father had already forgotten he'd been there at all—a reality he'd lived with for most of his life.

Indiana was quiet on the drive home, leaving Oliver to sift through the remnants of the night, and the thing that stood out above everything was how she hadn't let his father or Munro whisk her out of his sight. She'd stayed close, including him in the conversations. She'd listened to him, she'd smiled, she'd initiated physical contact.

She'd left no doubt she was with him, even though they weren't dating and she was free to enjoy Munro's—or anyone's—attention. Even though theirs was not a romantic relationship. This had been an experiment. A test of compatibility. A night without sex. He hated what it was, as much as what it wasn't. But he wasn't ready to examine why.

Pulling to a stop behind her Camaro in her driveway on Three Wishes Road, he put his BMW in park and opened his door, leaving the engine running while he circled to open hers. She took his hand and swung her legs from the car, then stood and let him go.

She held her clutch in both hands between them, as if using it as a shield, or warding him off, and he shoved his hands in his pockets to let her know she had nothing to worry about. He was

Merrilee Gatlin's son. He was an expert in being a gentleman.

"Thanks for the evening. Your father's absolutely lovely. I had a wonderful time."

"I'm glad you came." Really glad. "Though I don't know that I got to know you any better."

"That's okay. I got to know you."

He wasn't sure he liked things going that way. "I'll see you on Thanksgiving, then? If not before?"

She nodded, waved him off when he started to accompany her to the door, then waved again as she went inside, leaving him standing in her driveway, wondering why he didn't know whether the night had been a success or a failure.

Chapter Twelve

The days between Indiana's date with Oliver and the Thanksgiving holiday were insanely busy at the farm. Her pumpkins and winter squash and green beans went like mad, and her small market building was a veritable beehive of activity, with candied pecans and cranberry relish and other seasonal goodies in high demand.

She made the drive to Hope Springs twice, telling herself she needed to check on the cottage. Lying to herself, really, because Tennessee was in constant contact, keeping her apprised of the progress. Will, too, surprising her, in fact, by driving to Buda one morning, and hunting her down in the equipment-repair shop to talk to her about flooring options—something he could just as easily have done over the phone.

They hadn't spoken in person since she'd gone to his loft the week after Halloween, so looking up from a tractor that had just bitten the dust to see him walking through the shop surprised her. She'd watched his approach, taking in his long, lanky stride, the wolfish grin pulling at his mouth, twinkling in his eyes. A slash of hair falling over his forehead.

She realized that, as happy as she was to see him, her heart wasn't pounding, her fingertips weren't tingling. She wasn't hit with the urge to run into his arms, to have him lift her and twirl her and lower her against his body, to slide into his kiss. The realization left her torn, mourning what they would never have, celebrating the friendship they did.

In reality, her visits to Three Wishes Road were about seeing Oliver, though she'd missed him both times. On the second trip she did find a note taped to her front door, one he'd obviously left, because it was from his father. Orville was sorry to have been distracted during her visit to the gallery, and invited her to his studio to see his newest piece.

Oliver had scratched a quick accompanying

note of his own: "Let me know." That was all it said, and the only contact they'd had in the nearly two weeks between their gallery visit and the holiday. Which had her looking forward to Kaylie's dinner. Because that night she'd finally been given a glimpse into Oliver's life.

She'd met his father. She'd learned he was friends with Adam Munro. He'd confessed his snobbery, though she considered his list of sins to be more about excellent taste and less the snooty airs his mother displayed. Interesting, too, that his mother had no care for his father's show. Almost as interesting as the fact that he painted. Or had painted.

She wanted to know if she was right about why he'd given it up, when he'd given it up. The medium in which he'd painted. His subject matter. And she would have hours today to find out, because this holiday would be nothing like the past.

Last Thanksgiving, Indiana had spent a quiet day alone. She'd roasted a turkey breast, baked a pan of cornbread for dressing, made gravy, tossed a salad, and dug a fork into the center of a store-bought pecan pie while watching Kevin Costner as Robin Hood.

The year before had been spent similarly, though instead of a salad she'd gone to the effort to put together a green bean casserole. And the pie, which she'd eaten while watching Kevin Costner as Robin Hood, had been cherry.

The year before that, ditto to the turkey, gravy, and dressing. Broccoli casserole. Chocolate cream pie with a four-inch meringue. Kevin Costner as Robin Hood.

She didn't mind spending the day alone, though with Kevin on her TV, she never really was. But a whole pie to herself—because face it: Who bought half a pie, or a small pie, or only a slice?—was not a good idea, even if she was active enough that she could afford the calories.

The problem was that Thanksgiving came right after Halloween, and she always over-bought the M&M's and Tootsie Rolls. And Christmas followed almost immediately, the season arriving with cookie exchanges and vendor gifts: caramel popcorn, creamy fudge, iced gingerbread men, and Danish butter cookies. She was getting too old to eat her way out of one year and into the next and was thankful she'd have no leftovers.

Stepping from her car parked behind a dozen others, she wound her way to the back door of Two Owls Café, though technically where she was headed was simply Tennessee and Kaylie's home for their friends and family get-together.

Reaching up to smooth back her hair, then smooth down her skirt and her sweater, she took a deep breath before pulling open the screen door into Kaylie's kitchen. The room buzzed with activity, Kaylie and Dolly and Luna all flitting by, along with a couple of women Indiana didn't think she had met.

And the smells. Oh, the smells. Everything Thanksgiving should be was in this room. The rich, savory aromas of turkey and gravy, the yeasty scent of Kaylie's famous softball-size hot rolls, and that of pie dough, like buttery flour, and warm. Sweeter smells: yams and cranberries and desserts oozing lemon and coconut, sweet apple, spicy pumpkin, cherries both tangy and tart.

She was in heaven. Who needed Kevin Costner as Robin Hood?

"Indy! You're here!" This from Kaylie as she tossed a pair of elbow-length oven mitts to her dad. "Happy Thanksgiving!"

Mitch gave Indiana a smile and a wave as he tugged them on, then turned for the huge roasting pan and the turkey, a blast of heat and so many smells pouring into the room as he opened the oven door.

Indiana set her contribution to the meal—six bottles of wine in a rustic jute carrier—on the counter, and said, "What can I do?"

"Find a corkscrew, then find Tennessee. He should be in the main dining room," Kaylie said before being swallowed up by the crowd.

Indiana did as instructed, winding through the smaller eating areas toward the front of the house. But her brother wasn't where he was supposed to be. Instead, he stood looking out the open front door, his arms crossed, his shoulder braced on the jamb.

She nudged him with her hip, then held up the corkscrew and indicated the wine carrier she'd brought from the kitchen. "I come bearing gifts."

"And not a minute too soon," he said, wrapping her in a hug. "Glasses are this way."

She followed him into the largest dining room, where Angelo sat deep in conversation with Luna's parents at the end of the long row of tables. Two men Luna didn't recognize, and who most likely belonged to the women in the kitchen, stood talking in front of the room's picture windows.

Smiling at Angelo and the Meadowses, she waited while Tennessee opened a bottle and poured them both a glass without offering one to his guests. "Cheers," he said, downing half of his in one long swallow.

She didn't think she'd ever seen her brother drink anything but beer. Or drink as if trying to drown his sorrows. "What's going on?" she asked, leaving her glass on the table set up with the coffee and iced tea dispensers slated for use in the café, along with cups and glasses for both as well as for water and wine.

He turned his back on the rest of the room and lowered his voice. "You can't say anything. Not yet."

She did her best to keep a straight face though her stomach fell, and she had to swallow to find her voice. "You haven't given me anything yet not to say."

"We're going to tell everyone at dinner, but I wanted you to know first." He took a deep breath, rubbed at his forehead. "Kaylie's pregnant."

Pregnant? As in a new little Keller? As in more family to love? She jumped up and wrapped her arms around his neck. "Tennessee! That's wonderful!"

"Yeah. It kinda is," he said, but nothing in his voice or his expression—he was frowning when he should've been grinning like a loon—led her to believe *wonderful* was what he was feeling.

The door chime sounded, and she glanced over in time to see Will walk in, returning his wave as he headed toward the rear of the house, then giving her attention back to her brother. She guided him to an empty chair at the table's near end, then pulled her own around so they sat knee to knee. "Now, tell Sister Indiana what's wrong."

He leaned forward, his forearms on his thighs, his hands twisted together, his chin tucked all the way to his chest. If she hadn't just seen Kaylie in the kitchen, she would've sworn he'd just lost his best friend. "What do I know about being a husband, much less a father? I'm going to screw everything up. I just know it."

Ah. Silly man. "Socks will help with that."

"Socks?" He looked up, frowned, then rolled his eyes. "This isn't about cold feet."

"Sure it is." She refused to let it be anything else. "The cold feet of uncertainty. You didn't come into this world an expert at everything the way you are now," she said, earning herself an arched brow. "You'll be a master at diapers in no time. Just put on your socks and shoes, one at a time like everyone else. You'll be fine."

Sitting straight now, he crossed his arms over his chest. "So you're the one who got all the smarts in the family."

"Yep. That would be me," she said, and this time when the front chime sounded, it was Oliver walking through the door. She started to stand, stopping because her brother deserved better than a fraction of her attention. But then Dolly came into the room, shepherding everyone into their seats, giving Indiana time to do nothing but catch Oliver's gaze and smile.

The afternoon passed in a whirl of food and drink and conversation. There was turkey and gravy and cornbread dressing, homemade cran- berry sauce with pecans and whipped cream and red grapes. There was coffee and tea, water and wine, something for those who were expecting and those who were not. There were Two Owls huge hot rolls, and pumpkin muffins, and thick slices of warm honey wheat bread.

With so many at the table involved, talk turned often to the Caffey-Gatlin Academy, and then moved across the street to the Gardens on Three

Wishes Road. Dolly put dibs on the first crop of zucchini for the café. Luna begged for tomatoes. Kaylie's face blanched, and Indiana refilled the expectant mother's water, giddy with the news.

Tennessee chose that moment to rap his knife on his tea glass and stand. "Kaylie and I have an announcement—"

"I knew it," Dolly said, clasping her hands beneath her chin, her new wedding band sparkling in the candlelight. Tears welled as she said, "You've finally set a date to get married."

"No date yet, though it'll be soon," Tennessee said, his face, always ruddy from his time in the sun, coloring. "But that's not the announcement."

"We're having a baby," Kaylie said, and the words were barely out before the dining room erupted in cheers and tears and cries of joy and congratulations. "We're due late in May, so I'm hoping the café gets its sea legs before I'm too unwieldy to navigate."

"Listen to you," Dolly said, having left her chair to give Kaylie a hug, her eyes glistening, "worrying about Two Owls when you know your father and I will be here to handle every little thing."

Mitch appeared speechless, rubbing a hand back and forth over his crew cut, his own eyes growing red, his accompanying laughter gruff. "A grand-father. I'm going to be a grandfather. Aren't I too young to be a grandfather?"

Everyone laughed, Kaylie saying, "No, sir, you are not. And I'm going to expect you to spoil this little one rotten every day of his or her life."

Because he hadn't been able to do that for Kaylie.

The thought came unexpectedly, and had Indiana wondering if anyone in the room wouldn't change something in their past if they could. Maybe not Harry and Julietta Meadows. Luna's parents seemed to have a perfect marriage, a perfect life.

Then again, they'd suffered with Luna as she'd mourned the loss of her best friend in the tragic car accident that had changed so many lives. Yet like every person here, their eyes shone with happiness as they celebrated Tennessee and Kaylie's news.

Was the Meadowses' relationship stronger because of all they'd endured? Was Luna and Angelo's? Kaylie's childhood spent in foster care had been one of the saddest Indiana could imagine, but she'd moved on, eventually reuniting with her father, making a new life with Tennessee, establishing the business she'd dreamed of.

"And just think," Harry was saying to Mitch. "You'll have a grandkid the same age as my daughter. So if anyone around here should be feeling old, it's me."

The laughter started up again at that, Indiana recalling that Mitch and Harry had been in the service together not long after Kaylie and Luna were born. She thought about Dakota again, wondering if, wherever he was, he was married, settled down, a father with kids in grade school, or a newborn.

The thought of both of her brothers with families had tears welling in her eyes. Happy tears, yes, but also mournful tears for the time they'd lost, the milestones. If Dakota had children, did they fight over the turkey's drumsticks? Did they still believe in Santa Claus? Did the tooth fairy leave coins or cash? Did his boys play baseball, following in Daddy's footsteps? Did his girls love to dig in the dirt like Aunt Indiana?

Aunt Indiana. Oh, how she loved the sound of that. And now her brother would be Uncle Dakota, a realization that had the melancholia she'd been keeping at bay pushing into the room where it didn't belong. She didn't want it here.

There was so much here, in this room, to be thankful for. Just like there was so much in her life to be thankful for. She couldn't lose sight of that, of her business and now her bees, of Kaylie and Tennessee's news, of this bounty of food when so many had so much less, yet were still buoyed by the spirit of the day.

Just then, Oliver's phone rang, snagging Indiana's attention. He lifted a hand in apology to those at the table, then turned in his seat to take the call while the chatter went on around him. He didn't say much; he mostly listened, and the few words he did speak were terse and exact.

And it wasn't but moments later when he said, "I've got to go," and scooted back his chair at the same time he clipped his phone to his waist.

"Is everything okay?" Indiana asked, knowing from his voice, the tone as worried as it was sorrowful, what the answer would be.

"It's my father. Oscar's . . . He's had an infection, and it's worsened. I've got to go."

Around the table, murmurs of sympathy and prayers and best wishes followed Oliver to his feet. He placed his napkin across his plate and looked only at Indiana. "I'll see you later?"

Nodding, she replied, "Do you want me to come with you?" trying to remember what he'd told her—if anything—about Oscar being ill.

"I don't want to take you away from your family," was what he said, but Indiana heard more in his voice, saw more in the relief that filled his expression at her question. She pushed to her feet, turning to Kaylie. "I'll come back and help you clean up."

"You go on," Dolly told her. "Mitch and I will help Kaylie."

"Sure, sure," Mitch said. "If you can get back later, make it for coffee and pie. You, too, Oliver. If you can."

"Thanks, Mitch. Dolly." Oliver lifted his hand

in good-bye. "Kaylie, the meal was wonderful. Tennessee, thank you for inviting me to share it. And congratulations to you both."

"Thanks, and glad to have you, man," Tennessee said, pushing back his chair and leaning forward to shake Oliver's hand. "Let us know how things go."

Indiana smiled at her brother, then glanced at Luna and Kaylie, receiving concerned and knowing looks from both in return. She gave a small wave to the rest of the guests, meeting Will's gaze and receiving a nod. Once outside, Oliver said nothing. He simply took hold of her hand, squeezing it with his as they hurried together, a couple, to his car.

It took almost no time at all to reach the Hope Springs Rehab Institute from Two Owls Café, but even less time with Oliver driving. Indiana held tight to the armrest and the edge of the console, finally closing her eyes until the car slowed, and he turned into the lot and parked.

She reached for her door handle, but glanced over before stepping out of the car, and though Oliver had turned off the engine, he'd yet to move. Taking her cues from him, she waited, but the air grew still and the delay uncomfortable, and the pressure in her chest had her feeling incredibly sad.

"Oliver?"

"I know. I know. I need to go in," he said, his

hands so tight on the wheel she knew he was nowhere near ready to release it.

She reached over without thinking and brushed his hair from his forehead. His skin was cold, and dry, and she suddenly wished she had a blanket. "It's okay. Just take a minute. Or take as long as you need. I'm right here. I'm not going anywhere."

He looked at her then, the strangest expression in his eyes as they glittered in the parking lot lights, as if only just then was he really seeing her. As if only just then was he realizing something even she had yet to see, and then a shudder coursed through him and the look vanished.

She moved her hand to his shoulder, wondering what had happened, what had gone through his mind, or if it was best she not know. The possibility didn't stop her from asking, "Are you all right?"

"I just can't . . . I know what I'm going to find. What the outcome of tonight's going to be." He let his head fall back on his shoulders, and he laughed, a brutal, brittle, terrified sound. "I'm going to go home from here an only child. Even if I don't leave until tomorrow. Or a week from tonight."

Indiana almost couldn't breathe. Her chest was so tight, her throat so swollen, her stomach tied in such knots. And to think what Oliver must be feeling . . . "What can I do? Please, if there's anything, please tell me."

"Can you turn back time so that we don't have to be here now? My mother. My father. My brother most of all?"

And yet he didn't mention another word about himself, what he was feeling, all of the things he as the oldest son, the survivor, was going to have to face. "Are you ready?" she asked, squeezing his shoulder.

But he was trembling, and when he released the wheel, he reached for her, his hands holding her head and slamming his mouth against hers, the taste of his emotions bitter and tortured and salted with tears.

She didn't know what to do except kiss him back, give him the connection he needed, the life in the face of death she wasn't even sure he was looking for. And maybe he wasn't. Maybe all he needed was to feel something that wasn't so crushingly sad.

She wrapped her arms around his neck and brought him close; he leaned over the console, pressing her down against the cushy leather cradle of her seat. She wanted him with her, and told him so with her fingers at his nape and the base of his skull, rubbing circles, comforting him, soothing him.

He let her go, and fumbled at the base of her seat. It reclined with an electronic whir, and Oliver came with her, covering her, his upper body as heavy as his sorrow. She bore both weights willingly, inviting him in, giving him solace, giving him all that he asked for, with her lips, with her tongue, with her hands on his shoulders, in his hair, at the buttons of his shirt.

This made no sense, yet made perfect sense, and she would never have chosen this time or this place, yet she wouldn't change a thing, because he needed her.

He needed her, and for reasons that had less to do with bodies than with the tidal wave of emotions drowning them. He was breaking, and looking to be healed, or at least glued back together before he completely cracked.

This wasn't the sort of intimacy she'd known in the past, and it was glorious, exploding with emotions, fear and longing and regrets and the burrowing sense of nothing between them ever being the same again.

How could anything be the same after this? He fit her as if they were one, filled her and left room for no one to come between them. He made her ache and burn and pulled her toward a completion from which she feared she would never recover.

But it was too late to consider consequences, too soon to wonder where they went from here. All that mattered was this, this, *this* . . .

Then he rested against her, breathed against her, stroked her hair, and whispered against her, "I don't know what that was, or where it came from."

"Shh. It's okay. I know. It's okay."

"This was not the first time I wanted to be with you," he said. Then he looked down at her, the soft smile on his mouth almost reaching his eyes. "A bed would've been nice."

"A bed would've been," she said. "And more time."

"Next time. More time. For certain."

"Good," she said, holding his gaze, a flood of tenderness rushing through her, a flood of hope, a flood of possibilities. "Because I didn't want to think—"

It was all she got out before his mouth was on hers again, telling her not to think about anything but this: his lips and his need and his tongue and his promise. Then just as quickly he was back in his seat, adjusting his clothing before opening his door, coming around the car, and opening hers.

Once they were inside the facility, she asked, "What's the room number? I need to"—she waved a hand toward the restroom—"clean up a bit."

"Of course," he said, adding, "It's two forty-two. I'll see you there."

The words were automatic, his mind having switched gears to what lay ahead, and that was okay. That was expected. Her mind, on the other hand, was still reeling enough for the both of them.

What in the world had they just done?

Chapter Thirteen

As much as she longed to give Oliver whatever support she could, Indiana sat outside his brother's room in a chair one of the nurses had carried over after seeing her pacing the width of the hallway and back. She hadn't known Oscar Gatlin, though she'd known of him, his tragic accident, the death of Sierra Caffey in the same. One didn't spend time in Hope Springs and get to know two of the Caffey-Gatlin Academy board members without learning about the decade-old catastrophe.

Oliver had respected her wishes to give him this private time with his family, though the weary sadness in his expression as he'd walked away had nearly broken her heart. Still, it was better this way. She would've hated to intrude and give Merrilee Gatlin true cause to hate her, as opposed to the reasons the older woman had manufactured. It was best she stay out here. Where she belonged.

Because even if she and Oliver were friends, or had been friends—she had *no* idea what they were now—she wasn't family. And whatever had just happened in his car didn't change that. But wow. It had certainly changed her.

She might feel differently tomorrow, but when she could still sense him every time she moved, her thighs aching, other parts of her sore . . . There was no way this feeling, this experience, this premonition of nothing ever being the same again wouldn't linger.

How could it not? She'd had sex with Oliver Gatlin.

In. His. Car.

In what part of her world did that make any sense? With her history, her guilt, and the trauma of all she'd lost, why would she do something so incredibly reckless?

Because he needed you. And because you love him.

No. She didn't. She couldn't. How could anyone love someone they barely even knew? She'd met him a little over a month ago. That was it. They'd had breakfast. They'd had coffee. They'd shared Thanksgiving, and he'd taken her to see his father's show.

And yet . . . He'd been on her mind constantly. Not a day had gone by that she hadn't thought about something he'd said, or remembered a look that had flashed through his eyes, or wondered if she'd see him when she stopped by her cottage.

No. This wasn't love. This was a bit of infatuation. Maybe a crush. Something as simple as enjoying a man's company and his attention. As a friend.

But it wasn't, *it wasn't,* love.

And no matter what they'd done in his car,

tonight was not the time for such musings. His brother was near death, if not already gone, and she was only here should Oliver need her. And yet telling herself that didn't stop her from closing her eyes and remembering his desperation, his strength and his sorrow, the smell of him, the sweet intrusion of him . . .

She hadn't realized she'd dozed until Oliver woke her, kneeling in front of her where she'd curled into a contorted fetal position in the chair. Her back aching, she straightened, pushing her hair from her face. Sobs from inside the room registered, as did Oliver's solemn, damp eyes. "Oh, Oliver. I'm so sorry. So, so sorry."

The last of her words came out choked, and she pressed her hand to her mouth to catch them back, before cupping his face in her palms. Oliver shook his head, then reached up to tuck her hair behind her ear. "It's been a long time coming. Truth be told, he died ten years ago with Sierra. This last decade . . . He should never have had to endure all of this. And I don't want you to be sorry for that."

"I'm not," she said, but stopped because what *was* she sorry for? The words seemed so meaningless, so clichéd, and yet she was filled with an incredible anguish, a magnificent ache because of what Oliver had lost. "But I am. He should still be with you, whole and vibrant and full of life and—"

"What is *she* doing here?"

Merrilee's words echoed down the hallway, sharp and stinging and as hurtful as they were hurt. Indiana got to her feet, Oliver rising with her, and held first his mother's gaze, then his father's as she said, "My condolences, Mrs. Gatlin, Mr. Gatlin. I'm truly sorry for your loss."

Then, before Oliver's mother could do more than suck in a breath broken by a mother's pain, Indiana turned to go. She was not going to stay and make things worse. Behind her, she heard Oliver speaking to his parents; then she pushed through the door into the rehab center's main corridor, defying the urge to run.

Seconds later, the door whooshed open again; then Oliver was beside her, taking her by the elbow and slowing her to stop. "She doesn't mean anything by it."

"Of course she does." He knew it as well as she did. "But she's devastated, and I'm not going to judge her for anything tonight."

"Thank you," he said, pulling in a deep breath that had him shuddering. Then cupping the back of her head and pulling her close. "Thank you."

For not judging his mother? For the sex? For being here? She wanted to know, but not so much that she was going to burden him with having to answer. Instead, she nodded against his chest, feeling his heart pound beneath her cheek.

His arms came around her then, and she

wrapped him similarly in hers, and they stood in the quiet hallway together, neither saying a word, neither moving. This she could give him. This was easy, this human connection, this private, compassionate communion.

Nothing in this moment was about what had happened hours before in the front seat of his car, yet she couldn't help but remember the feeling of his being over her, being inside her. Being a part of who she was as if he were meant to be with her.

As if they were meant to be together. To be one.

After a long moment, he dug in his pocket, and as he stepped away, handed her the keys to his BMW. "You can get yourself home?"

"Of course," she said, her fist closing around the fob. "I mean, I'm staying at Tennessee and Kaylie's tonight. I'll leave your car there, or I can bring it to you, or pick you up—"

He lifted his index finger and placed it against her lips. "Thank you. I'll see you soon." Then he cupped her nape and brought her to him, pressing his lips to her forehead and lingering, breathing, his hold tight and possessive and absolutely needy and raw.

She breathed him in, all the rich, exotic scents that made him who he was. "You'll let me know about the arrangements? And if there's anything I can do?"

"I will, but you know my mother."

Still . . . "Anything."

"You're here. And that's what I need."

Strangely, she believed every word.

The morning after his brother's passing, Oliver stood in front of a blank canvas for the first time in more years than he could remember. His father was the artist in the family. His father who was rarely home, and always consumed with whatever piece he was sculpting when he was. As little hands-on parenting as Oliver and Oscar had received from their mother, they'd been given even less by the famous Orville Gatlin.

What he *had* provided both of his boys with was an education in the arts, an appreciation for the arts, and more than a little bit of artistic talent. Oscar's had been the gift of music, though their father hadn't sung or played or composed. Oliver had painted. Oils. Until he'd stopped. Right about the time Oscar had no longer been able to run his fingers over a piano keyboard, or draw a bow across his cello's strings.

Convenient timing, that. And obvious. Oliver hadn't needed a therapist to point out why he'd given up the thing in his life that he'd most enjoyed at the same time his brother's body had ceased to function. He didn't deserve such an easy outlet for expressing his grief, or his guilt. He should've paid more attention to Oscar's life, where he went, what he did. Whom he kept company with other than Sierra Caffey.

Oliver had never objected to Oscar dating Sierra. He'd liked Sierra. She'd been good for his brother. Oh, he'd hated her later, after the accident, blaming her when he should've been blaming himself, but the years his brother and Sierra had spent as a happy couple, Oliver had been totally on board.

Their mother was the family snob, unable to see how happy her son was despite her constant meddling in his life, meddling Oliver should've put a stop to. It should make Oscar's passing easier, knowing he'd been in a good place, wanting for nothing, loved by a gorgeous girl when he'd gone down that ravine.

But it didn't. Because Oliver hadn't been half as attentive as he should've been.

He hadn't butted in, even after his brother had come to him concerned about the steering in his car. He'd left Oscar to do his own thing. Just once, just that once . . . Why couldn't he have been more like their interfering mother, and less like their father, who couldn't bring himself to be involved? If he had . . . He'd just put his brother in the ground as surely as if he'd been the one driving.

"I'm so sorry, Oscar. I'm so, so sor—" It was all he could get out for the pain ripping at his heart, for the fists closed around his throat and choking him, for the tears burning gullies down his face.

He cried for his brother, great gulping sobs

that had him crouched down and hunched over, one hand on the floor for balance, that tore through him like glass, jagged. Broken. Shards and splinters and . . . How was he ever going to forgive himself and move on? His brother was gone. Oscar, who should've been playing Carnegie Hall by now, but thanks to Oliver . . .

Ages seemed to pass before he was spent; then he stood, using his T-shirt as a towel to dry his eyes and his face. He stared at the easel and the table where he'd laid out his paints after arriving this morning.

He'd been thinking about painting again for a while now, seeing Indiana passionate about IJK Gardens, and Luna about weaving, Angelo about woodworking, Kaylie about her café, and had arranged with Luna to rent part of the loft where she stored her loom. He still had a studio at home; it hadn't been touched since the last time he'd used it. He could've had it stripped clean and outfitted and worked from there.

Considering what he was getting done here, he should have. Or emptied his office in the River Bend Building and used that. Except he didn't want to share this part of his life with anyone. Not his mother. Not his father. Not Indiana Keller. Not yet.

The canvas mocked him. The paints mocked him, too. Twelve hundred square inches of stretched Belgian linen. Charvin Fine Oils in Absinthe

Green and Anise and Cassel Earth. And yet all he could do was stand here and stare through bleary eyes at nothing. Ten years. His brother had hung on to a worthless life for ten years, and Oliver couldn't even make himself pick up a brush.

He'd try again tomorrow. Then he'd try again the day after, and the one that followed. He'd keep trying until he made it happen. Until he got it right. Or until he had to admit there was nothing left to try.

Chapter Fourteen

The day of Oscar Gatlin's funeral, Indiana drove to the Second Baptist Church in Oliver's BMW with every intention of returning the car. The service was held on Sunday afternoon, which seemed rather unusual, but the family, with Oscar in limbo for ten long years, hadn't wanted to wait another day.

These bits of gossip Indiana had learned from chatter at Kaylie's, where she'd spent part of the Friday holiday pitching in with Luna and Dolly on the prep work for the Two Owls opening. She'd also learned that the Hope Springs Funeral Home was unable to accommodate the expected crowd, ergo, the church.

For all her unpleasantness, Merrilee Gatlin had many friends, and Orville had acquaintances throughout the world, both attested to by the abundance of plants and flowers lining the walls of the church's vestibule and those of the auditorium. Lilies and chrysanthemums and ivies and ferns. Then there were Oliver's business associates and social colleagues, and Oscar's friends from school. Friends who included Luna Caffey.

Luna sat near the front of the church, tucked up beneath Angelo's shoulder on her left, with her father almost as close on her right, both men ready to hold her together should she break. Kaylie and Tennessee had taken the pew behind Luna's parents, with Indiana on her brother's other side. She hadn't known Oscar; she was here for Oliver. Just as Kaylie and Tennessee were here for Luna, who'd known Oscar well.

As Indiana listened to the minister, the choir, and friends of the Gatlins speak, she was unable to look away from the woman she thought might have known Oscar better than his family. The woman she was certain mourned the loss of her friend as much as his parents did their son, though, finally glancing from Luna's tear-streaked cheeks to where Oliver sat grim faced and still, she had no doubt the loss of his brother was killing him.

In the pews set off for the family, his mother held his arm and leaned against his side, while his father hunched forward, his hands between his knees, his head bowed. Oliver wore sunglasses with his suit and faced forward, stoic. She had no way of knowing if his eyes were closed, if he blinked away tears, if he was looking at the casket and the high school portrait of Oscar on one end, or at the people who'd come to pay their respects.

She doubted he could see her, but she trained her gaze between Luna and her father, Harry, and willed Oliver to know she was here if he needed her, if he wanted her, for anything. Yes, he had his parents, but he looked so alone—taller than both where they sat, stronger than either, a buttress bearing a monstrous weight—that Indiana found her eyes watering, her chest tightening, and wished so very much she could go to him.

She wanted to hold his hand, to sit beside him and bring his head to her chest, to stroke his hair from his face, to soothe him. She wanted that so very much because of how he'd reached for her in his car, and how ruined he'd appeared when he'd knelt to wake her after Oscar's death. He'd needed her. He'd wanted her. Surely now was no different . . .

Except it was, because she was the one needing, the one wanting, the one desperate to draw him close. Seeing him like this, knowing what he was suffering, the pain he was in . . . *Please let me take away his pain.* The thought tore through her, and when she caught back a sob, his head turned.

She wasn't loud; others in the church were openly weeping, but he'd heard, or sensed her above the rest.

He shouldn't have; her sorrow was that of an outsider. But that wasn't true, because her sorrow was all for him. It came from a place inside so deep she thought when she stood she might crack, that pieces of who she'd been would fall away, that nothing would remain but a woman desperately, wholly in love.

And with no idea what to do about it.

When, coffee mug in one hand, blueberry muffin in the other, Indiana walked out onto the porch of her cottage three days after Oscar Gatlin's funeral, one single thought came to mind: What would Merrilee Gatlin think if she saw her son's BMW parked in Indiana's driveway?

There'd been no chance to talk to Oliver or return his car before the funeral—he'd been busy with his family, and at the service, behind his dark glasses, withdrawn, separate—and Indiana hadn't attended the private burial, or paid her respects following at the Gatlins' home. The family had made it clear they wanted to see no one but their oldest friends, their closest friends, and Indiana knew she'd been excluded.

She'd phoned Oliver once the Friday after Oscar's Thanksgiving Day passing, hanging up when the call went to voice mail; she'd wanted to talk to him, not his phone. She'd called the Saturday before the Sunday-afternoon funeral. The phone had been answered on the first ring by a service, but she'd waited until last night to leave a message. He hadn't called back.

Something told her he wasn't at home; no matter how much he loved his mother, Indiana couldn't see him having the patience to put up with Merrilee when his own suffering was as great as hers. He had no reason to be at the Caffey-Gatlin Academy, and if he *had* stopped by the arts center for anything, she couldn't imagine he wouldn't have walked across the street and picked up his car.

That left her one place to go looking, and if he wasn't at Luna's loft . . .

"How did you know I was here?" he asked when she arrived a half hour later. He turned for the kitchen area, leaving the smells of paint and turpentine and stale clothes and unwashed skin in his wake.

Strangely, the combination wasn't entirely unpleasant. It just wasn't what she'd come to expect from the well-dressed Oliver she'd known. This one, dirty and disheveled, hadn't said a word when she'd buzzed him from the lobby and announced herself, just allowed her access to the private elevator.

"I didn't," she said, following him. "I guessed."

"Good guess."

"It wasn't completely random. Tennessee

mentioned before Thanksgiving that you'd rented the space." She glanced toward the far end of the loft, where Luna's loom had been during the Caffeys' wedding reception. It now sat in the center of the large room, and a partition separated the section set up for Oliver's use. "How are you doing? I've been worried."

And probably with good reason. She was pretty sure he hadn't showered since the funeral. She was also pretty sure he was still wearing the same dress shirt, untucked and mostly unbuttoned, and suit pants, which hung loose on his hips, though he'd lost the jacket and tie, as well as his shoes, socks, and belt.

Either he was sleeping in the clothes, too, or he had nothing with him to change into. Though she knew the loft's water was working, so why hadn't he used it? And why did he look so good when he was so incredibly undone? "When's the last time you had anything to eat?"

He circled the kitchen bar, littered with empty wine bottles, and shrugged. "I've been busy."

Hmm. "Too busy for food?" Or a shower? Or clean clothes?

"It happens," he said, reaching for a full bottle in the case on the floor. Then reaching for a corkscrew and a glass.

She wasn't the connoisseur he was, but even she knew the flute, most likely left from Luna and Angelo's wedding reception, was the wrong glass for the merlot he poured. "I'd be happy to pick you up something to eat. Or cook for you if there's anything you'd like?"

"And then?" He swigged down half the flute's contents, then backhanded his wrist over his mouth. His gaze burned into hers, his eyes too bright for being so bleary, and unaccountably mean. "Are you going to wash my clothes? Clean up the bathroom? Climb into my bed?"

On second thought, he seemed to be perfectly capable of screwing things up on his own. She didn't need to be here to see it happen or, she told herself—her stomach growing tight as it rolled—stay to bear the brunt.

"I'm more a front-seat-of-the-car kind of girl," she said, leaving his keys on the bar before heading back the way she'd come. She would walk back to Three Wishes Road before she'd put up with this.

She was reaching for the elevator's call button when he caught up to her. He reached out, but stopped himself from grabbing her hand, and held up both of his in surrender. Held up the empty flute, too.

"I'm sorry. I'm so sorry. I don't even know where that came from."

He was grieving, and filled with guilt, and most likely harboring doubts about what they'd done in his car when he should've been spending those minutes, the last of Oscar's life, inside. All of those things allowed forgiveness to come easily, though the sting of his words remained.

She hung her head, wondered how long the welts would last, if they would itch as they healed, if they'd scar. Weighed how involved she wanted to get, when she was already up to her eyeballs and probably had been since that first morning when he'd advised her not to bother Hiram's bees.

Breathing deeply, she looked up, bracing herself for what she'd see. The bracing didn't help. His misery sliced into her, the knife ragged and dull. Sorrow was etched in his expression as if he'd used a razor blade at the corners to draw crow's-feet. His nose was cupped by deep parenthetical grooves. No doubt his mouth was as well, but his dark beard hid the bottom half of his face.

He was a mess, physically, emotionally. The fact that he hadn't been in touch since leaving her with his keys should've worried her long before now. What was wrong with her that she hadn't looked for him sooner? Had she truly been too caught up with her search for Dakota, and the Gardens on Three Wishes Road?

She understood wanting to be alone to mourn one's loss, to process one's loss, to come to terms with life going on yet never being the same. She also understood there came a point when being alone became its own kind of burden. Oliver had hit that point.

"Why don't you get cleaned up? I'll fix you

something to eat; then you can show me what you've been working on. I know Luna leaves clothes here. I imagine Angelo does, too. He's a little taller, but you're a little broader. It should even out."

Oliver nodded at her rambling, a furious up and down that had the ends of his hair falling forward. When had it grown so long? No matter. It was more important to get something into him, even a can of chicken noodle soup, than to worry what his mother might think about the shaggy look of his hair.

And really. His mother? Where in the world had that come from? she mused as water ran into the loft's tub hidden only by a room screen. She rummaged around in the kitchen, coming up with a soup pot, and a container of fresh tomato basil in the fridge, along with one of chipotle sweet potato. Obviously someone had been by, and most likely it had been Luna.

She poured the tomato basil into the pot and lit the gas burner beneath, stirring as the soup heated, then rummaging further and finding a loaf of crusty artisan bread. The refrigerator yielded both butter and chèvre—yes, definitely Luna— and she set them on the bar along with bowls and spoons.

By the time the soup was warmed through, the sounds of water splashing and skin squeaking against the tub had been replaced by those of fabric rustling. Not that the image of Oliver getting into clothes was any easier on her nerves than the one she'd conjured of him being wet and naked, but at least he was no longer either of those.

Then he walked from the living quarters of the sectioned-off loft and into her line of sight. She'd been right about the fit of Angelo's clothes. The jeans were snug on Oliver's hips and thighs, the hems dragging around his bare heels. And the T-shirt, an athletic gray number nearly worn through, showed off his upper body in ways cashmere and designer cotton never could.

She thought of him hovering over her, pressing her down, his body heavy and hard. She thought of sleeping with him in the bed behind the kitchen, no car seat, no clothes, no family tragedy waiting just outside a locked door.

"You look . . . better," she said, her gaze falling back to the soup as she struggled to slow her jerky breath.

"I smell better, too. Trust me on that."

"I will," she said lamely, because she didn't trust herself.

He took a seat on one of the bar stools as she ladled soup into his bowl. "That smells good."

"It was in the fridge, and the date's good. I'm guessing Luna brought it by."

"She did. She told me before the funeral that it would be here if I needed it. I guess she knew this

212

wasn't going to be an easy week to deal with."

And Luna, having been a high school friend of Oscar and Sierra Caffey, would know.

As Indiana watched, Oliver dipped his spoon into the soup and began to eat, falling silent as he did. She circled the bar to take the stool beside his, breaking off a chunk of bread and smearing it with cheese. It wasn't even noon, and she wasn't sure she'd ever had soup for breakfast, but she dug in, suddenly starving. Luna had good taste.

Oliver finished his first bowl and headed to the stove for a refill. He lifted the pot to ask if she wanted more, but she'd eaten several meals the last few days and he obviously hadn't. She'd do best to just get out of his way. Carrying her bowl to the sink, she left him to eat, and used the time to wander toward Luna's loom.

Now that she was here, she wasn't sure what to do. She'd been worried, wanting to make sure he was okay, but even though he seemed to be so, more or less, she wasn't comfortable leaving him. She didn't think he would do himself harm, but it was obvious he had no intention of caring for himself either. She couldn't bear the thought of him wasting away, thinking himself not worth saving.

And what did that say about the true depth of her feelings for him? They hadn't talked about the sex, and she didn't know what he was feeling, or how to label their relationship . . .

Should her heart be breaking at the thought of his mistreating himself so? Or was she only reacting—over-reacting?—to his pain and unable to process her own?

Until she saw the canvases spread out in front of her, she hadn't realized she'd moved away from the loom and into his studio. Her gaze took in the painting leaning against the wall, and the one still on the easel. Both similarly colored. Both identically sized. Both depicting the same subject matter, which had her pressing her fingers to her mouth to cover her gasp.

He'd painted her bees. Of all things. She'd expected something dark, something brutal, cathartic slashes of anger and sorrow and ugliness. Not bees. Not soft colors of butter and cream and sunshine and honey. Not transparent wings, or segmented legs, or fuzzy thoraxes, or oversized compound eyes.

The paintings were airy and bright and happy, with grassy backgrounds, and floral back-grounds, and so busy she could feel the buzz along her skin. They weren't a literal depiction; they were abstract, but the subject matter was absolutely clear.

It should never have come from the man she'd walked in on earlier.

The man standing behind her now.

But it had. "Why?" she asked, her eyes watering.

"Why what?" His voice scratched up his throat, and his feet were bare, and she felt his warmth and wanted to turn and bury her face in his chest. "Why did I come here to paint? Or why did I paint your bees?"

He'd come here to be alone. To mourn the loss of his brother. To find what comfort he could without the barrage of condolence calls and potted palms and casseroles arriving daily at his parents' home. She knew that without his having to explain. It was the rest . . .

"I don't understand."

He moved to her side, his hands in his pockets, his hair swinging at his neck, and shrugged. "I don't know that I do, either."

"I expected something . . . darker, I guess." Gah, how lame did that sound? When had sorrow come to be equated with black? And if he didn't understand, how could she? "I thought that's why you were here."

"To be dark?" he asked, and smiled at the question, as if entertaining her same thoughts.

They were a pair, weren't they? Caught up in the crazy-making that was sex and death and crooked little families. "Well, to work out what happened with Oscar. Though I suppose that's a cliché, isn't it, painting grief and sorrow as dark?"

"Those aren't about grief and sorrow," he said, nodding toward the canvas, the tone of his voice, fluid like honey, pouring over her, sticking to her, coating her, staining her, and sweet. "They're about you."

"Me?" she asked, fearing the answer would open the curtain to reveal the elephant in the room, the one sitting on her chest making it impossible to breathe. "Why me?"

"I think you know," he said, his gaze a magnet pulling at hers.

She swallowed, said the words. "Because of the sex."

He nodded, waited, sighed, then walked away from where they were standing, leaving her alone, abandoning her. "It shouldn't have happened."

And just like that . . . wow. Because he didn't like her? Because he thought she was going to want more from him? Because he hadn't enjoyed what they'd done? This wasn't what she'd come here for. This wasn't what she'd wanted to hear him say.

"Maybe I should just go."

"Did it scare you?" he asked as he turned. "Having sex with me?"

She looked at him, his unkempt hair, his unshaven face, his thighs she remembered from him pressing his body to hers. "I wouldn't say scared—"

"I would."

"I don't understand," she said again. Coming here had obviously been a huge mistake, the two

216

of them on different pages, unable to connect. And why did that surprise her? They came from different worlds. And that one thing, above any other, would never change. "Do Gatlins not have sex in the front seat of cars?"

He swallowed, his throat working. "Not in front of hospitals where their brother is dying."

"I'm sorry." What was wrong with her? "That was uncalled for."

But instead of responding, he said, "I don't know what we're doing. I don't know what *I'm* doing." He snorted. "When I finally got into Oscar's room that night, my mother asked me where I'd been, what had taken me so long, and I almost told her."

"Oliver!"

"She knew I was at Two Owls," he said as he shrugged. "She nearly went apoplectic when I told her I was eating Thanksgiving at the café. She knew it shouldn't have taken me that long to make the drive. Then later, when she saw you in the hallway . . ."

Indiana screwed up her nose. "I'm sorry that went over the way it did."

"That was the last time she and I talked."

And again, she didn't understand. "You were both at the funeral. I saw you holding her, walking her to the limo after the service."

"I didn't go to the cemetery or back to the house. I came here. I just couldn't . . ." He ran his hands back through his damp hair, held it away from his face. "You and me . . . I have to know. Is this a thing?"

Her heart clambered into her throat at his question. "More than sex, you mean?" Like the relationship she didn't have time for? Wasn't sure she wanted? Wouldn't know what to do with because she'd never learned what it meant to be loved, even though she was certain she loved him with all of her heart?

"Yeah. I guess."

Way to sound enthused. "I'm not after your money, Oliver. If that's what you're thinking."

But he was shaking his head, frowning, wisps of longer hair with a mind of their own not wanting to settle. Leaving her aching to reach up and smooth them down. "That never crossed my mind."

"Even though it crossed your mother's?"

He dropped to his haunches, let his wrists dangle over his knees, and rocked. "The last ten years . . . Oscar's accident changed everything. The person I've been, the person you first met . . . I don't even know what I'm trying to say."

He was trying to say that he'd suffered an enormous tragedy. That he was only just coming out on the other side, and he was not unscathed. Did he not think she could relate? She had no idea where her brother was, whether he was alive or dead. That didn't compare to Oliver losing his, but surely it gave her enough insight to be trusted. To be confided in.

Unless he didn't want the burden of caring for someone else, the possibility of losing someone else. Of loving and being hurt, because wasn't that what happened when one gave away one's heart? The least she could do was make it easier on him. "Halloween. Thanksgiving. They were blips out of time, okay? We can still be friends. At least, I hope we can."

"Friends." He said the word with a huff, and she started to object, but then he added, "I don't even need one hand to count the number I have. I haven't kept up with anyone from high school or from Rice."

"And work?"

"I advise people on how to invest their money. That doesn't exactly lend itself to friendships."

One question answered. "What about the arts center? You've got Tennessee. Luna and Angelo. Kaylie, even."

He got to his feet, his mouth lifted in a private sort of smile. "I can't believe I gave Luna so much hell about the arts center. It's going to be such an amazing place when all's said and done."

"I'm worried about you." The words came out before she could stop them, but she wouldn't have taken them back if she could. She *was* worried. And maybe his knowing that somebody

body cared, that he wasn't alone, would keep him from sinking into further destructive behavior.

"I'm okay. Really." He shook his head like a dog shaking a bath, and breathed deep. "Let me get some sleep. The food helped, thank you. I'll be better after I sleep. What are you doing tomorrow?"

"I'll be at Two Owls. It's opening day."

"That's right. Maybe I can see you after?"

"Sure," she said, wondering why the anticipation that clutched at her heart felt more like dread than excitement. "If that's what you want."

"Yes, Indiana. It is."

"I can't deal with morning sickness today," Kaylie said the next day, her hand pressed to the base of her throat as she leaned against the kitchen island. "I just can't."

"And that's why we're here to help." Luna poured Sprite into a glass of crushed ice and set it in front of her, searching for a straw while Dolly helped Kaylie to one of the island's stools.

Indiana readied another stack of plates to carry to the buffet table, watching as Mitch checked the third batch of casserole dishes to go in to bake. The kitchen at Two Owls Café smelled like onions and chicken and cheese, like fresh greenhouse tomatoes and chilies, like yeast rolls still warm from the oven, and salty butter, and all of the herbs and spices in Dolly's vinaigrette.

Nearly six months to the day after the date Kaylie had originally planned to open Two Owls, the café had finally flung wide its doors to the residents of Hope Springs, and the food service had been nonstop since ten a.m. Indiana was picking up every tiny chore she could, which mostly dealt with the dishes: scraping the dirties, loading the dishwasher, hand-washing the overflow, seeing to the supply of cleans.

Dolly had put her two teen granddaughters to work as hostesses, managing the seating arrangements, while Tennessee was on call this first day in business to help with moving tables for larger groups. The noise level was deafening, with every seat spoken for, and the porch inundated with the overflow crowd.

But it was the kitchen where all the action was. And poor Kaylie wasn't having a bit of fun enjoying the fruits of her labors. "I don't know what I was thinking, opening during the holiday season. I had no idea I'd be pregnant, of course, and now with the wedding plans . . ."

"Are you kidding?" Indiana left the plates where they were and wrapped an arm around Kaylie's shoulders for a quick hug. "Do you know how tired everyone is of eating turkey leftovers? You couldn't have picked a better time."

"Oh, I could've picked a better time. Like one when I didn't feel the need to vomit," Kaylie said, her face pale, her hand shaking as she reached for the glass of Sprite.

"We've got this, Kaylie," Mitch said, turning from the oven to check on his daughter. "You should go upstairs and lie down. Take care of yourself and my grandchild."

"If I feel this bad tomorrow, trust me. I'll leave the show in your very capable hands. But I just can't do it today. Not today."

Because she'd been waiting months for this day to arrive. Years, really. Two Owls Café had been Kaylie's dream for ages, and she'd devoted her life to making it happen. Indiana wanted to burst with the admiration she had for her sister-in-law-to-be. "Then back-burner all thoughts of the wedding until tomorrow."

"Tomorrow, when I'll still have morning sickness and the date will be that much closer?" Kaylie shook her head, then stopped, and held it with both hands as if to keep it in place. "Ten and I must be insane, thinking we can pull together a wedding in a month. And a Christmas wedding? When everyone already has plans? And now we only have three weeks—"

"Then let me do the wedding," Indiana heard herself saying. "I can't cook. All I'm good for here is washing dishes. But I can plan like nobody's business."

Kaylie looked up, her expression so hopeful and so exhausted and so very green, Indiana wouldn't have taken back the offer for a million bucks. "Are you sure? It's so last-minute—"

"Which is why it makes perfect sense to hand it off. You've got your hands full here."

"Indy's right," Dolly said, dumping rolls from an oversize muffin tin into a basket lined with linen napkins. "I'll give her all the notes you and I have already made. And I'll be available for anything she needs help with."

Since Indiana had no experience planning a wedding, she welcomed the offer. Dolly had never let a detail get away from her since Indiana had known her. "Thank you. And now I'm going to deliver these plates and get out of the kitchen and everyone's way. I'll check back in a few to see what might need to be done."

By the time she made her way through the crowd and the house and out Kaylie's private back entrance, her mind was buzzing with the scope of the task she'd just taken on. And the buzzing made her think of her bees and laugh. She knew as much about wedding planning as she did beekeeping, and yet here she was, tackling both.

Ah well, she mused. What was one more distraction, since according to Kaylie and Luna she was latching on to anything she could to keep from dealing with the issue of the men in her life? Though Thanksgiving in front of the rehab center had pretty much made that decision for her, hadn't it?

Or maybe not, because seeing Oliver at Luna's loft yesterday hadn't solved anything. Had, in fact, only left things more up in the air than before. He'd said he wanted to see her. He'd said he was okay. But all he'd done since his brother's death was paint bees. Her bees. She didn't think he'd dealt with Oscar's passing at all.

Weddings. Not funerals. She flipped the switch on her train of thought.

Location.

Invitations.

Flowers.

Cake.

Those were the basics, and she would need to talk with Dolly and Kaylie about a guest list—not to mention a budget—before she got too deep into the particulars. Obviously, Apple's Flowers & Gifts would be her first stop for flowers, and Butters Bakery would be on tap for the cake, but as far as the rest of the food and drinks . . .

Sitting on the hood of her Camaro, her stylus and smartphone in hand, Indiana looked up from jotting her first rash of notes, her stomach clutching at the sight of Oliver's BMW pulling to a stop on Chances Avenue.

The street was nearly impassible, cars lined up on both shoulders, but he handily parallel parked in a space she wouldn't have thought he'd fit. That car. Would she ever be able to look at it again without thinking of what they'd done in the front seat? As far as looking at him . . .

It was so unfair, the confidence in his walk, his movements so fluid and effortless as he traversed the uneven surface of the crushed-shell drive. He was wearing his own clothes today, new clothes, it looked like, giving her cause to wonder if shopping had been the lesser evil than that of going home.

Eventually he was going to have to go home. Eventually didn't everyone?

Before she let that bit of cryptic pondering go any further, she asked, "Did you want lunch?" and canted her head toward the full parking lot and the cars overflowing onto Second Street. "It may be a while."

He shoved his hands in the pockets of the khaki cargo pants that hung low on his hips. "I figured you'd be busy inside."

"I was, and I'll go back in a few to wash more dishes." She gestured with the stylus and phone, wishing that looking at him didn't make her feel like a schoolgirl with a crush. "I volunteered to plan the wedding."

He nodded before asking, "Kaylie and Ten's?"

Was there another one? "She's got the café, and she's dealing with morning sickness. Just seemed the least I could do."

His gaze, when he searched her face, was curious or concerned or even censuring, as if he was invested in how she spent her time. "Even though you've got the cottage to renovate and the annex going in and your search for Dakota ongoing?"

Not to mention whatever this is with you? She shrugged, then tried to laugh. "Who needs sleep?"

"I obviously did," he said, scratching at his nape. "I crashed after you left, though some of that was thanks to the wine. I only woke up a couple of hours ago."

"You're feeling better, then."

His hair fell around his face as he looked down, as he scuffed at the driveway gravel, as he hunched his shoulders in the wrinkled oxford button-down he wore, and did everything he could to avoid meeting her eyes. "If better means like I need to spend some time getting my act together, then yeah."

As opposed to spending some time with her.

"So you didn't want lunch." Or really to see her, like he'd said he would yesterday when she'd left him at the loft. She swallowed, her throat tight as she cleared it.

He gestured with his chin toward the road where he'd parked, as if the warehouse district, and not acres of woods, was on the other side of the street. "I've still got soup. And crackers. Though I think I should probably stay out of the wine."

That, at least, was good to hear. "Does that mean you'll be living at the loft?"

He held her gaze, his sharply focused on her and intense, as if making certain she was with him, listening. "I want to paint. I need . . . to paint."

She nodded, finally looking down at her phone's screen but seeing nothing. "I guess I'll see you when I see you."

"Indiana—"

"It's okay. Really." Though of course it wasn't, or else she'd be able to speak without her voice breaking, without her tongue swelling to fill her mouth. Without her chest hurting like he'd punched her with his fist instead of words as complicated as they were simple.

"It's just . . . Oscar. And everything." He breathed deeply, exhaled slowly. "I mean, I'll be at the arts center from time to time. I'm not going to totally disappear."

She thought it might be easier if he did. "Listen," she said, sliding off the car and pocketing her phone, "I need to get back inside and check on the dishes."

"When I said I wanted to see you today, I meant it."

Her smile, when it came, was resigned. "I think that was the wine talking. But really. I've got a ton of things going on, and so do you. Maybe if the timing were better—"

"The timing—" He cut himself off before saying more, and she was glad that he did.

She didn't want promises or platitudes. All she wanted was honesty. "Do you want me to send your wedding invitation to the loft, or to your house?"

"The loft is fine," he said, adding, "I'll see you there, I guess, at the wedding, if not before."

The wedding was in three weeks. Three weeks. She should be able to get over him by then, yes? "Good luck with figuring things out," she said, turning for the house and refusing to look back to see if he was still there. She didn't want to know if he was waiting, if he was watching her, if he'd already gone.

Then again, she wouldn't be able to see anything anyway. Not with buckets of tears filling her eyes. Tears she swore would be the last she'd ever cry over any man.

Chapter Fifteen

A very busy three weeks later, twenty-one days—but who was counting?—of not seeing Oliver, twenty-one days during which the work on her Three Wishes Road property got serious, Indiana found herself standing in the vestibule of the Second Baptist Church thinking back, of all things, to Oscar Gatlin's funeral. It had been held in this same building, and though she'd been here a half dozen times since, getting ready for today, that was the one that stuck with her.

She didn't think she'd ever been inside a church for a sadder occasion.

And today might very well be the happiest event to bring her into one.

Such a juxtaposition. The end of a life. The beginning of a life, the one Tennessee and Kaylie would share as well as the one they'd created. Being here today of all days, Christmas day, a day of so much celebration and spiritual reverence and even secular communion . . . It was almost more than she could stand, and her hands shook from the excitement, as much as the worry that she'd forgotten something vital and the wedding would fall apart.

Sensing movement to her right, she looked over at Kaylie as she exited the anteroom where she'd dressed. Her dress was a simple, long-sleeve sheath in a beautiful white satin, with glass buttons from her wrists to her elbows, and from her nape to the small of her back. Luna came with her, adjusting the decorative bow at her hip, as did Dolly, who saw to her intricately knotted chignon. Mitch, who'd been pacing across the room from Indiana, stopped and looked up and simply stared at his daughter. His eyes reddened as tears welled, and his reaction had Indiana on the verge of crying, too.

"Oh, Daddy," Kaylie said, a crack in her voice as she swished over the floor toward him. "Don't make me start crying again. I finally stopped long enough to get my makeup done."

Mitch pulled a handkerchief from his pocket to wipe his face, then touched the back of one hand to Kaylie's cheek. "My precious girl. Look at the beautiful woman you've become. What did I ever do to deserve you letting me back into your life?"

"You're my father," Kaylie said, pressing her forehead to Mitch's when he bowed close. "You don't have to do anything but be you."

The silence in the room was so all consuming, Indiana swore the pounding of her heart could be heard. She, Dolly, and Luna all knew the story of Kaylie's reunion with Mitch, her belief that he'd abandoned her, the truth that he'd nearly been broken by his decades-long effort to find her. There wasn't a dry eye among the five of them, or enough air in the room to breathe without struggling, but the show had to go on.

"It's time," Indiana stepped forward to say, getting a nod from Kaylie as she lifted her head from her father's then stood on tiptoe to brush her lips against his cheek. That done, Dolly fussed over Kaylie's veil and the red and green ribbons in both her snow-white roses and her hair.

Luna moved to stand in front of the vestibule doors, waiting for Indiana and Dolly to open them. Indiana counted down the beats of the music playing—the bride and groom had chosen to use Eddie Vedder's "Longing to Belong" as the wedding processional—then gave Dolly the signal. Though out of sight of the guests, Indiana could hear the rustle of movement as heads turned, and Luna, as maid of honor, began her walk down the aisle.

Indiana timed the progress of the song, then glanced around the door to see Luna move into place in front of the sanctuary. Tennessee was waiting there, too, and Indiana's throat grew tight as she smiled and gave Mitch the go-ahead. He nodded, but he didn't move until Dolly, hidden by the door, reached over to nudge him from behind.

Kaylie held tight to Mitch's arm, and Indiana was certain it was to keep him from losing his footing and falling to the floor. She didn't think she'd ever seen a father of the bride more nervous than his daughter. Neither had she seen a groom look like he was about to throw up every meal he'd eaten the last three days. Poor Tennessee.

But a wife! And a baby! What an absolutely thrilling day! She wanted to burst with the joy tickling down her spine like a zipper, and gripped her stylus and the smartphone that held her event notes as tightly as she could to keep from running down the aisle to give her brother a hug. To tell him she was there and loved him. To beg his forgiveness for Dakota's absence.

Mitch moved to stand beside Tennessee, acting as best man after giving his daughter away. Luna stood in the mirror position beside Kaylie. Dolly came close to Indiana's side and each wrapped an arm around the other's waist as the music waned and the minister began to speak.

It was a blur of words: faithfulness, companionship, sickness and health, better and worse, and love. Words Indiana knew neither bride nor groom needed to speak or to hear. They lived them. Daily. With so much conviction she couldn't think of another couple who so honestly epitomized the same.

She wasn't even sure she would be able to. What did she know about *better?* She was an expert on *worse,* yes, but her experiences with love were all failures. And not even romantic love, but familial love, which should've been easier, yes? Being born into a family, growing up with siblings who shared the same parents and the same blood?

Yeah. She'd done a great job of loving Dakota and Tennessee, letting one go to prison, letting the other also vanish from her life. She was a gold-plated prize, a catch only good for releasing. Why in the world she was letting herself get so close to Oliver, thinking about Oliver, dreaming about a future that included Oliver . . .

They had no future, unlike Kaylie and Tennessee. She would never be able to make him happy, or give him what his art obviously did: that completion, that sort of fulfilling satisfaction. She hadn't even figured out how to do any of that for herself. Thirteen years since her life had imploded, and what did she have to show for it?

A business, yes. A successful one of which she was extremely proud. But that was it. Shouldn't she own a home that wasn't one step up from a tar-paper shack? A vehicle more suited to a twenty-eight-year-old woman than a sixteen-year-old boy? The home-and-car-owning thing was material and shallow, but the rest? The friends? The husband and kids?

She was alone. She would stay alone. And with good reason.

She didn't deserve anything else because she'd ruined what she should've taken care of.

How could anyone ever argue with that?

The service was over all too soon, Indiana hurrying out of the way of the newly married couple as Dolly swept them into the anteroom to give them a few minutes with family. Mitch and Indiana joined them, all five sharing hugs and kisses and relieved chatter and tears. Then Luna was there. Then Angelo. Then Harry and Julietta Meadows. But no Oliver, no Will.

And no Dakota.

"The car's out front to take you to the reception," Indiana finally found her voice to say. "Just keep your heads down as you run and you won't have to worry about getting bird seed in your eyes and going blind."

"Thank you for everything, Indy," Kaylie said,

laughing and crying at the same time. "I can't even imagine how I would've managed any of this. I am so happy we're sisters."

"What the wife said." Tennessee's words earned him a great big grin from his new bride. "I have no idea what all you did, but taking over for Kaylie . . ." His voice going raspy, he pulled Indiana into a hug, crushing her stylus and her smartphone and the prettiest dress she'd ever owned. "I love you, girl."

"Oh, Tennessee. I love you, too," she said, and nearly strangled on the rush of choking emotion his words caused.

Once the newlyweds were gone, and the building emptied of guests, she walked outside and sat down on the church's front steps, heedless of the mess she was making of her dress. Heedless of the damage the concrete might do to the heels of the shoes she doubted she'd ever wear again. Heedless of the duties she had left to perform. Luna had volunteered her loft for the reception, requiring Oliver to clear out for the day. The caterers didn't need their hands held, and Luna would be there to answer any questions they had.

Surely she wouldn't be missed . . .

"Are you okay?"

Blotting a fingertip beneath both of her eyes, she looked up at Oliver's welcome question.

It was the first time she'd seen him all day; she

hadn't even known he'd come to the wedding, and a flood of tension seemed to pour from her bones as he sat down on the steps beside her. She wanted to lean against him, to fall asleep in his arms. To keep him close until the end of her life.

But the last twenty-one days remained between them, so instead she said, "I'm wonderful."

He leaned forward to look into her face. "You're crying."

"They're called tears of joy," she said, her voice breaking with a need to fall apart she was having a hard time keeping contained.

"That doesn't sound like joy."

What was she supposed to say? That she was both happy and sad for her brother? That if she hadn't made such a colossal mistake as a teen, Dakota would be here to celebrate, too? How was it possible to be so ecstatic and so completely miserable at the same time? She couldn't possibly explain.

And even with all that his family had suffered, she didn't think he could truly understand the loss she was mourning. This was her grief, and oh, but it was so unbelievably unbearable today. She wanted to be anywhere but here. Her face ached from smiling, and any minute now she was going to break.

Again she thought about leaving. "I want cake."

"Cake," he repeated, as if making sure he'd heard her right.

He had, but that didn't keep her from elaborating, because she was desperate to get out of here. "White cake. Chocolate cake. Gobs of icing."

He draped his wrists over his knees and watched the cars leave the church parking lot. "I assume you're talking about the reception."

"No." She glanced over, blinking hard against the tears threatening to wash her away. "Let's play hooky. For a little while at least."

His gaze held hers; then he took in her face and the state of her hair, and he smiled. "Would you rather go to Butters Bakery?"

From what she'd heard, Peggy and Pat Butters kept the bakery open part of Christmas Day for others who, as they, had no family, and might need a cup of coffee or a friendly face.

She nodded, giving him her hand to pull her to her feet, and priding herself for not falling into him and using his coat as a Kleenex while she cried. "Do you think I'm insane?"

His smile was the absolute last straw. "I think you're a little bit manic with emotion. And maybe hungry for cake. But nothing there says insane."

"You're a good friend, Oliver Gatlin," she said as they traversed the rest of the steps, Kaylie and Luna's words coming back to haunt her. "And I hope you have a really big wallet, because you have no idea how much cake I'm going to want."

"Tight as that dress is, I'm not sure where you'll put it."

He'd noticed her dress. *He'd noticed her dress*. The dress she'd modeled in front of the dressing room mirror while wondering if he'd like it. She'd even wondered once if his mother would approve, but already had enough crazy in her life with the wedding plans.

"Lucky for me, it comes with a jacket designed to hide a multitude of sins. Including broken zippers."

Too bad it couldn't do anything for broken hearts.

Oliver had been late to arrive at Second Baptist for the Flynn and Keller wedding, and his timing pretty much reflected his interest in the event. He was happy for Kaylie and Tennessee, of course. Happy for Mitch and Dolly, too. But if not for Indiana, he wouldn't have come.

And he wasn't happy about that at all.

She'd gotten under his skin a whole lot deeper than he liked. His painting her bees . . . Yeah. That had come out of nowhere, and had never been meant for her to see. Maybe when he hadn't been such a wreck he could've dealt with what he'd painted, and why. But he still wouldn't have wanted her to have seen it.

It was hard enough to look at it himself.

The first pieces he'd painted in ten years, ones he'd been driven to after his brother's death, and his chosen subject matter wasn't the least bit cathartic. It was about sex, and Indiana, and the sweet buzz she'd left on his skin that he couldn't shake.

But it was also about all of the things in his life that were changing, and how Indiana, even more than the loss of Oscar, was responsible. Or at least had influenced it all . . . her inclusive nature, her empathetic nature, her kindness and enthusiasm and ability to laugh at herself, and at him without malice.

For years, for his entire life, he'd lived under the same roof with a woman who couldn't be more Indiana's opposite. But until spending more time with Indy and the group at the Caffey-Gatlin Academy, and less in his office at home, he hadn't realized the severity of his mother's domineering personality. Or how much worse she'd become in the ten years since Oscar's accident, a change not completely unexpected.

And as he pulled to a stop in the Butters Bakery parking lot, he wasn't sure what he was supposed to do with that knowledge. Or with the seed of resentment wanting to take root in his heart. It wasn't like he'd had a gun held to his head, keeping him at home.

Indiana waited for him to open first the car door, then the one to the bakery. The smells of sugar and vanilla assaulted him, but he wasn't about to complain. Not with the look of euphoria lighting Indiana's face. Her eyes, as much gray as they were blue, sparkled as if reflecting a flute of champagne. And her smile, her lips colored a deep rose for the occasion, was just as bright.

"Do you smell that?" she asked, walking the length of the long glass display case holding thick slices of cake, tiny single-serve pies, cupcakes, cookies, macarons, and a refrigerated section with a dozen iterations of cheesecake.

Honestly. He didn't think he'd ever seen so many.

He gestured toward a small bistro table with two chairs he thought might collapse beneath their weight. "What do you want?"

"One of everything," she said, twirling to sit, her skirt a froth of lace that brushed her knees in a way that was more provocative than the bumblebee outfit she'd worn at Halloween, the figure-hugging dress she'd worn to his father's show, the skirt he'd lifted to her waist in his car at Thanksgiving. The cowboy boots and sundresses that drove him crazy.

He shook his head and left her there while he went to order, cruising the cases as he might wine bottles at an auction. Since one of everything was out of the question—their table wouldn't hold but six plates—he chose the desserts by flavor, and had to make two trips to deliver all the goods.

"This will have to do," he said, coming back a third time with two lattes, crossing his legs and drinking his while Indiana wielded her fork, slicing into one dessert, then another, pulling the fork from her mouth slowly, licking at the tines.

"Mmm. I would say this is better than sex, but it's probably safer if I say this is just what I needed. Thanks."

That had him wanting to cringe. "I'd rather you not use our . . . encounters as any sort of sexual benchmark. I wasn't at my best on either occasion."

She took her time cleaning the back of the fork, her eyes cast down, color rising to stain her cheeks. Then she reached for the single salted-caramel macaron sitting alone in the center of a very small plate. "I was wondering if we were ever going to talk about it. The sex."

"We talked about it. The day you came to the arts center. And the day you found me painting your bees."

"And if that isn't some kind of double entendre . . ."

"Indiana—"

Her eyes snapped when she looked up at him. "No, Oliver. I'm a grown woman. I enjoyed being with you. But I'm not using what happened as anything but what it was. Sex that we both, I hope, enjoyed."

"Thanksgiving. In the car. I wasn't thinking straight. I wasn't actually thinking at all. I was more"—his gut clenched as he formed the words—"forceful than I would've been otherwise. I need to apologize for that."

"That wasn't force," she said, cutting a bite from a slice of white cake iced with lemon buttercream and filled with lemon curd. When he opened his mouth to respond, she stuck the fork inside before he could get out a word. Or tell her he didn't like lemon. "That was force."

He chewed and swallowed, finished off his latte, then said, "I just wanted to be sure that night wasn't an issue."

She went back to grazing with the same fork she'd fed him from. It was strangely intimate, though why he thought so when they'd been nearly naked—

"The only issue we have is your hair," she said into his musings.

"What do you mean?"

She gave him a look, and he reached up, running the fingers of one hand along the side of his head, frowning when he hit a tangle. Had he even brushed it today? "I guess I need a haircut."

"And maybe a shave?"

This time he did a better job hiding his surprise, though he did rub at his jaw several times. Wow, but he was some kind of mess. "I've been busy."

Her gaze fell to the placket of the wrinkled shirt he wore beneath his suit coat, and she nodded toward it. "You're missing a button."

He pulled the coat front closed, only to realize it wanted to swallow him. "And?"

"And you've got paint on your hands."

Enough. "What's with the third degree?"

She shrugged, ate one more bite of the three-chocolate layered cheesecake. "Talking about the way you've let yourself go is easier than talking about sex."

"Let myself go?" Was that what she'd thought he'd done, when the truth was he'd lost himself so completely in his painting that rarely did he remember to eat.

"I suppose it's an artist thing. Never shaving, rarely bathing, only wearing pants when company comes by."

"Now you're just being silly."

"Like I said. It's easier than talking about sex." She stabbed what was left of the key lime pie with her fork. It stood upright as she blotted her mouth with her napkin. "I should put in an appearance at the reception, I guess."

He supposed that was the signal that she was done. With the cakes. Possibly with him. He fought against the fist squeezing his throat and said, "I'll drive you."

"And you'll put in an appearance, too?"

He shook his head. "I think I'm close to overdosing on sweetness."

She got to her feet with a look that said *Your loss,* and if she'd said it aloud, he wouldn't have been able to argue. He wasn't able to do so convincingly, even in his own mind, because there seemed to be a knife in his gut, slicing open a big gaping hole.

They made the ride to the warehouse district listening to Zooey Deschanel and M. Ward singing Christmas classics, but the trip was short, leaving little time to defuse the tension that had followed them from the bakery into the car. He hated this. *Hated* it. He didn't want to make her uncomfortable, or leave things between them so unsettled. But neither one of them was in a position for the sex to lead to anything more.

Or maybe he had it all wrong. Maybe what they needed was time together and sex done right. Maybe what each of them needed was someone to lean on, someone who understood how long it took and how hard it was to come back from the losses that had flattened them.

He wasn't the only member of his family to have had Oscar ripped away, yet not once in the last ten years, even before Oscar's death, had either of his parents hinted at an awareness of the chasm left in his life. Indiana shared her worry over her absent brother with Tennessee, but she was the one so torn apart that she'd hired an investigator to find him.

Was he missing something here? Had his inability to get past Oscar's suffering retarded the rest of his emotions, too? No doubt this was where friends—if he had close ones—would tell him to work out this uncertainty with a therapist's help. Maybe a decade ago doing so would've made a difference. These days, he called it a good one when he got out of bed on the first try, and that was something he would never want Indiana to see.

Guiding his car to the curb in front of the warehouse housing Luna's loft, he braked to a stop and shifted into park, but he left the motor running. Indiana dropped her gaze from the street in front of them to her lap, tendrils of her upswept hair curling against her nape, others cupping her ear. Which reminded him . . .

"Here," he said, reaching into the backseat and handing her an eight-inch square box wrapped festively in paper with glittery snowflakes, and a bow of sheer ribbon that glittered, too. Such forced gaiety. Such manufactured merriment.

She took the package from his hand and smiled when she looked over. "You could come in. Give this to Kaylie and Tennessee yourself."

Of course she'd think that, he realized, shaking his head. "That's not a wedding gift. That's for you."

"Me," she said, and when she looked over this time she was frowning. "Why?"

He shrugged, not wanting to make more of the gesture than the gesture itself. "It's Christmas."

As if needing to let the words sink in, she stared

down at the box she held, slipping one finger through the bow and back out. "I didn't get you anything. And you paid for all the desserts."

"Just open it," he said. He didn't want some kind of quid pro quo relationship with this woman. He liked her too much for this to be a game of one-upmanship. He liked her a lot. He was scared by how much he liked her. The ways he liked her.

And that was why he couldn't let the day go without telling her how much, even if he couldn't put it into words and had to let the gift speak instead.

"Oh, Oliver," she said, as she broke the boutique's red seal and pulled back the green tissue paper to reveal the scarf inside. "This is one of Luna's. A Patchwork Moon original." She lifted the corner with the tiny moon label, rubbed first it, then the woven fabric between her forefinger and thumb. "It's gorgeous, and it's so, *so* soft, and the colors are so perfectly me. But then you knew that, didn't you? You painted my bees with almost the same ones."

He'd hoped she'd like the many shades of yellow, with the one of orange, and the interspersed bits of knotted black. "I didn't know if you had one."

"I don't. I've wanted one forever, even before I got to know her, but wow." She brought it close to her face, as if wanting to nuzzle against it, but she didn't, closing her eyes instead and returning it to the box. "I know how much this cost. I can't accept this."

"Of course you can. I don't look good in yellow, and my mother doesn't wear anything but Chanel." He wasn't going to take no for an answer, reaching over to pull the scarf from the box by one end.

She took it from his hand, lifting it to the car's roof, with still more to come from the box. "This is gorgeous," she said, and he said, "Here," reaching for the center and using it to measure the loops he made around her neck. When he was done, the ends hung artfully on either side of the draped cowl, just as Luna had shown him they would.

"It's perfect," she said, laughing, a giddy, joyous sound that almost made him believe in holiday magic. "But I don't think it goes with this dress."

"It goes with you," he said, because that was all that mattered. It was the reason he'd commissioned the scarf. The reason he'd been so anxious to see the look in her eyes when she put it on. She was right. It was perfect.

She snuggled her face into the fabric bunched closest to her face. "Thank you."

"You're welcome."

Another few seconds ticked by, and she asked, "Are you sure you don't want to come up? I mean, aren't you staying here?"

He was, but he refused to be a damper on a

party that meant so much to her. "I need to go see my folks. Stay with them a couple of days. Check on my dog."

"Susan."

"Susan," he said, the car still running, Indiana making no move to leave. "Do you want me to take you back to the church for your car? Or to the cottage? Or to Buda?"

She shook her head, though he knew she'd weighed each option as she did. "I'm staying at Kaylie's house this week while she and Tennessee are gone. It's just me and Magoo."

"The café is closed?"

"Till after New Year's, yes."

"Would you rather I take you there?"

"I'd rather you come into the reception," she said, the honest longing in her voice nearly gutting him. "Just for a little while."

"Indiana—"

She held up a hand, silencing him as she pulled in a breath that had even her fingers trembling. "This has been the strangest Christmas I can ever remember."

He didn't want to leave her like this, breaking, sad. "Listen—"

"No," she said, adding, "I can't," then pushing out of the car before he could walk around and help her. "Thanks for the cake. And for the scarf." Then she slammed the door and whirled away, hurrying inside the building.

He sat there idling for a very long time after she was gone, wondering if his car would always smell like cake and sex and turned earth, and if he'd ever get over Indiana.

INDIANA

Robby Hunt was a man in training wheels, slightly built with what could only be called a pretty face. He was nonthreatening and safe. He was the feminine familiar, not the overtly masculine unknown. I wasn't the only girl who thought him the most gorgeous boy in school, on a physical dreamboat par with Justin Timberlake. I imagine he shaved, but doubt he really needed to until he was twenty. If then.

Other girls, girls like Shelley James and Thea Clark, preferred man-boys, boys like Tennessee and Dakota, who matured early. My brothers were the jocks with the wide shoulders. Their letter jackets swallowed the girls who wore them. I think Robby and I probably wore the same size. Though he went to school with my brothers, and hung out with my brothers, I thought of him as another one of my friends. My girlfriends.

So it didn't make a lot of sense that he was the boy I decided to use for practice.

Watching Thea with Dakota had given me all sorts of ideas. My head was full of them, but they were fantasies. They were pretend. They were no more real than the illustrations in *The Joy of Sex*. I'd seen when Shelley had smuggled her parents' copy of the book to school. And the brief glimpse of a porn movie I caught once through Tennessee's not-quite-closed bedroom door was just as illusory.

I'd learned as much about the birds and the bees from health class as I had from my mother. She was good enough to buy me tampons, with biodegradable applicators, of course, but orgasms were something I discovered for myself. I knew what went where, though had no clue as to sizes and shapes, or how something so supposedly hard could possibly be a comfortable fit for either party.

Rather than ask—my mother or my health teacher or my school nurse or my friends who'd done away with their virginity as soon as they could—I decided a hands-on lesson would be best. And since Robby was nonthreatening and safe, and a boy instead of a man, I chose him, as I would any girlfriend, to show me a new skill. Or maybe I should've thought of him as my tutor, though that would imply he knew what he was doing.

He had no more experience than I did. This I discovered the night I intercepted him outside near our garage door. I'd heard Dakota on the phone. I knew Robby was coming over for pizza and video games. Tennessee worked two nights a week making deliveries, and would drop off orders gone wrong. This subterfuge was all done behind our parents' backs; we'd already been served plates of sprouts or something.

I was supposedly waiting for the pizza that night, but *pizza* was my safe word; its arrival would guarantee my assignation with Robby didn't get out of hand. Of course, Robby had no idea we were assignating (yeah, not a real word, I know) when he arrived to find me leaning against the corner of the garage, my hands behind me and my shoulders back to emphasize my perky assets, my T-shirt riding just above the waist of my denim shorts.

It took him a minute to get out of his car, though after seeing me there, he did cut his headlights. I was breathing so hard I just knew he'd be able to tell. When he finally opened his door, my mouth was so dry I doubted I'd be able to say anything. And I'd been standing in the same position so long, my muscles were aching.

"What're you doing out here?" he asked, and I was glad I had a ready answer.

"Waiting for Tennessee and the pizza."

He let that settle, then said, "Thought that was Dakota's job."

"Usually." I propped the sole of one sneaker against the garage wall, and sorta swung my knee side to side. "He was finishing his Spanish homework. I told him I'd wait."

"Huh." Robby came closer then, walking slowly, his hands in the pockets of the jacket he wore. "Aren't you cold? Wearing shorts?"

They showed off my legs and that was the point. "I wasn't cold inside. But, yeah. I would've changed if I'd known it was going to take him so long to get here."

He'd just about reached me, and my heart was beating pretty fast, and whether it was nerves or cold, I didn't know, but I watched his gaze fall to my chest. I wasn't wearing a bra, and my nipples were hard, and honestly, I'd had no idea the difference it would make when it was a boy responsible for all these things happening in my body rather than me doing it to myself.

He raised one arm and braced it on the wall above my head; then he stepped so that one of his legs was between mine, and likewise. As friends, we'd never been this close, or close in this way. We'd sat next to each other on the couch watching TV, and I'd reached across him to grab more popcorn from Tennessee's bowl, resulting in "accidental" contact.

This wasn't accidental at all. He'd gotten my message, even if I wasn't fully aware of sending it, or what it was. The dark night, the clothes, and the pose . . . They all seemed like something Thea Clark would do, and wasn't that my goal?

To be like Thea? To be less self-conscious, more self-confident? To go after what I wanted? To be noticed instead of invisible?

I can see all of that now, of course. How needy I was for attention. How desperate to feel something, anything, instead of being shunted aside for one cause or another because I had everything a girl my age could ask for, didn't I? A bed to sleep in, food to eat, clothes to wear, dogs and cats and friends? And yet the one thing missing from that list was the one thing I wanted most. The one thing I didn't know how to ask for: to be loved.

Robby made me feel all manner of things that night with the way he looked at me, the way he kissed me, his lips along my jaw and my neck.

Only then it got scary. Robby pulled me around the side of the garage and said, "All ya gotta do is slip one leg outta your shorts, hook it around my waist, and we'll go to heaven."

He'd really said that about heaven.

I shook my head. All sorts of shivery things were getting tangled up in my stomach. I came very close to throwing up.

Just then, Tennessee pulled into the driveway behind Robby's car, and flashed his brights as always. And though we were blocked by a hedge, Robby wasn't having any of my jumping away.

And then Tennessee honked. "I need to get the pizza."

"We'll finish this later."

But we didn't. Not that night. Dakota had heard Tennessee honk, and he reached the car before I did. For the rest of that night, Robby and I had a chaperone, though he made certain I sat beside him when we crowded onto the couch.

I could barely swallow the pizza I managed to chew. I had no idea what movie we watched in that room lit only by the TV.

I'd been wrong. So very wrong. Robby Hunt was very threatening. He was not safe at all.

And I loved it.

Chapter Sixteen

The new year, fresh with its starting-over, clean-slate, what-happened-in-the-past-stays-in-the-past promises, was, so far, sucking as badly as the old. And not just the most recent old, but all of the olds Indiana had told good-bye since she was fifteen. At least *her* year was sucking, all two weeks. It didn't help that she'd put on five pounds since Christmas, and all of it cake.

Two Owls Café was thriving. The work on the Caffey-Gatlin Academy was almost complete. Same with Luna and Angelo's barn renovation. Those Keller Construction projects had been well under way before she'd hired her brother to remodel her cottage and erect the greenhouses for the annex on Three Wishes Road. Of course they came before hers.

But now the rain was mucking up everything. The part of the property cleared had yet to be filled and leveled, and resembled a series of tar pits; clumps of the gooey mud clung to her boots from her earlier walk around the site. The thought of Hiram seeing what she'd done to the place where he'd lived . . . No, he hadn't kept the place in pristine condition, but it had been his home. In its current incarnation, it wasn't even fit for the bees.

Any day now they'd be packing their bags and flying the coop, er, hive.

She didn't have time for this. She wasn't in a big hurry, but she *was* busy with her farm in Buda, and spring wouldn't be delayed. So why was she spending so much time fretting over a tiny little cottage, and an annex that was less about heirloom vegetables than it was about being closer to Kaylie and Tennessee?

Why, too, was it so hard for her to come out and admit that particular truth? Couldn't she just tell her brother and sister-in-law that she was tired of being alone? That she loved them dearly and wanted to be close? After so many years on her own, she wanted more? Shared holidays and quick cups of coffee and shopping trips and a smile and a wave when they passed on the street?

And nothing was happening with her search for

Dakota either. Or at least, not happening the way she wanted it to. Kaylie's investigator delivered regular reports, but those reports did nothing but depress her further. Her brother had worked for six months in Seattle, but left no forwarding address. He'd been in Portland, in Boise, in Missoula, Montana.

He'd fished for salmon. He'd built houses. He'd felled trees. He'd roasted coffee beans and even pulled espressos as a barista. He'd wrangled cattle. Dakota. The high school baseball star who'd loved him some muscle cars. On horseback. Wrangling cattle. Some things really did need to be seen to be believed.

She wanted to know where he was now. She needed to know. She ached with it. She had to make sure he was okay, that she hadn't ruined his life, because for thirteen years she'd been unable to get beyond the certainty that she had. That he hated her for what she'd done. Even though he didn't know what she'd done. Nobody did.

But she knew.

"You're all wet."

She looked up from where she was sitting on the back steps outside the cottage's kitchen door. Will's appearance wasn't surprising, though she hadn't heard him arrive. "Thanks," she said. "I wasn't aware."

"You're also muddy."

She glanced down at the goop stuck to the

vamps of her boots. "Again. The obvious. I appreciate having it pointed out."

He crossed his ankles and dropped down to sit beside her.

Company loving misery? "And now you're all wet and also muddy."

"I've been worse," he said, and shrugged, leaning back on his elbows.

Worse. Oh, good. They could talk about him instead of her having to examine even more of her life. "Are you ever going to tell me about it? Prison?"

"Probably not." He straightened his long legs out in front of him and crossed his ankles. "It's one of those things no one else needs to know."

"Yeah," she said, because he'd come closer than she liked to reading her mind about her past with Robby.

"I do wonder sometimes what in the hell I was thinking."

"I doubt you're the only one to ever feel that way," she said, deflecting whatever questions he might ask by adding, "I had no idea this acreage was in such bad shape. I should've done more research, but I jumped because . . ."

He let his head fall to the side, his hair falling, too, and looked at her. "Because the mountain wouldn't come to Muhammad."

She huffed, unable to stifle a grin. "I'm assuming you mean Tennessee."

"If you'd called me, I would've come."

The words fell between them, tumbled around, bounced, and demanded their due. "This can't happen, you know. I mean, I'd thought it might . . ."

"But you really didn't want it to."

Was he right? "I don't know you. You won't let me know you."

"And Oliver Gatlin will."

"It's not about Oliver. Not really." Except . . .

Hadn't everything been about Oliver Gatlin since that first morning on Three Wishes Road? Or maybe even sooner. Since they'd brushed against each other at Luna and Angelo's reception? Even that night there'd been something there. She'd gone home with it, the feel of his arm, his scent. The picture of him talking to Angelo and Harry Meadows.

"You can tell yourself that," Will said, "but the truth would be along the lines of, 'It's all about Oliver. Really.' "

She hadn't meant to fall in love with him. That family . . . She would never fit in, and she didn't need Merrilee, with her pearls and her pumps and her handbag that had cost more than Indiana's Camaro, to tell her that particular truth.

She'd bring Oliver the same trouble she'd caused Tennessee and Dakota. The same trouble she'd brought down on Robby Hunt. He was no innocent, but if she'd been content to be who she was at fifteen . . . If she hadn't been swept up in the exotic unknown that had been Thea Clark . . . She couldn't hurt another man. She just couldn't.

He'd told her to never be sorry . . . "Will—"

"Don't. Just be honest," he said, pulling his knees toward his chest, and sitting forward to drape his wrists over them. "If anything, be honest."

He stared at the muck between his boots, his hair wet where it hung in thick hanks from his bowed head. Had someone been dishonest with him? Had he been the one who hadn't been truthful? Was he being dishonest now, feigning this dejection that had her wanting to reach for him, to soothe him, when she knew her instincts were right?

Why couldn't she take him at his word? Why was being forthcoming so difficult with him? "The day we met, at Kaylie's place. Do you remember that?"

The corner of his mouth teased upward. "I was unloading some two-by-fours, I think. Had them on my shoulders and walked around the side of the house. There you were, talking to Kaylie and Ten. I think that was the first time you'd seen him in a while."

"It was. I was pretty caught up in all that emotion." And it rose in her now, the same rush of so many things she'd had no idea what to do with.

"But it didn't keep you from noticing me."

Noticing him. When did she not notice him? He walked through a door, he exited his truck, he appeared from around the side of a house unexpectedly. He was impossible not to notice, but his charisma wasn't enough. He was off in a way she would never be able to deal with long-term. And she was too old for short-term to be an option.

She looked down at her lap, her skirt soaked nearly through, her thighs beneath the fabric of her tights covered with chill bumps, though she didn't think she was cold. Wet, yes, but this was Texas, and January didn't always require warm clothes. "You didn't say much. With your mouth, anyway. But your eyes . . ."

"I'd been out maybe a week? First there was Kaylie and Luna. Then you." He reached down and swiped his palm over the toe of one work boot, then swiped it across the walkway cement to clean off the gunk. "Keeping my mouth shut is probably what kept me out of trouble those days."

"And now? You've been out, what?" She counted back to the previous March. "Ten months? What keeps you out of trouble now?"

She waited for the obvious response: he stayed out of trouble to keep from going back in. But he surprised her, saying instead, "I'm in more trouble now than you can imagine."

"Will—"

And then he threw back his head and laughed, water from the leaves of the backyard trees, their limbs creating a canopy over the cottage, dripping onto his face, and him not seeming to care at all. As if the possibility of bark or bugs or water-logged bees falling into his open mouth hadn't occurred to him, when she couldn't think about anything else.

Except what sort of mess he'd gotten himself into. "Can I do something? Can I help?"

"Trust me, Ms. Keller. You've done more than you can possibly know."

She was caught too off guard to find any sort of response.

"But yeah," he said quickly. "If you want to do something, you can listen."

"Okay," she said, pulling her skirt over her knees and huddling in on herself.

"You've got a brother here who, I've got to say, is nuts about you moving to Hope Springs, even if he hasn't told you." He held up a hand when she started to interrupt. "And I know you want to find the one who walked out of your life, but don't forget about Tennessee."

"I would never forget about Tennessee." She frowned. How could he even think that?

"Good. Now make sure he knows that," he said, catching and holding her gaze. "Don't let everything be about Dakota."

"It's not," she said, but didn't argue further because she couldn't do so and know she wasn't telling a lie.

He nodded. Whether he believed her or not . . . "That's all. I just wanted to say it before I split."

Splitting didn't sound like he was headed to work. And then it hit her, her pulse blipping, though she shouldn't have been surprised. "You're leaving Hope Springs."

"Eventually. Manny's working on finding me another job. It's time to move on."

"Because you're still bored?" *Please not because of me. Please.* "What about your loft?"

He shrugged as if he hadn't counted on her question. "If I decide to come back, I'll have a place to lay my weary head."

"Will—"

"Do me a favor," he said, his hands on his knees as he readied to stand. "Be nice to Gatlin. I think he needs it worse than I do."

"We're friends," she said, because she was not going to talk about Oliver. "Just like you and I are friends."

"No," he said, his accompanying laugh sharp. "I don't think so."

"You can think what you like," she said, and braced for his argument.

But he didn't argue. He reached for her instead, pulling her to him, settling his mouth over hers, and urging her lips apart. She stiffened, her eyes open, shocking herself with her lack of response. Oh, how far she'd come with knowing herself and what she wanted.

Whom she wanted.

He was laughing to himself when he let her go and stood, looking down to where she sat, still stunned. "See? That's how you kiss a friend. Remember that the next time you kiss Gatlin."

Though Indiana had hoped to spend Valentine's Day in Buda, away from the only man the day brought to mind, too much was happening on Three Wishes Road for her to abandon Hope Springs, which put her across the street from the Caffey-Gatlin Academy—where Oliver's car was parked in the newly poured front lot.

Oh, she couldn't avoid him forever. And she wasn't even sure avoiding was what they'd been doing since Christmas, but a month and a half made for a really long silence. Especially between two people who purported to be friends. Friends had one another's best interests at heart. Friends stayed in touch. Friends were whom one turned to in times of need, even if that need was as simple as a cup of coffee and a laugh.

Their friendship was one of the reasons she'd missed her brothers so much. Oh, they'd had the same garden-variety spats as most siblings eventually did, but she'd been able to count on both without fail. The failure had come later, her failure, her fault.

What she did know was that neither Thea nor Robby had been a true friend, but it had taken too long for her to realize that particular truth. Sad, really, when she'd lived with the two best examples of what friendship meant that she'd ever known.

Tennessee was better than anyone she knew at caring for others. Problem was, he wasn't so good at caring for himself—much like she wasn't so good at caring for herself. Much like Dakota hadn't thought of himself at all when he'd picked up that baseball bat.

Huh. And she'd always wondered how many things they had in common . . .

Having parked and left her car, she headed for the front steps and climbed them to the porch. Two boxes sat at her door, both UPS deliveries. She picked up both, recognizing the one from Amazon as the latest Jo Nesbø novel she'd ordered, but the other . . . She pushed into the house, setting the boxes on the kitchen countertop.

Inside the white cardboard were two layers of Bubble Wrap, and inside the Bubble Wrap two layers of thin brown paper, like that from a grocery bag, but lightweight and imprinted with the logo of the sender—Lockets and Figs—with whom she was unfamiliar. Once she pulled that paper aside, she found the box.

It was white and square and about the size of her palm. The top fit snugly to the bottom and was held in place by a flat bow of silver ribbon. She pulled both ends, then lifted away the box top to be met with cotton padding and a tiny bifold card. The outside was engraved with the same logo as the box and the paper.

But the inside . . .

With the box in one hand, the card in her other, she walked to the small bistro table she'd bought to have in the house and sat. Her hands were shaking when she opened the card to read it again, her heart in her throat causing her much breathing grief. She blew out a breath like she would a whistle, and forced her eyes to examine each word.

> **"The bee is more honored than other animals, not because she labors, but because she labors for others."**
> **Saint John Chrysostom**

That was it. No salutation. No signature.

It didn't matter. She knew whom it was from.

She didn't recognize the name of the jeweler, but the piece itself told the tale. The delicate chain was made of tiny, lace-like links, and the dainty little bee dangling on the end was, she was certain, crafted of onyx and topaz and diamonds and gold. It was gorgeous. It was extraordinary. It was too much for a gift between . . . friends.

No off-the-shelf baubles for Oliver Gatlin. Uh-uh. She'd bet her whole crop of honey this piece had been custom-made. Meaning he'd commissioned it weeks ago. More than likely before the wedding and the reception and all the in-between cake.

And he'd given her a Patchwork Moon original for Christmas, which had her wondering how original it really was. Had he bought it off the shelf in the Austin boutique that sold Luna's wares? Or had he made the request, even though Luna rarely took on special orders?

Two months ago he'd thought enough about her to buy these gifts, to have at least one of them specially designed, and considering the colors in the scarf, quite possibly both, and at some cost. Yet she'd only seen him in passing since Christmas, when she'd left him sitting in his car in front of Luna's loft after gorging on the desserts he'd paid for.

That day in Butters Bakery . . . The things they'd left unsaid . . .

Once she'd made it upstairs to the reception, she'd stood by the loft's windows, blinking back tears, and watching until he'd pulled away. She'd only been able to see a sliver of his car's roof, and she'd had to stand on tiptoe to peer down at the street. He'd sat there in the idling vehicle for ten minutes, then burned rubber when he'd left.

Only when he pulled away had she realized she was shaking. Her hands, her knees. Her heart that wanted so badly to break. How had she let herself get so weak that she completely let down her guard?

This was frightening, and it tore her up because what she felt for Oliver cut to the core of who she was. Who she'd been since fifteen and her course set with the opposite sex. Robby's assault had happened almost half her lifetime ago, and yet it ruled every choice she'd made since. A part of her knew she'd given too much power to that one boy, and that one night.

Yet how could she not?

Nothing about her seduction of Robby had compared to the tales Thea Clark told of the boys she'd had her way with. Thea's stories had sent sparks tickling through Indiana's body. She'd expected the same electric charge to happen from Robby's touch, and it had, though the rest of her expectations couldn't have been any further off base. Then had come the night of his attack, when fear had sluiced through her veins, as cold and cutting as ice shards.

Even now the emotion clutched hard, pulling her down, drowning her. She couldn't let it, *she couldn't let it,* and she stood, pushing up so swiftly her chair rocked back and fell to the floor. Leaving the bee in its box on the table, she exited the house, slamming through the back door before making her way to the closest greenhouse. It would be warm in the greenhouse, familiar, soothing. It would be safe. And her salvation.

She had starter plants at her Buda farm growing in biodegradable planting pots while waiting to be transferred into their permanent homes here. And here she had all the components of her growing mix, plus the trays for the larger pots.

Who cared that it was a holiday meant to celebrate romance? She was not a romantic. She was practical. She got things done. She didn't let emotions get in the way of anything, and oh, she was such a liar. Emotions were eating her alive, crowding out logic and leaving her a mess. She hated being a mess. She hated it so very much.

She was sifting potting soil when he drove up. She'd heard the low thrum of his expensive import, wondering at first if she was hearing her bees, and what had their drone sounding so loud. She was being ridiculous, worrying the way she was, but since finding the dead one on her porch last month, she'd felt like a helicopter parent.

It took him a few minutes to find her, and waiting for him felt like a torturous game of hide-and-seek. She couldn't breathe; she couldn't think. She held her trowel so tightly her fingers lost all feeling. The cottage was unlocked, and she imagined him walking through the unfinished rooms, peeking into each, seeing the garage sale finds she'd moved in so she wouldn't have to sleep on the floor between furniture pads, or eat standing up at the sink.

Seeing the discarded wrapping paper and packaging on the kitchen counter.

Seeing the bee in its box.

What would he think, the way she'd left it there, not ignored but not appreciated? Except she did appreciate it. More than she could put into words. She just didn't know what she was supposed to do now . . .

"Hi," he said, walking up behind her, having latched the door behind the influx of cool air. "It smells good in here."

"It smells like dirt." And now it smelled like him, spicy, earthy. Privileged.

"I'd say it smells like you," he said, "but I don't want you to think you smell dirty."

She smiled at that. "I've been known to. But I know what you mean. It's on my boots. I'm forever wiping my palms on my jeans or skirts. It gets under my fingernails. Even when I wear gloves, it gets under my fingernails." Good grief, but she was babbling. "I don't know how that happens."

He moved to her side, leaned a hip against her worktable, shoved his hands in the pockets of his navy pants. Pants he wore with a pinstripe dress shirt beneath an argyle-patterned sweater in colors of heather and plum. Clothes from his old life, though his hair brushed his chin now, and he hadn't shaved in days.

"I've never noticed," he finally said, his gaze falling to the shovel in her hand. "And you've always smelled good."

She couldn't do this, be casual, be flirtatious,

tease. He'd been clean shaven when he'd kissed her, and the way she wanted to feel his beard . . . She couldn't. *She could not.* "About the necklace—"

"I know we left things up in the air at Christmas," he said, turning to brace his backside and the heels of his palms against the table. Getting dirty. Not caring. "And I'd forgotten until today that this would be arriving. But I haven't forgotten about you for one minute." He paused, waited for her to look over. "And I've missed you like mad."

Oh, her heart. Her stomach. Her heart. She did her best to breathe. His eyes were clear and bright, the circles beneath hardly visible at all. He looked good. So very good. She'd missed *him* like mad, and suddenly she found herself wanting to cry.

Why couldn't life be simpler? "You sound like you're in a better place than you were in December."

He nodded, his hair falling forward. "I am. Eating right, getting enough sleep, working out."

She could tell. "And painting."

"And painting."

Her eyes on her trowel and the dirt on the table, she thought back to the first new work he'd done. "More than bees, I hope?"

But he didn't answer. He just stood there, waiting, staring, as if he knew he'd eventually get his way. That she'd stop what she was doing and pay attention to him. And she did.

"Thank you," he said, smiling as he caught her gaze. "I've been painting, yes. More than bees, and I'd really love for you to come see what I've done."

She listened to what he said, the words he used, the tone of his voice. But she also saw a plea in his eyes that left her thinking she had a decision to make: Did she follow her head, or her heart?

"Why don't you tell me about it?" she heard herself saying, because now was not the time to determine the rest of her life.

"It's all abstract," he finally said, "but then you saw my idea of bees. And it's all about Oscar and Sierra. Musical notes mostly. Cellos and pianos. It'll all go in the arts center. The classrooms. The reception area. The board agreed."

And Luna hadn't told her? Then again, it was Oliver's triumph, and his to share. "That's wonderful."

"So you'll come see?"

"I'll try." Oh, that was lame. "I'm so busy." And that even more so. "I might not be able to until they're finished and installed across the street." She added a laugh. It didn't help. In fact, she feared it may have been the nail in the coffin of the effort he was making to either salvage or define what they'd had.

He nodded, knocked his fist against her table before pushing away. "I guess I'll see you at the Meadowses' for Easter."

"I guess you will," she replied, then because she really wasn't a bitch, added, "I'm happy your painting is going so well. I really am. And thank you for the necklace. I don't . . . You shouldn't . . ." Gah, she didn't even know what to say. "It's too much. Really, Oliver. It's too much for—"

"It's not too much for anything," he said, taking several backward steps toward the door and shrugging. "In fact, it's nothing. It's nothing at all."

Chapter Seventeen

The Easter barbecue at Meadows Land, the sheep farm owned by Luna's parents, Harry and Julietta Meadows, was an annual tradition, though this year's was Indiana's first to attend. Mitch, Kaylie's father, manned a fifty-five-gallon pit, and Harry, Luna's father, manned one even larger, and the tables were piled high with so much food it seemed criminal.

There was chicken and sausage and brisket and ribs. There was potato salad—mustard-style, mayonnaise-style, warm German-style—and a macaroni salad with shredded radishes and ham. There was a tossed salad, a Jell-O salad with Red Hots, and a pea salad with cubes of cheddar cheese.

There were baked beans. There were mustard greens. Loaves of white bread and yellow-squash casserole and deviled eggs sprinkled with bright red paprika. And all of that before Indiana even got to the table laden with drinks and relish trays and desserts. So, *so* many desserts, and icings in every possible pastel to match the season. She thought she might just sit down and start loading her plate right there.

There were also kids everywhere dressed in their Sunday best, holding baskets at the ready. And there was Luna Meadows Caffey in charge of the annual Easter egg hunt. She'd wrangled the group like a boss, having hidden all the eggs and prizes herself this morning, and was now holding the little monsters at rapt attention as she explained the hunt's rules. Also at rapt attention was Angelo, his expression as he watched his wife hold court as impatient as those of her subjects. It was a very personal impatience, and Indiana blushed.

Of course, she might've been more in a mood to enjoy it all if Oliver wasn't staring at her from the far side of the Meadowses' big yard. The expression on his face—hungry, expectant, restless—stirred emotions she'd thought long settled. Long because she hadn't seen him but in passing since Valentine's Day, and here it was closing in on the end of April.

At this rate, maybe they'd get their act together by Memorial Day. July 4th, even. Because it was obvious from the flutters tickling their way up her spine there was something very real lingering between them, something that refused to fade with time. It was worth holding close, this *something,* she was certain of it, and she didn't have it in her to give up.

She'd driven over with Kaylie and Tennessee, and brought every one of the heirloom tomatoes from her greenhouse annex ripe enough to pick. The same tomatoes that had been destined for the Downtown Buda Farmers' Market, but that she'd decided would make the perfect contribution to the community meal; she couldn't pipe decorative frosting or deviled egg yolk to save her life.

"Indiana? Could I take those tomatoes off your hands?"

She supposed she did look rather lost, standing and holding the wicker basket. All she needed was a pair of ruby slippers, and to click her heels. The idea that she was so close to having everything she wanted, that she was almost home . . . She gave Dolly Pepper a smile. "I need to wash them. I just picked them this morning. And I hope you have a knife so I can slice them. I meant to bring one . . ."

Dolly gestured in the direction of the house. "Why don't we do that real quick in Julietta's kitchen? And maybe that young man will find something else to stare at while you're inside."

Good grief. Had everyone noticed? "Is it that obvious?"

"That he's crazy about you?" Dolly held open the back door and smiled. "I'd say so."

Indiana's cheeks heated. "That wasn't really what I meant."

"Well, he is." Dolly followed her into the kitchen. "Same as he was at Thanksgiving."

Setting the basket on the counter next to the sink, Indiana said, "I'm just about to decide that it's impossible for men and women to be friends."

"Oh, sugar, that's not the case at all," Dolly said, echoing what Kaylie had told her. "Though granted, it works out a lot better without attraction to muck things up."

"I didn't mean for any of . . . *this*," she said, gesturing with one hand and not even sure she knew what she meant, "to happen."

"One rarely does," Dolly said, setting a large colander into the sink, the simple gold band on her left hand reminding Indiana of the older woman's unexpected romance. "It's just the way of things, lightning striking when you least expect it." She motioned for Indiana to get started. "How 'bout you wash and I slice?"

While Dolly found a cutting board, a long, serrated knife, and a large white plastic platter, Indiana turned on the faucet, looking out the window above the sink at the children scrambling through the ankle-high grass searching for treasures. "I'm not sure who's having more fun, Luna or the kids."

"Oh, Luna. Without a doubt. If she and Angelo decide to have a family of their own, she's going to be an amazing mother. But then, it would be hard for her not to, with the example Julietta has set." Dolly reached for the first tomato. "And Kaylie will be the same, with her foster mama looking over her shoulder every step of the way. May Wise was a wonderful mother."

"Nurture over nature?" Which Indiana had to believe in with her history at home.

"Absolutely," Dolly said. "Did you know I once met your parents?"

"Really? Where?" Because she couldn't imagine Drew and Tiffany having reason to cross paths with the down-to-earth Dolly.

"Rick, my son, was in several classes with Kaylie when she lived with Winton and May. There was an educational fair, I guess it was, in Austin one year." She paused, cocked her head, and frowned while she thought. "I chaperoned Rick's class trip with another parent. Your parents had come as part of your school's group."

Indiana remembered the bus ride from Round Rock, but couldn't recall much else about the trip. "Was it seventh-grade English maybe?"

Reaching for another tomato, Dolly nodded. "That sounds about right."

"That was so long ago. I can't believe you would remember meeting my folks."

Dolly took a deep breath and blew it out while drawing the knife blade through a palm-size Mexican Red Calabash. "They were a hard couple to forget."

Uh-oh. "Let me guess. They were more interested in quizzing the kids about the source of the food in their bagged lunches. And lecturing about the recyclable nature of their paper bags versus their plastic. Ahead of their time, my folks."

Shaking her head, Dolly made a little sound Indiana wasn't sure she could interpret. "I kept thinking what it must've been like for you and your brothers at home."

"To tell you the truth, not as bad as you might imagine," she said to set the older woman at ease. And really. Except for the lack of parenting, it hadn't been. Though it was much easier to see that looking back now.

"It's absolutely none of my business," Dolly rushed to say, turning, contrite, to squeeze Indiana's wrist. "That was totally out of line. I'm so sorry."

"Don't be." But speaking of out of line . . . She watched the running water sluice over the last tomato, the thin skin of the plump fruit nearly vibrating. "Do you know Oliver's parents?"

"Orville and Merrilee?" Getting back to her knife, Dolly nodded. "Sure. They probably moved to Hope Springs about the same time Rick's father and I did."

And? she wanted to add, but it was bad enough that she'd been as nosy as she had. "Orville's quite nice."

Dolly chuckled. "Does that mean you've had the pleasure of meeting Merrilee?"

"I've met her, yes," she said, and this time Dolly laughed.

"Not much of a pleasure, was it."

"It was so unexpected I didn't know what to think. It was before Oscar passed. She came to my office in Buda. Totally out of the blue."

"*She* came to see you." One hand on her hip, Dolly held the knife in the other and, staring at Indiana, repeated, "Merrilee Gatlin came to see you. In Buda."

"It did seem strange . . ."

"What in the world did you ever do to her?" Dolly asked, laughing again, but this time with less humor than before, leaving Indiana to scan the yard, looking for Oliver.

"*I* didn't do anything. Except mention to Oliver that I was going to look for Dakota."

"Ah. And what did Oliver do?"

Dolly's response had Indiana wondering what the other woman knew that she didn't. "He hired the Gatlin family's investigator."

"To find your brother?"

Indiana nodded. "Is that weird? I mean,

considering at the time Oliver and I had only talked a couple of times."

"Oh, honey. No wonder he was looking at you like he wanted to eat you up. You know he wouldn't do that for just anyone. I can only imagine what his mother had to say."

"Mostly to leave him alone. It seems I don't have the right pedigree."

Dolly huffed. "Merrilee doesn't even have the right pedigree. Not that you heard that from me."

"Pray tell," Indiana said, doing her best not to laugh at herself. Was she really standing here in Luna's family's kitchen gossiping with Kaylie's stepmother about Oliver's mother?

"Orville is the only one in the family to have come from money. Or to have made any money. To use Merrilee's yardstick, he married beneath his station. And she's done her absolute best to make sure he never regrets it, or that anyone would ever guess how far beyond the wrong side of the tracks she grew up."

Indiana felt a pang of sympathy for the older woman. "She's done a good job. I would never have known."

"To tell you the truth, I'm not even sure her boys were ever aware."

"Huh. I wonder what happened to make her so ashamed of her background."

"You mean besides the background itself?" Focused on the spiral of tomatoes she was

278

arranging on the platter, Dolly shook her head. "If there was a particular incident, I've never heard."

"And how does your nurture-over-nature theory come into play here? I didn't know Oscar, but Oliver seems quite well adjusted." If not a little bit interfering. And possibly somewhat full of himself. Both traits that sounded just like his mother.

"I'd say it was their father's influence that had both boys turning out so well, but Orville was always an absent father, the way he got wrapped up in his work. I don't know this firsthand, of course, but gossip will be gossip."

And apparently that was all there was going to be for now. Dolly rinsed her knife and the cutting board, stacked both with the colander on a towel. Then she picked up the tomatoes and gestured toward the door. "Let's see if one of the kids has found Luna's golden egg, shall we?"

He found her sitting on the stoop of what had once been Luna's weaving shed, and before that a shearing barn her father had actually used. It was far enough from the Meadowses' house to have offered Luna privacy while she worked, yet not so far that Indiana could be accused of abandoning the party.

"I've been looking for you," Oliver said, staring down.

One side of Indiana's mouth lifted as she raised her gaze to his. "And now you found me."

He moved to sit beside her without asking, and braced his elbows on his knees. "Did you want to be alone?"

"It doesn't matter," she finally said, toying with the hem of her sweater.

He watched her thumb and forefinger rub at the fabric. "Are you not having a good time?"

"I was. I am."

"Which is it?"

"I don't know." She shut her eyes, dropped her head back against the shed's closed door. "It's so dumb. But I see Kaylie with Mitch, and Mitch with Dolly, and Angelo with Harry Meadows, and I hate that Dakota's not here to know everyone, and share in these friendships and enjoy the holidays."

Her words had him bristling. This was where he was probably going to regret everything that came out of his mouth. But he couldn't keep it in any longer. He'd known this woman six months, and he couldn't recall a single time they'd been together that she hadn't bemoaned her brother's absence.

He got that. He better than anyone, good Lord. And because of that he didn't want to see her let her missing Dakota ruin her life the way he'd let Oscar's tragedy ruin his. "He's probably somewhere with his own group of friends, biting off chocolate rabbit heads and chasing 'em with barbecued ribs."

"I don't care. I want him here." Petulant and sulky and a testy crab. "With me and Tennessee. With Kaylie. He doesn't even know he's going to be an uncle. He needs to be here. Not"—she waved one hand—"wherever he is. Which I still don't know. And I'm beginning to wonder if I ever will."

He studied the ground, the tufts of grass between his shoes, the tiny ants scrabbling down between the blades, then lifted his head to look toward the party. "Why can't you appreciate the family you have here? The friends? Why does everything have to revolve around your brother, who obviously doesn't want to be a part of your life?"

The gears in her head, insulted and shocked, were whirring so loudly he swore he could hear her words even before she spoke. "Why would you say that? You don't know anything about what Dakota does or doesn't want."

He knew Derek Wilborn hadn't been able to find more than a faint trail. And any man who didn't care about being found didn't go to such lengths not to leave one.

"And I do appreciate the family I have here," she said before he could respond. "The friends, too."

"But we're not enough, are we?" he asked,

turning to look at her, though her gaze was cast down and away from his. "We never will be." *He* never would be.

"I don't know what you mean," she said, shaking her head.

"Sure you do." He stood, shoved his hands in his pockets. "I'll bet a day hasn't gone by since we first met in the academy's driveway that Dakota hasn't been on your mind."

Finally she looked at him, still sitting, but lifting her chin, her head tilted back and her eyes angry. "A day hasn't gone by since I was fifteen years old and this close to being raped that Dakota hasn't been on my mind."

He scrubbed both hands down his face, cursed under his breath. What was wrong with him? "I'm sorry—"

She waved a hand in a weak attempt to blow him off. "I don't expect you to understand."

Was she kidding him? He moved in front of her, dropped to his haunches, waited for her to look at him. "You're not the only one to have lost a brother, Indiana. And at least as far as you know, yours is still alive."

"But I *don't* know, do I? My investigator can't find him. Your fancy investigator can't find him. Maybe he's not alive at all."

"Fancy investigator?" he asked, frowning. "What's that supposed to mean?"

"Nothing. I don't know. I just . . . I don't know,"

she said, picking at the fabric covering her knees.

He stayed there for several long moments, not speaking, not reacting. He wasn't sure how to react, or what to say. He understood her frustration over the lack of progress in her search, but her giving up seemed to come from a much deeper place. "Indiana—"

"What are we doing here, Oliver?" she asked, her cloud of dark hair bouncing around her face as she turned on him. "I mean, really. Are we friends? Am I an experiment or some sort of goodwill gesture for you? We're certainly not lovers. Or is this about getting back at your mother somehow?"

This? What did she mean by *this?* "Hold on—"

She got to her feet as he did the same. "Why? Why should I hold on? What do I have to hold on to? You give me expensive gifts. You take me to see your father's show. You buy me cake when I ask for it. You kiss me. You—"

She stopped herself before saying more, and he imagined her blurting out an expletive he'd never heard her speak. One that described the way he'd used her. One he deserved.

She was right. They were not lovers. And the desire to be so sawed at his insides, leaving his breathing jagged, his need for her desperate and achingly harsh.

"We haven't had a lot of time together—" was what he finally started to say.

"Six months," she said, cutting him off.

"Except we've only seen each other a handful of times."

"No. I mean, a man I work with, one of my mechanics . . . He told me once that six months is all anyone needs to know how they're going to fit in a relationship. He didn't believe in these multiyear engagements or long cohabitations. Might as well be married, he said. If you don't know after six months, then you're never going to know."

"Do you believe that?" he asked.

"I told him he was being ridiculous, but when I think about the couples I know in successful relationships . . ." She shrugged. "Those first months have been awfully intense."

He couldn't argue with that. "We should probably talk. About . . . things."

"Isn't that what we're doing?" she asked, reaching up to clear a strand of flyaway hair from her face.

"Yeah, but not here," he said, glancing at the festivities, then back. "Unless you'd rather stay."

She seemed to consider his request, then said, "How much time do you need?"

"To talk?" Or was she referring to the six-months scenario?

"Never mind," she said, and waved him off, then hugged herself tightly.

"I've never been in a relationship before." The

words came out of nowhere and expanded to fill the cavernous space between them. He hadn't meant to make the confession, though strangely, he didn't mind having her know.

"What?"

He shrugged. "I had girlfriends in high school, and two or three in college, but then Oscar's accident happened and it was easier to put my head down and forget there was a world outside."

She narrowed her gaze. "You haven't dated since Oscar's accident?"

Where did he even begin with all the ways his life had changed that day? "Have I been celibate all this time? No. But a relationship's always felt like too much . . ."

"Responsibility?"

That made him sound like a jerk. Probably because he was a jerk. Look how he'd failed his brother. Look at the grief he'd caused in the lives of those around him in the years before he'd discovered the truth of that tragic weekend. "Silver spoon, remember? I live up to the self-involved hype."

"No. You don't. You're about the least self-involved person I've ever met." She smiled then, truly smiled, as if it were easier than dealing with the drama. "I'm going to credit your father's influence for that."

"Ah, but you've only seen him on display," he said. He didn't like talking about his father. "He would go weeks at a time without coming home. And it wasn't like he was traveling. He was too wrapped up in his work to shower or get a haircut or even eat. Forget remembering he had a wife and kids."

"I'm sorry. I had no idea."

He huffed. "I don't even know where that came from."

"Obviously from some deep dark place inside." The woman was way too perceptive. "Which makes me wonder what other skeletons you've got hidden."

Because telling her the worst of the secrets he kept wasn't on tap for today, he said, "You show me yours and I'll show you mine."

"Oliver Gatlin. Are you flirting with me?" she asked.

If he was, he feared he was doing so to deflect her prying, and that really wasn't fair. Sighing, he asked, "Isn't it kinda late for that?"

"Because we've already had sex, you mean?" She shook her head knowingly. "You obviously haven't been watching Luna with Angelo, or Kaylie with Tennessee. And really. Do you not pay any attention to Mitch and Dolly when they're together?"

He liked this woman a lot. "Like I said. I'm not so good with relationships."

"How would you know if you've never been in one?"

"Something tells me I'd be in one now if I was any good," he said, unable to be anything but honest.

Honest or not, his comment wedged itself between them, and she frowned. "Since I haven't been in one either, I'm not sure I like your logic."

And then she backed away, one step, two, and on the third she turned, leaving him standing alone in front of the shed.

He hadn't known that about her, and it surprised him. Then again, like him, she had a lot of emotions tied up elsewhere, and until she freed them, until he freed them . . . He watched her join the others, thinking she was way too perceptive.

And deciding he didn't like his logic, either.

Chapter Eighteen

A week later, and after closing time, Indiana arrived at Two Owls Café bearing gifts, and for no reason other than she wanted to see a friend. That said friend happened to be her very pregnant sister-in-law made her anticipation of the visit that much brighter. She absolutely loved Kaylie to death. And who wouldn't?

Indiana had bonded with Kaylie the first time they met. That day was supposed to be about her advising on the Two Owls garden, when really it was all about her reconnecting with Tennessee.

But she owed that reconnection to Kaylie, and Kaylie would always hold a special place in Indiana's heart because of the part she'd played in the reunion.

Today, however, it was just the two of them, Indiana bringing the first of the zucchini from the Gardens on Three Wishes Road for Dolly's zucchini bread. Or so was the story she'd given when she'd called. The reality was that she needed girl time with her favorite girl before she fell completely apart.

"How're you doing?" she asked, joining Kaylie in her second-floor sitting room. She'd left the zucchini in the kitchen with Dolly, where she and Mitch were cleaning up after the day's buffet.

"Just peachy," Kaylie said, resting the book she'd been reading on the swell of her belly as she reclined against the pillows in a chaise lounge. "If peachy means like a bowling ball bag."

"When does the doctor think your lane will be ready?" Indiana couldn't help but ask.

Kaylie smiled at that, shifting higher in the seat. She set her book aside, and pulled a basket of baby clothes closer. The woman did not know how to relax. "A week. Maybe two. At this point it's all up to the ball."

Indiana sat on the ottoman that put her closest to her sister-in-law. The parents-to-be hadn't wanted to know the baby's gender, preferring the surprise, so most of the baby things Kaylie had at hand were gender neutral in color. She reached for a hooded towel in a bright spring green and folded it.

"Not that you have much choice, but hang in there. You really look great. For a bag," she said, causing both of them to laugh. "I left the zucchini in the kitchen, which is a mess, by the way, though I'm guessing that's a really good thing for Two Owls."

"It is." Kaylie took a deep, grateful breath. "I don't know what I'd do without Dolly and Mitch. They've pretty much taken over running the café."

"I'm sure they don't mind."

"I know," she said, smoothing the wrinkles from a second hooded towel. "But I've worked so long and so hard to make this happen, and now I'm nothing but a big fat lump on a log."

"Wait. I thought you were a bowling ball bag."

"You left out big and fat," Kaylie said, her mouth twisted.

Indiana smiled. "The big and fat are temporary, and aren't even you. That's all little Keller."

"Or not-so-little Keller," Kaylie said, then before Indiana could respond, added, "Dolly mentioned Oliver seemed rather infatuated with you at Easter."

Infatuated. Somehow that word just didn't fit. It was too simple. Too one-sided. Too shallow, even. Yet no other came to mind, and Indiana sighed. "Honestly. I never meant for any of this to happen. Oliver is . . . complicated," she said, and left it at that. "But I don't think it's things with him as much as with Dakota that are turning me into a bitchy mess."

Kaylie folded a tiny yellow onesie, taking her time as if she weren't quite ready to let go of the subject of Oliver. "Ten's not been the easiest man to live with of late, either."

"Because of Dakota? Or because he's anxious about you and the baby?"

"Some of both, I'm sure, though he doesn't really have any reason to worry about the baby or me. The doctor says we couldn't be a more textbook pregnancy if we tried."

"Still. This changes everything about both of your lives. And as natural as childbirth is, there can be complications."

Kaylie twisted her mouth to the side. "Thanks."

"Sorry," Indiana said with a wince, "but you know what I mean. Tennessee loves you. Until he gets you and the little one home, he's going to worry."

"And he'll keep worrying about things like the best schools, the safest cars, the healthiest foods. And he'll keep worrying about Dakota." Kaylie reached for a drawstring sleeper. "Has there been anything new from Martin?"

Indiana shook her head, recalling her last conversation with Kaylie's PI. "I don't think I ever told you that he's not the only one looking."

"What do you mean?" Kaylie asked, and Indiana pulled in a deep breath.

"Apparently the Gatlins have a PI on retainer. Don't ask me why," she said with the wave of one hand. "But Oliver put him on the case, too."

"Huh. Did you know? Did he ask you about it?"

"I found out after the fact." Indiana smoothed a tiny white T-shirt over her knee. "And all he'd asked was if I wanted him to vet Martin or recommend anyone. I said no."

Kaylie stacked the sleeper on top of the onesie, looking at the laundry instead of at Indiana. "So rather than doing either of those things . . ."

"Exactly. The spirit rather than the letter." Such a Gatlin way to operate. Or so she'd thought before getting to know him.

"He must care for you a lot," Kaylie said after a long moment spent watching Indiana fumble through folding the T-shirt.

"I think it's just a man thing," she said with a shrug, giving up. "Wanting to be right. Taking charge."

Kaylie took the garment from her hand. "A man doesn't spend that kind of money on a woman he doesn't care for."

Indiana kept silent about the Patchwork Moon scarf, and the Lockets and Figs bumblebee necklace. "He was just being nice."

"Indiana—"

"Okay. He cares for me now, but that happened

a long time ago. We'd just met. We certainly hadn't—" She stopped herself but was too late with it.

"Tell me something," Kaylie said.

"Maybe." It was the only response Indiana was willing to make.

But Kaylie ignored her feigned reluctance. "If you and Oliver are . . . together like that, have you gotten over Will?"

There hadn't really been anything to get over, had there? "Will thinks I need to be thankful for the brother I have in my life." When Kaylie remained silent, she added, "And he's not the only one."

"Oliver, too?"

Indiana nodded. "Oliver I understand. He lost his only brother. It makes sense he'd push me to not forget about Tennessee. What he doesn't get is that not for a minute, no matter what happens with this search for Dakota, will I ever forget about Tennessee."

"You should see the look Ten gets on his face when he talks about you," Kaylie said, her eyes growing misty. "I'm not sure if he's ever told you what it means to him to have you back in his life."

It took several emotional moments for Indiana to find her voice and be able to work her very tight throat. "Do you think they're right? That I'm taking Tennessee for granted? Or relegating him to second class because I want to find Dakota?"

"He wants to find Dakota as much as you do. And if he feels you're treating him like a second-class citizen, he would be the last one to complain, because he treats himself the same way. Whatever wrongs you want to make right with Dakota, Tennessee has just as many of his own. All I ask is that you do this together. Tell him about Oliver's investigator. Let him know anything either man finds out."

At the sound of the elevator engaging behind him, Oliver closed his eyes, took a deep breath, and set down his palette and brush. He hadn't spoken to Indiana since Easter because he hadn't known what to say to her. The way they'd left things had pretty much sounded like the end of whatever they might've been working toward.

And that on top of his butting into the business of her and her brother . . . Yeah, he couldn't imagine she had anything to say to him. Apologizing for his tone was one thing, but he couldn't apologize for his words. That didn't make him right. It was her life, her situation. Her brothers. But he was not going to change his mind.

And yet, wasn't he just as guilty as she was? He'd put his life on hold the moment he'd heard the news of Oscar's car tumbling down the ravine. What right did he have to lecture Indiana on how she was living hers? Except it hadn't been a lecture, had it? But more his taking another tack to try to fix her pain. Which brought him around to asking what right did he have to do that? Oh, that answer was easy.

He loved her.

The thought shuddered through him, gripped him hard, squeezed until he had to struggle to draw a breath. Yeah. Loving her didn't give him either of those rights. But loving her made him want to do anything he could to stop her from hurting. The fact that she was the only one who was able to do that . . .

He shook his head and tabled the thought. The elevator had arrived, and he'd just realized, just admitted, just accepted that he loved Indiana Keller.

What in the world was he supposed to do now?

Wiping his hands on a rag, he turned toward the door, his hands stopping, his feet stopping, his heart nearly stopping when his father stepped out. The only words he could think to say were, "What's wrong?"

The older man looked him up and down. "Other than you needing a haircut, nothing that I know of."

Indiana's voice came back to him: *What's going on with your hair?* "This coming from a man wearing a ponytail?"

"Susan misses you," his father said, setting the dog he held tucked under his arm on the floor.

The miniature poodle, who looked more like a

terrier, ran circles around Oliver's feet, then sat and looked up, her stubby tail wagging through the dust on the floor. He opened his arms and she jumped, landing against his chest, and it was hard not to smile when her tongue went to work against his cheek.

"All right, all right," he said, putting her down and wiping his face on his shoulder. "Did you bring her food and her leash, or just the dog?"

"It's all in the car. Didn't want to haul it up if you told Susan to take a hike."

He would never say such a thing to the dog, and his father knew it. "She can stay. It'll be nice to have the company."

"And a reason to breathe some fresh air a couple of times a day?"

Oliver indicated the open windows. "I breathe it all day long."

"A reason to take a shower, then."

"And how often have you been so wrapped in a sculpture that you skip a shower or two?"

"Smells like you've skipped at least a dozen."

Huh. He didn't realize things had gotten so bad. Good thing Indiana hadn't stopped by. Not that he'd given her a reason to . . .

"How long are you planning to hide out here?" His father's question came from halfway across the loft. "Your mother's worried."

Oliver shook off thoughts of Indiana. Or he tried. But the ones that replaced them were no better. He'd been here now for six months, painting, thinking, coming to grips with the years he truly had spent hiding. He'd gone home at least once every week. Or he had until Easter.

When Indiana had told him six months should be plenty of time to know what he wanted.

"I'm not hiding out. I'm working."

"On bees?"

Yeah. About that. He walked to where his father was standing, and took in the canvases stacked against the loft's brick walls.

"They're not all bees."

"They all look like bees. Yellow, black. That says bees to me."

He'd used more colors than yellow and black, and the orange that he'd had Luna weave into the scarf. She'd told him she didn't do special orders. He'd told her it was for Indiana, and offered to pay her enough for three. She wouldn't take money save for the one, and she made him tell her about what Indiana made him see.

All he could think to tell her was about the property on Three Wishes Road and the morning he and Indiana had first talked. How excited she'd been about becoming the care-taker for Hiram Glass's bees. Or maybe it was her excitement over owning the acreage and expanding IJK Gardens into Hope Springs. He didn't know what parts of the morning were memories, and what parts impressions.

He did know she'd been wearing her cowboy boots and a sundress, and he'd thought what a strange combination. He couldn't imagine any woman he knew being comfortable in what he'd come to accept as Indiana's uniform. The boots, anyway. The weather determined whether she wore dresses or T-shirts and jeans.

Neither could he imagine any woman he knew being comfortable getting her hands dirty— literally—while coaxing a harvest from the ground. And she'd seemed just as at ease, or at least as efficient, dealing with his emotional grime. No one had ever done that for him before. No one had ever been there for him before. Not in the way Indiana had. There was no one else. Only her. Just her.

He turned to his father. "I'm hiding. And I'm painting bees. What do I do now?"

Orville stared at his oldest son, his only son, his gray eyes knowing, his smile knowing, too. "That one's easy. You tell her that you love her. But not until you take a bath."

Chapter Nineteen

Mid-May found Indiana in her favorite place: up to her elbows in potting soil. The peaty, rich smell always calmed her, as did the feel of the dirt on her skin, nourishing, comforting, grounding.

She'd been thinking that Kaylie was right: Tennessee deserved to know about Oliver hiring an investigator. It was explaining why he would do so that was going to be tough.

Dakota had been gone for more than a decade. She, his sister, the reason he'd gone to prison, the reason he'd had to abandon all his plans for his life, had only decided seven months ago to look for him. Oliver hadn't needed that much time; he'd put his man on the case within days of hearing about her search. Neither man had found success, but that wasn't the point.

The point was . . . how could she explain to Tennessee what she couldn't explain to herself: Oliver's involvement? Unless Oliver returned the feelings she was having so much trouble with. Especially after the way they'd left things at Easter . . . Why hadn't he come to see her? Why hadn't she called him? *What is wrong with us?*

It was then that her phone rang, and for once she welcomed the intrusion. "Tennessee?"

"Kaylie's in labor."

"Now? At home? At the hospital?"

"It started last night. We're at the hospital now."

"She's okay?"

"She's close. If you want to be here for the main event—"

"I'm on my way."

Fifteen minutes later, clean and dressed, her hair mostly damp, she grabbed for her wallet and keys and phone, her gaze caught by the bumble-bee necklace lying on the top of her dresser. She closed her eyes, willing away the mixture of emotions and thoughts of Oliver that she was struggling to reconcile. All that mattered was that he was Kaylie's friend. No, all that mattered was that Indiana wanted him to know. To hear his voice. To possibly see him.

"Indiana?" he said when he answered her call.

"I thought you might want to know that Kaylie's having her baby. Tennessee just called. Well, he called fifteen minutes ago, but I was up to my elbows in potting soil and had to clean up. Anyway," she said, wondering why she thought Oliver would care about the dirt under her nails, "I'm headed for the hospital. If you want me to call you later—"

"Would you like me to come and wait with you?"

Her pulse jumped, even though he wasn't coming for her. "Yes. I'd love that. Thank you."

"Then I'll see you soon," he said.

Her pulse jumped again, her stomach flipping, too, though she was probably reading too much into his offer. Unless she wasn't. Unless he was as anxious to see her as she him. Unless they'd both been waiting for an excuse to pick up where they'd left off, or to try again, or just go back to the beginning and start over.

Oliver's accusations at Easter . . . He was right.

She had let her obsession with finding Dakota consume her. Oh, it didn't feel that way, but logic and reason told her the truth. All she had to do was look at the time she spent worrying.

She couldn't do it anymore. She just couldn't. She'd put things in motion with the investigator, and she had to accept that what would be would be.

The drive to the hospital from Three Wishes Road was short, as was every drive in Hope Springs, and Indiana arrived moments ahead of Luna, waving for her to hurry and join her as Angelo parked the car.

"Can you believe it?" Luna asked, grabbing Indiana's hand. "It seems like just yesterday she told us she was expecting."

"Thanksgiving was"—she quickly counted on her fingers—"six months ago. But, yeah. You're right. Like the blink of an eye." Except Christmas had come and gone, the new year, too. Valentine's Day, Easter. Soon it would be Memorial Day. She had to stop fretting about time passing. About missing Dakota. About missing Oliver most of all.

Minutes later, Angelo joined them in the waiting room outside labor and delivery. "Can we go in? Are we too late? Have you talked to Ten?"

"I don't know about going in," Indiana said. "I haven't seen Ten yet. I'm not even sure how to let him know we're here." She turned then, looking for someone to ask, but Oliver was walking down the hall toward her, and that was that. The buzz of the hospital faded.

How had she let him walk away? How had she survived this last month without seeing him?

How was it possible to have missed him this much when she wasn't even sure they were friends?

He reached her quickly; his steps were long and purposeful, his jeans worn, the tails of the button-down shirt he wore flapping and tattered. And his hair. He still hadn't cut his hair. It fell into his eyes, over his eyes, and he pushed it back over his head with both hands, clearing his beautiful face.

He was so, *so* beautiful. So beautiful. She'd never known a man could be described with that word, but it fit Oliver Gatlin in ways nothing else would. His brows were drawn together in a concentrated frown, his lips pressed similarly tight. But his hips rolled as he walked, loose and confident as his steps brought him close.

"Any news?" he asked, coming to a stop in front of her.

She shook her head, and then she stepped into his body, wrapping her arms around him because it had been too long, and she needed him, and having him here was like the rest of her life coming home. She caught back a sob, and he tightened his hold. She let him, even knowing he had no idea what was going on in her mind.

"I'm glad you're here."

"I wouldn't have missed it for anything."

She was so close to telling him she loved him. Oh, the time and the place was horribly wrong, except it really wasn't. It was perfect. A new life coming into the world . . . How could such a joyous event not put her own life into perspective? A life she wanted to share with Oliver.

Though whatever declarations she wanted to make would have to wait, because her phone buzzed at that moment with a text from Tennessee. She read it, turned to Luna and Angelo. "They're taking her into delivery. It shouldn't be too much longer."

It was two hours later when Tennessee appeared at the waiting room door and ushered them into Kaylie's room. Oliver walked in behind Indiana, and she held their joined hands in the small of her back as she approached the bed in the center of the room. She glanced up at her brother; the expression on his face, the dampness reddening his eyes, stole Indiana's breath.

Standing next to Kaylie's bed, Tennessee braced a forearm on the raised mattress, and with his free hand reached down to touch his daughter's cheek. Georgia May Keller. Seven pounds, ten ounces, nineteen and a quarter inches long. Her skin was flawless, her hair sparse but an obvious golden sort of red like her mother's.

Indiana leaned back into Oliver where he stood behind her, so solid, so strong. So understanding of what she needed from him. Never in her life would she have imagined herself this much in love. Thinking of the possibility that Oliver might feel for her what Tennessee obviously felt for his wife . . . She brought up a hand, pressed her fingers to the base of her throat, measuring the rhythm of her pulse.

Two soft knocks on the door had all heads turning. The handle moved. The door opened. Light from the hallway spilled into the room, and the man who'd knocked followed. He closed the door. He came closer. He stuffed his hands in his pockets and hunched his shoulders in a gesture so familiar, Indiana had to fight the dizziness threatening to take her to the floor.

Then she had to fight all the bodies in the way to get to him. She slammed into him, wrapped her arms around him, sobbed into his T-shirt, and sputtered his name. "Dakota!"

The room got crazy after that with gasps of joy and disbelief and excitement. Tennessee joined her, his arms going around her and their brother both, the three of them rocking and shaking, their hug filled with laughter and hard-beating hearts and joyful sobs and words that made no sense but were nonetheless understood.

"Where did you come from?" Indiana asked once the sibling huddle had disbanded. "How did you get here? I mean, how did you even know to come here tonight?"

He hooked an elbow around her neck and walked with her toward the bed. "Later, little sister. Right now I'd like to meet my sister-in-law. And my niece."

Tennessee made the introductions, a good thing, since Indiana wasn't sure she had it in her to say anything else without breaking down. If not for Dakota's arm keeping her standing, well, she wouldn't be. She was certain. Her legs were shaking. Her stomach was tumbling. Her palms were sweating so ridiculously she'd dampened her skirt trying to keep them dry.

He'd come out of nowhere. After all these years, he'd walked into her life as if he'd never been away. Except it wasn't that simple. It had to have been costly getting him here. It had to have taken many hours and many miles and many, many phone calls to track him down. She had such a monstrous debt to pay, and she met Oliver's gaze as the thought went through her mind, because monstrous and debt left her little doubt his man had been the one to come through.

Oliver stood at the foot of the bed, his gaze on the baby, not on Dakota and not on her. His hands were shoved in his pockets, his shoulders hunched, his hair falling like a curtain on either side of his face. He reached up and raked it back, rubbing at his whiskered jaw, then smearing his thumb beneath one eye.

And then, as if he was as overwhelmed as she

was, he moved toward the door. When Dakota let her go to pick up tiny Georgia May, Indiana joined Oliver. She couldn't let him leave the room without thanking him, and she reached out a hand, placing it in the center of his chest. She felt the beat of his heart, then flexed her fingers and pulled away.

It was hard to find her voice to ask, "Are you okay?"

He nodded toward the bed. "She's gorgeous, isn't she? And so tiny. I don't think I've ever seen a newborn who's only hours old."

"It's pretty amazing." She stepped to his side so she could see the knot of people speaking quietly, the smiles, the tears, Kaylie's glorious exhaustion that left her doing little but watching. But most of all her gaze was for her brothers. All three of the most important men in her life were here. Could this day be any better? "I'm so glad Dakota got to see her. I can't even believe that he's here. When he walked through the door, I thought I might faint."

He reached for her shoulder, squeezed it, then leaned to drop a kiss to her temple. "I'm going to go, let you be with your family."

"You don't have to," she said, grabbing for his hand, torn between her family and her future.

"Yeah. I do," he said, nodding toward the other visitors, adding, "We all do," as Indiana glanced toward the bed.

"I'll see you soon, sweetie," Luna was saying, cupping her hand over Kaylie's forehead to brush back her hair. "You take care of this gorgeous little bundle, and see that this man here," she added, glancing up at Tennessee, "takes care of you."

"That's not even a worry," the proud father said, shaking Angelo's hand before the couple headed for the door. Oliver stepped into the hallway with them as they left, lifting his hand as the door closed between them.

She wanted to catch him and say good-bye. She wanted to introduce him to her brother. But she had every piece of her family here with her, and she couldn't bring herself to leave. Not when the very thing she'd been hoping for had finally come to pass. Her brother was home. Her family, complete with the newest little Keller, was reunited.

So why did it feel as if the most important part was still missing?

Oliver squeezed Indy's shoulders, leaned to drop a kiss to her temple, then walked to the door to close it behind Luna and Angelo, stepping into the hallway as he did. The Keller family deserved this reunion and didn't need outsiders intruding. Not that he was necessarily an outsider. He just wasn't part of the family in the same way Kaylie was, though perhaps one day. Maybe even one day soon.

He had to admit surprise at having reached this

point, not with one of the women his mother had pushed on him, but with one who he imagined would prefer a day spent digging in the dirt to a night spent mingling at a Gatlin fund-raising soiree. He wondered how Indiana would fit in with the rest of the attendees, and imagined her standing out—not because she didn't belong, but because she wouldn't care.

Then again, she'd most likely fit in with no problem. She was like that, sociable and gregarious in ways he wasn't sure he'd known another woman to be. Honest ways. Authentic ways. Nothing about Indiana Keller was for show, and he was pretty sure he'd fallen in love with her because of her genuine nature even more than the cowboy boots she wore with everything, and that would make his mother insane.

His poor mother. He loved her dearly, and knew having to let Oscar go had devastated her. It had devastated him, a sibling, not a parent. His mother's interference in his life over the years had been in a large part her way of holding tight to the only son she could interact with, projecting her dreams for Oscar onto him without considering he and his brother were not the same person. They never had been. And even had Oscar survived the accident and grown into his full potential, they never would have been.

They were that different. That individual. That unique. And his mother had never, even when

Oscar was a thriving child, been able to see that.

He understood some of her blindness. It came from the strict, nearly abusive mores under which she'd been raised, the life of poverty she'd lived, the desire to escape, wanting to be more than her family circumstances allowed. Meeting his father while working her way through college as a waitress. Marrying his father because she'd wanted a way out, not for anything close to love. She had no idea he'd learned any of this, of course, and he had no intention of telling her. But the knowledge had gone a long way through the years in giving him patience.

Movement at the end of the hallway had him glancing that direction, where Will Bowman stood in quiet conversation with the Caffey couple. As Oliver looked on, Luna and Angelo said their good-byes, Luna with a lingering hug, Angelo with an extended handshake, leaving Will alone. Leaving Oliver to wonder . . . Hmm. What was going on?

He glanced from Will toward Kaylie's closed door, wondering about the convenient timing of Dakota's arrival. Had his own efforts turned up the missing Keller sibling, Oliver doubted he could've arranged such a heartwarming tableau.

Bowman, on the other hand, with the connections Oliver had recently learned the other man had, the access he would have to investigators . . . Huh. It seemed he may have been able to work the miracle Oliver had not, yet it was more than clear Indiana had given Oliver the credit. As soon as he could, he'd set her straight.

Will was walking toward him now, his head shaking slowly. Oliver frowned, not sure what to make of the gesture. And then in a voice as weary as the dark circles beneath his eyes, Will said, "Don't tell her."

He held Oliver's gaze keenly, until Oliver let go of the door handle and nodded. "She thinks it was me."

Will shrugged with a laziness Oliver didn't buy. "Let her think that."

But that wasn't Oliver's way. "I can't."

"For now, then," Will said, shoveling his hair out of his face. "Just do it for now."

"You'll be back to tell her the truth?"

Will answered with a snort. "You know I'm leaving?"

"I do now. And if you don't come back and tell her, or write and tell her—"

"It doesn't matter, dude. Really, it doesn't."

"Yeah. It does. I love her. I'm not going to lie to her."

"Fine. Just give me time to split. A week. I'll wrap things up as quick as I can."

"Where are you going to go?"

He grinned, raised both hands, and began walking backward down the corridor. "I'll go everywhere, man. I'll go everywhere."

Then he spun and pushed open the door to the emergency stairwell, disappearing as the warning buzzer sounded, bringing two burly orderlies to investigate the breach.

Oliver started walking the other direction, thinking the two were wasting their time. They wouldn't see so much as a flash of Will Bowman's black hair.

Chapter Twenty

Nine months ago, when Indiana had purchased Hiram Glass's overgrown fifteen acres, and wreck of a cottage, and thriving hives of bees, she never would've imagined that her first overnight guest would be the brother she hadn't seen since the day he'd walked out of prison.

In the ten years since, she'd done her best not to think about that day. About the ride to Huntsville she'd made with Ten, their parents out of the country and too involved to get back. Waiting anxiously for a glimpse of the brother she'd been responsible for sending away.

She hadn't realized until it was too late that the man with the broad shoulders and buff chest, the big biceps and crew cut, the man getting into the cab parked three car lengths in front of them was Dakota. That was the picture she'd carried with her all this time.

Her brother. Leaving. Gone.

His hair was longer now, his face without a shave for at least a couple of days. His body was even more fit than it had appeared in the brief glimpse she'd gotten that day. What had changed the most were his eyes, the deep lines cut into his temples, the dark circles carved beneath. There was sorrow there. Worry, too. Resignation.

As happy as she was to see him, those changes made her sad. She had caused whatever he had suffered. Her need to be noticed. To be wanted. To be as important as the climate and the glaciers and the clubbed baby seals, and Thea Clark . . . Could she possibly have gone about seeking attention in a worse way?

Because wasn't that why she'd toyed with Robby? She'd seen Thea do the same with Dakota, Shelley James do the same with Tennessee. How sad that she'd ruined so many lives because she'd been looking for love. And she'd done so in all the wrong places, a thought that had her groaning aloud.

"If I'd known it was going to take you this long to make coffee, I would've just asked for a glass of water."

"Oh, it's done," she said, shaking off the bleak musings. She would learn to live with what she'd done. The consequences. The whys. All that mattered now was having Dakota home.

Except when she turned to hand him the mug

she'd just poured, she stumbled. Dakota grabbed the coffee before it spilled, but he was too late for her. She spilled everywhere: on the floor, curling in on herself as she leaned against the cabinets, onto herself, crying a veritable flood of tears that soaked her, then soaked her brother as he sat beside her and pulled her into his lap.

"I'm so sorry for what I did. What I caused to happen. I ruined your life."

"Indy, no. Just stop." Dakota stroked her hair from her face, held one arm wrapped around her. The hand of the other pressed her head to his chest. "Robby Hunt was a piece of shit. Tennessee and I both knew that. But he got us what we wanted. Cigarettes, beer. Pot. That's all we saw. We never saw the ugly side of who he was, and we should have. We never saw what he might do to you until it was too late."

"It wasn't all his fault. I tried to seduce him. Not the night in the kitchen when he attacked me, but before." She sucked in a deep breath, shuddered as she released it. If Dakota walked out on her now, so be it, but she had to confess the truth of her part in Robby's sins. "I wanted a boyfriend. I wanted a boy to think I was sexy. The way you thought Thea Clark was sexy—"

"Thea Clark? Indy." He shook his head when she pulled back to look at him, and gave a gruff sort of chuckle that held little humor at all. "That was nothing but sex. I was sixteen. She put out. I don't know what about that you thought was sexy."

"You wanted her. I wanted that from someone." And that was all she could bring herself to say. How pathetic to have felt so *un*wanted.

"Oh, Indiana." He closed his eyes, let his head fall back against the cabinets. She slid from his lap to the floor, crossing her legs, staying close.

It was hard to wait. Hard not to make him talk. Hard not to shake him until the words poured out because she couldn't go on without hearing them. Thirteen years. What had happened to him while she was finishing college and establishing IJK Gardens and trying to convince herself she was worth forgiving for the things she'd done wrong?

"The day you walked out of prison, I didn't even recognize you," she finally said. "Your hair was short"—it was long enough now that he wore it banded at his nape—"and you'd obviously worked out a *ton* in the six months since I'd seen you, because I didn't recognize your shoulders, these shoulders," she said, squeezing the ball of muscle, then squeezing his biceps. "It was too late when I realized it was you getting into the cab in front of us. Tennessee tried to follow, but we were blocked in, and then you were gone.

"I've thought about you every day since. I've pictured you doing all sorts of things. Fishing in Florida. Fishing in Alaska. Working the oil fields in Alaska, or North Dakota, or South Texas, though if you've been that close all this time I'll have to hurt you." He grinned when she said it, but he didn't interrupt, and so she went on. "I imagined you as a tour guide in Colorado. Rafting trips. Hunting trips. I never thought of you sitting behind a desk. It's always been something physical. I guess because of how you swung that bat—"

"That bat was a very long time ago," he said, one big hand rubbing at his forehead. "I don't like thinking about it because of what that night cost me, but mostly because of what it cost you."

"What it cost *me?*" Her stomach tumbled. She thought she might throw up. What in the world was he saying?

"I made the choice to swing," he said, reaching for one of her hands, holding it, bouncing it on his thigh. "You did not make the choice to have Robby assault you—"

"You don't know everything." She bowed her head, her voice soft. "I teased him. I led him on. I—"

"Uh-uh. I didn't come all this way to listen to you take blame for that night." His voice was deep, raspy. Firm. "There's one person to blame. And he's not in this room. I don't blame you for anything. I could never blame you for anything."

When she looked up and met his gaze, she thought she might break into a million pieces. Oh, the sadness simmering in his eyes. His lashes were long like Tennessee's, but his eyes were a golden brown, and the tears welling in them, spilling from them, slipping down his cheeks burned her as if she were the one in pain.

What had he gone through while he'd been away? What could he possibly be suffering from? "I love you, big brother. So very much."

He nodded, lifted the hem of his Henley pullover, and wiped his face. Then he sniffed and he smiled and he actually ruffled her hair. "You're not bad yourself. For a kid sister."

"So are you going to tell me where you've been? What you've been doing? Why in the world you left instead of coming home? And how in the world you managed to show up when you did? Talk about perfect timing—"

A sharp rap sounded on the front door, interrupting; then the door opened and heavy footsteps echoed from the living room before Tennessee appeared in the cottage's eating area, frowning down where Indiana and Dakota sat on the floor. "I'm not sure I want to know what's going on here."

"What are *you* doing here?" Indiana asked, following Dakota to her feet.

"Kaylie kicked me out," he said. "Said she needed sleep and I needed to be with the two of you."

"How did you luck into a gorgeous, sensible woman like that?" Dakota asked, grabbing

Tennessee to him for a lingering, backslapping hug. "Especially looking at how you turned out."

"If I had a clue, I'd figure a way to sell it," Tennessee said, his eyes misty, his voice as gruff as their brother's. "Now, fill me in."

Dakota's hands went to his hips as he looked from Tennessee to Indiana. "Indy's trying to convince me she's to blame for the swing that changed Keller history."

"I *am* to blame," she said, anxiety rising inside her like a flood. She was drowning with the need to atone for her sins. Unable to breathe through the band of guilt drawing tight around her chest.

"You are not," Dakota said. "And I don't want to hear those words come out of your mouth again."

"I should've been the one to do it," Tennessee said. "I was still a minor. I wouldn't have gone to prison—"

"You don't know that," Indiana butted in to say. "You were seventeen and could have easily been tried as an adult and served just as much time."

"Hey." Dakota held up a hand. "We're all here now. We're together. Nothing else matters."

"But we've lost so much—" Indiana began.

Dakota cut her off with a shake of his head. "We haven't lost a thing. Yeah, there's a decade in there we spent apart, but who says Ten and I would've made a go of Keller Construction the way we'd planned? I like to think he pulled it together because I wasn't here, and because giving parolees a leg up—and yeah, I know about that—was more important than the two of us trying to make a go of a family business."

Was that really the way he saw their ruined lives? This wasn't just some show for her benefit? "What happened to you out there in the big bad world? I don't remember you ever being so . . ."

"Mellow?" he said, a laugh rolling up from his chest. "It's a long story."

And finally, *finally,* they had time. She walked back to the coffeepot, poured two more cups. "So was it my investigator who found you? Or Oliver's?"

"I was in a little town in your namesake state, and I'm clueless as to who the dude was or where he came from."

"It doesn't matter. You're here now." And then she was struck with the most terrible thought ever. "You're going to stay, aren't you?"

"For a while, yeah."

"No, no, no. Don't say that." Her knees nearly gave out at the thought. "We've got years and years of catching up to do. I can't even think about you leaving again."

"Chill, baby sister." His grin pulled wide through the scruff on his face, his dimples so familiar. "I'm not going anywhere yet."

Chapter Twenty-one

Oliver hadn't gone home after leaving the hospital, but had driven all the way to Dallas before realizing where he was. He'd just needed to go somewhere, anywhere. He'd needed to breathe. He'd needed time and space to reflect. About birth and about death. About life and about love. About families. Parents, brothers. A wife.

He'd reached the ripe old age of thirty-two without thinking about getting married. Without thinking seriously anyway. Without thinking it was what he wanted. His mother wanted it. As long as he wed the right woman. Pedigree counted. Education. Social status. The Gatlin name wasn't up for grabs to just anyone.

How many times had she drilled those things into him? Funny, that, because the name belonged to his father. His mother had taken it as her own with no pedigree or education, and a negative social status. She'd brought nothing to the table except a strong desperation to escape the circumstances of her life.

She'd never told him anything about her background. He'd learned some from his father, but discovered most on his own. Having Oliver know what he did would embarrass her. Humiliate her. She was such a proud woman, so incredibly

318

imperious, yet she would never understand how admirable her accomplishments were.

She'd overcome so much to make the life she wanted. A life that suited her. A life that had probably saved her. Yet he couldn't remember her ever appearing to be happy. Perhaps she found the emotion a weakness, or she was more concerned with keeping what she had than allowing herself to enjoy it.

She'd certainly never considered what would make him or Oscar happy. They'd had Belgian Malinois guard dogs, not pets. They'd played tennis, not football. When all he'd wanted to do was paint, she'd insisted he get his degree, then after Oscar's accident, insisted he focus on a career that wouldn't consume him.

And her matchmaking efforts . . . He didn't want to think about those, but how could he not? He didn't want what she and his father had. He wanted what Tennessee shared with Kaylie. What Angelo had found with Luna. Even what Mitch Pepper enjoyed with Dolly, both older, and wiser, this second time around.

And he wanted all of that with Indiana Keller. The idea that she might possibly be his for the rest of his life had him struggling to breathe, had him wondering if his heart would give out before he saw her to tell her. He floored the BMW's accelerator and shot like a rocket down the highway into the night.

He couldn't possibly get back to Hope Springs fast enough. He needed to be there now.

It was almost midnight when he arrived at the cottage on Three Wishes Road. Lights were on as expected; he couldn't imagine Indiana not staying up with Dakota. And Tennessee's truck was in the driveway as well.

He wondered how that conversation had gone, Kaylie most likely ordering the three Keller siblings out of her room so she could rest, and so they could get to know one another all over again.

Thinking back, he realized it had been seven months since Indiana had first mentioned her plan to find her brother. Seven months. He was pretty sure he'd fallen in love with her over breakfast at Malina's that morning. But Will asking him not to tell her that he was the one who'd found Dakota . . .

If things went the way Oliver was hoping, that secret wasn't one he'd be keeping for long. He'd promised to give Will a week, and he was a man of his word. But he was not going further into this relationship without a policy of full disclosure. Which meant he was going to have to do a lot of coming clean.

Indiana answered his knock with a loud, "Oliver! Where have you been?" and grabbed his arm and tugged him forward. "I left Kaylie's room and you were gone. I must have called you a half dozen times."

He took a single step inside and breathed in the scent of citrus that always hung in the air. But he smelled coffee, too, and what he thought might be biscuits and gravy. Comfort food for those needing comfort.

"I went for a drive. I needed to think. I turned off my phone."

She cocked her head and considered him curiously while pushing her hair from her face. "That sounds ominous."

"Not ominous. Just . . ." He shrugged because he wasn't sure what else to say. A loud burst of male laugher erupted from the kitchen, reminding him she had important company, and the things he wanted to say to her could wait. "I'll come back. I don't want to intrude."

"You're not intruding," she said, grabbing his shirtsleeve and nearly dragging him into the cottage's front room. "You need to meet Dakota properly. And I need to thank you properly for the best gift I've ever received."

His promise to Will weighed heavily, but it was a promise. "We'll talk about that gift later. And as much as I want to get to know your brother, you need this time with him, and with Ten," he added, hearing the voice he recognized above the unfamiliar one. And then, because he obviously wasn't thinking straight, and he didn't want to mess up the thing that had brought him here, he said, "I'll catch up with you tomorrow."

"Oliver. You're not making sense. Why come here if you're just going to leave?" She was frowning, her arms crossed in that way she had of showing her displeasure. "You look like crap, to be honest, and I don't just mean the hair and the clothes and the bags under your eyes. Are you okay?"

The fact that he knew that about her stance and that she recognized that about him made him smile. "It'll keep," he said, though really it wouldn't. The things he needed to say . . . He took a deep breath, blew it out, took another, and shoved his fists in his pockets. "Or you could come outside with me. Just for a few."

This time she considered him with a wary regard, and really, he couldn't blame her. The last few months he'd hardly been himself, and yet . . . That wasn't true. He'd been his real self. His true, artistic self. And he had this woman to thank for giving him his life.

"Fine," she said. She called toward the kitchen, "Be right back," then followed him onto the tiny porch, her boots scuffing across the surface. The screen door creaked and latched behind her, and she led him down the steps to the swing she'd set up on a frame in the yard. It wouldn't fit on the porch.

Nothing would fit on the porch, save for the small potted rubber tree he'd kept from Oscar's funeral, one sent by the staff of the Caffey-Gatlin

322

Academy and that he'd left without mentioning when visiting her on Valentine's Day.

Why it had seemed to fit here instead of at home . . . Then again, the house he'd lived in all these years hadn't felt like home in ages. He'd stayed because he needed to be where Oscar couldn't be. For his mother. To a lesser extent his father. Mostly for himself.

But this tiny little nearly uninhabitable cottage where Indiana spent most of her time, yeah. It felt like a home. And when he was here, no, when he was with her, he felt like he was exactly where he belonged.

She dropped to sit on the swing, and kicked it into motion. As always, she wore the only pair of cowboy boots he'd ever seen on her feet. Except for Kaylie's wedding, and the various holiday functions they'd both attended the last few months, they were *all* he'd ever seen on her feet.

He wanted to ask her about them, how long had she had them, did they have a special meaning, but realized all his questions were just a distraction when the whole of his future was on the line.

"Oliver?"

He shook his head, dropped it back on his shoulders, flexed his hands in his pockets as if he could grab the right moment and squeeze it into submission, because this wasn't going the way he'd planned.

"Hey. You." She stopped the swing, nudged his ankle with the toe of her boot. "What's going on?"

"I want very much . . . I would like very much . . ." He stopped and cleared his throat, hoping the words he was looking for would fall into the space that was no longer clogged, because they weren't coming. They just weren't coming—

"Oliver. What is it?" she asked, planting her boots on the ground.

"Indiana Jane Keller, will you marry me?"

She held his gaze, a long, lingering moment of his willing her to say yes, of her saying nothing, of her eyes tearing up so that he didn't want her to say anything at all.

He should've known better. He'd met her when he was someone else, before he'd grown into his skin. He couldn't blame her for refusing him, for wanting what she thought she'd signed up for rather than the truth.

"I can't."

"Because of Will?" he asked, not sure why he would use the other man as an excuse.

"Why would you ask me that?" But she didn't give him time to answer before adding, "No. This has nothing to do with Will."

"My mother, then."

"Oliver, please." She stood, hugged herself, rubbed her hands up and down her arms. "It's not your mother. It's just . . . There are some things about me, things I've done . . ."

Funny. He'd never been on the receiving end of the "It's not you, it's me" rejection cliché. "What about you? What don't I know? What don't you want me to know?"

Eyes closed, she let her head fall back as she shook it, then turned and gave him a sad smile. "Do you realize we've known each other almost seven months?"

And wasn't she the one who'd talked about knowing in six if a relationship was going to work? "Look, I know it seems as if I don't know who I am, what I'm doing with my life. The painting . . . I'd given it up for a long time—"

"Oh, Oliver, no," she said, and grabbed for his arm, squeezing his wrist, then his hand, then releasing him. "I love that you're painting. I'm so far beyond happy about it that I can't put it into words. When I said it was me, I meant it. You're right that there are things I don't want you to know. That I've never wanted anyone to know. Things no one does. Not Tennessee or Dakota. Not Kaylie. Not Luna."

"Then tell me," he said, and moved closer.

She countered by circling around to stand behind the swing. "I can't—"

"Yeah. You can," he said, and moved in, grabbing the chains and rattling them, the noise an echo of the commotion churning in his gut. "I'm not going to let you use some horrible secret you've been keeping get in the way of the best thing that's ever happened in my life. I'm not going to give you up, give *us* up because you refuse to come clean."

"What if I do come clean?" she asked, her voice soft, her head bowed. "And what if it changes everything?"

"It won't."

"You can't know that," she said, looking up again, her eyes wet and glistening in the light from the moon.

"I can know that. I do know that. Nothing you tell me will change how I feel about you."

"You say that now . . ."

Knowing the next few minutes would define the rest of his life, he responded in the only way he could. "Then prove me wrong."

Chapter Twenty-two

Indiana had known for months this day would come. That if she wanted a future with this man, she'd have to tell him the story of her sexual assault, not just hint at cryptic bits and pieces. That night in her family's kitchen with Robby . . . It wasn't something she liked to think about, much less talk about, but neither was it something she could keep from Oliver any longer. Not with the relationship she wanted.

The trust. The openness. The honesty. The truth.

Circling to the front of the swing, she sat, and waited until he sat, too, close enough to touch but neither of them making a move to do so. She wanted to run her fingers through the hair at his nape where it caught on his collar, dip them beneath the fabric and feel the heat of his skin. His shirt was wrinkled, the sleeves rolled to his elbows, the tails loose, buttons missing. She loved so much the way he looked wearing jeans. She loved seeing him so undone.

She loved him. The thought nearly brought her to her knees. Her eyes burned, fighting glorious, joyful tears. "Do you remember the morning last year when we ate breakfast at Malina's? That first time we sat down and actually talked?"

He was sitting forward, his elbows on his knees, his hands flexing as if he wanted to reach for something, or whale on something. Maybe shake them both until they figured this out. "You told me about Dakota going to prison for defending you."

Okay. Here we go. "What I didn't tell you was that he would never have had to defend me if I hadn't given Robby the idea that I welcomed his advances."

He looked over, his expression gentling. Almost paternalistic. Close to condescending. "Indiana—"

"No," she said, as she pushed to stand. She

327

would not have him so handily dismiss the guilt she'd carried all these years. "You have to listen. You can't interrupt. You can't tell me what Robby did was not my fault. Because it was. I know it was. You weren't there."

"I don't have to have been there," he said, and sat straight, stretching his arms across the back of the swing. "You could've stripped out of your clothes and invited him into your bed. But the second you said no, that was it. If he did anything but walk away, it was assault."

"I didn't strip out of my clothes. I didn't invite him into bed. But I flirted with him, and I teased him. I let him touch me. This all before things went wrong." She thought about the night behind the garage, her efforts to be provocative. "I was so young and so stupid. I couldn't imagine things would go that wrong," she said, and buried her face in her hands.

"Indy. Oh, baby." Oliver got to his feet and reached for her, but she made herself back away. "You don't need to tell me any of this. None of it has any bearing on how I feel about you." He paused, waited until she looked up at him, then added, "I love you."

"How can you say that?" How could anyone love her after what she'd done? With the garbage she brought with her? And that had her wanting to laugh. Love was the very thing she'd wanted. But no man had ever given her that gift. She'd made sure of that, pushing them away. Until Oliver, who'd pushed back . . .

Her fingers were stiff like sticks of ice when she rubbed her hands up and down her bare arms. "I led him on. I'm the reason he spent all that time in the hospital. I'm the reason Dakota went to prison. They were friends for so long, Robby and Dakota and Tennessee—"

"Stop right there," he said, and this time when he took hold of her, she let him, reaching out and making fists in the fabric of his shirt. "I don't have to know this Hunt kid's history with your family to know he wasn't a friend. Attempted rapists are not friends."

She wanted to believe him. She'd told herself the same thing for years, but her voice was weak and small and without conviction. So all she could do was nod and hope he had more faith than she did.

"I want you to listen to me. To hear me. And I want you to think about what I'm going to say."

She nodded again, desperate for a reason to keep from speaking and further ruining what should've been the happiest night of her life. He'd asked her to marry him. *Dear God. Oliver Gatlin proposed!* And all she could think about was the assault that had messed up her life and Dakota's life and Tennessee's life . . .

He lifted her chin, holding her so she couldn't look away. "You and I have both lived our lives based on having failed our brothers—"

"It's not the s—"

"Don't tell me it's not the same, because it's exactly the same. And we've both been wrong not to realize our brothers were the ones to make their choices. So you flirted with Robby. So you tempted him. You did not put that bat into Dakota's hands any more than I forced Oscar behind the wheel of his car."

No. No. She shook her head. How could he compare their two situations? Dakota would never have picked up that bat if not for her. But Oscar . . . She thought back to what she knew of the younger Gatlin's accident. Oliver didn't have anything to do with his brother's tragic end . . . did he? "Oliver? What aren't you saying? What haven't you told me?"

He closed his eyes then, and set her away, scraping both hands back through his hair before walking to the cottage to sit on the steps. "I knew something was going on with Oscar and Sierra. But then something was always going on with those two, so I didn't pay any more attention than I usually did, and I should have."

When he paused, she joined him, anxiety gnawing at her stomach as if eating her in two.

"The weekend of Oscar's accident, I'd come home to go to the Longhorns game. I went to school at Rice, but one of my best friends from high school played for UT. I'd actually been

330

home since late Wednesday night. And I'd heard Oscar complaining more than once about the steering in his car feeling off."

Indiana closed her eyes and swallowed the dread rising like bile up her throat. She knew Oscar had lost control of his BMW while driving along the Devil's Backbone. Knew, too, having heard the story from Luna, that Luna had been following in her car, and had witnessed him going off the edge of the ravine before she herself had crashed.

"Friday morning he asked if he could use my car," he said, back to flexing his hands. "He was supposed to attend a music workshop that weekend, but hadn't had time to get his looked at. If he asked either of our parents, he'd get lectured about car ownership and responsibility and have to stay home. I guess I thought I was teaching him a lesson by giving him the same answer—not to drive without the go-ahead from our mechanic.

"Plus, I had a lot going on that weekend, and I didn't want to risk breaking down using his. I mean, he could've rented a car. I don't know why he didn't rent a car. Or why I thought it was my place to act like a parent instead of a brother." He shook his head. Back and forth. Back and forth. But Indiana didn't dare move. Whatever he'd walled up inside had to come out, and she couldn't do anything but wait.

Oliver finally went on. "He came to me. My

brother. I could've helped him out. I *should've* helped him out. He was anxious and all kinds of hyper and worried, obviously about Sierra and getting married and the baby, though I didn't know that's what it was at the time. But I did know that he wasn't himself. And I should've helped him out. Instead, I did my thing, he did his, and only one of us came home again."

He bit off the last words, but she was sure he'd rushed to keep his voice from breaking. His breathing had grown choppy, and even now where he sat beside her, she sensed his tension, as if he were trying not to shake.

But rather than reach for him, she gave him time, gave him space, and then hoping she wasn't making things worse, she asked, "Do you know for sure it was his steering that caused the accident? Did accident investigators or mechanics or whoever examine his car?"

Calmer now, he shrugged. "They may have. Once it was clear Oscar wouldn't have an easy recovery, I went back to school. I didn't want to know what my parents found out. I didn't want to hear from them at all, or talk to them. I put my head down. I did my work. It was the only way I was able to get through. Because if I stopped to think about Oscar asking to use my car . . ." This time when he shuddered, she placed her palm between his shoulder blades and rubbed him there. "Not knowing became easier because knowing wouldn't bring him back, and the thought that his accident was my fault—"

"It wasn't your fault. It was his car. His decision." She knew so little about the events of that day, or even about the tragedy at all. But this she knew: Oscar Gatlin had deliberately chosen to get behind the wheel of his car.

Just like Robby Hunt had deliberately chosen to assault her.

She'd said no, but it hadn't stopped him. Like Oscar, yet so unlike Oscar, he'd made his decision. Oscar hadn't heeded his brother's admonition that he not take his car. And Robby hadn't listened to her.

Oliver had done his part. She had done her part. And yet here they were, both weighed down with guilt over decisions others had made. Robby had known better, and as cruel as it seemed, Oscar had known better, too.

Why was that so hard to accept?

"It wasn't your fault," she repeated, then added, "Any more than what Robby did, even what Dakota did, was mine."

It took him a minute, but Oliver turned and smiled, if a bit weakly. Then he brought up his hands to cup her face and rested his forehead against hers. "Do you know how good it is to hear you say that?"

"I wish it felt a little better than it does," she said, because saying it was the easy part. Believing it completely . . . That was going to take time.

"You'll get there," he said, and she arched a brow.

"I know you're not speaking from experience."

He laughed at that, moved to wrap his arm around her shoulders and pull her close. She let him, she even helped him; close to Oliver Gatlin was the only place she wanted to be.

"So how did we get here, to this point, living less than authentic lives?" she asked, because even with all of her career success, she'd always known her past would have to be dealt with.

"I don't know about you, but mine feels pretty damn authentic."

"Now maybe, but has it always?"

"Yeah. It has," he said, his free hand holding both of hers in his lap. "I made the only choices I could at the time. Probably not the best choices, but my choices. That's as authentic as it gets."

He was right. She was who she was because of all that she'd gone through. If she'd made different decisions, there was no telling who she'd be now. "And thank you so much for Dakota."

"Yeah," he said, and cleared his throat. "About that . . ."

"What about it?"

He came close to answering, she was certain of it, then said instead, "I'll tell you next week."

"Okay." And then she remembered the question

he'd asked her, not that she'd ever really forgotten, happiness filling her, a buoyant balloon of joy, as she added, "Yes."

"Yes?" he asked, his brows creased, a deep vee marring his forehead.

"Yes, Oliver Gatlin. I will marry you."

He started to smile, held back, and asked, "That's it?"

Wasn't it everything? Oh, wait! The best part!

She jumped to her feet, spun in a circle until dizzy from the stars, then stopped and climbed into his lap. With her knees straddling his thighs, she cupped his face in both hands and lowered her mouth to his, whispering against his lips, "I love you, Oliver Gatlin. I love you with all of my heart."

INDIANA

The night Robby Hunt decided I hadn't been serious the times I told him no, I was sitting at the kitchen table doing homework. The incident on the side of the garage had been only one of my several aborted seductions. The most intimate. The most confusing because of how I wanted to pretend it had never happened, and how I wanted more.

I can't imagine I was the only girl to ever face that conundrum. Because here was the thing. Boys would be boys. But girls? We had to deny becoming sexual beings.

We couldn't explore or discover our own changing bodies without labels or censure. God forbid we be allowed to misbehave, or be studs instead of sluts, or earn extra heartthrob points as word of our conquests hit the streets. No one wanted a girl with experience, one adept at what she was doing, yet everyone wanted a boy who knew his way around.

Robby didn't know his way around any more than I did. We'd both received our sexual instruction from movies and books, from exaggerated locker room tales, and learned our moves from the same. Those lessons had been dosed, of course, with hormones and imagination, and liberally so. That's why my heart skipped several beats when it was Robby who came into the kitchen that night, who pulled the pizza from the oven with a dish towel.

Who then moved to stand behind my chair, his fingers brushing my shoulders as he gripped the frame. "Homework?"

"Algebra." I closed my eyes and tried to slow my dead-giveaway breathing, but it was hard to do with how crazy-fast my heart was beating. We'd been here before, in this place where he wanted to touch me, and I wanted him to touch me, but never with my brothers so close.

He trailed his fingers along the chair back to my neck, through my hair, then leaned down and rubbed his mouth to my ear. It was wet, his breath hot. I wanted to like it, and in a way I did, but all I could think about was Dakota or Tennessee coming down and catching us.

It was when Robby slid his hands down my arms, his thumbs skating along the edges of my breasts, that I decided to move. And he decided not to let me. To wrap an arm around me and hold me to the chair. To dip his free hand into my shirt, then beneath my bra. It wasn't like he hadn't been there before. It just hadn't happened in a brightly lit kitchen.

And it wasn't going to happen in this one. I was not going to risk being discovered. Before I could make that clear, however, he used the barrier of his one arm to scoot me and my chair from beneath the table. I didn't even get a chance to stand. He flung his leg across my lap and straddled me, his weight, though slight, enough to keep me in my place.

I think he liked that, me being trapped, helpless —though I wasn't really; I was the only thing stopping me from calling out—my chest rising and falling, my eyes, I'm sure, quite wide. I figured he was testing some sort of limits, and any second would let me go. I doubted he'd want to be busted holding me down should either of my brothers come to check on the food.

I was wrong on all counts. And he was stronger than I'd realized.

He reached behind me and pulled open the

kitchen door. Then he grabbed hold of both of my wrists and stood, kicking the chair away and dragging me outside. The only thing I could think to say was, "The pizza's getting cold."

"The pizza will keep. This won't." Then he stuffed the dish towel into my mouth, and brought my hands shackled by his to the front of his jeans.

I didn't know what he was thinking. That I was going to willingly have sex with him outside? With both of my brothers upstairs? But it became clear pretty quickly that my being willing didn't play into his plans.

No matter how hard I fought, he held tight, and my wrists felt as if he were crushing them. The bones grinding. The skin burning as he twisted this way and that. I stumbled backward, hoping to fall, to bring him with me.

Surely he'd have to let me go to catch himself if I tripped him. But I was wrong about that, too. He landed on top of me, and he pinned my wrists over my head with one hand. With his other, he worked open his jeans. And when I finally wanted to scream for real, I couldn't.

But I struggled. Oh, I struggled. Sliding around beneath him, kicking with my feet, pummeling him with my knees, bucking with my hips, though since I was still wearing the track pants I'd put on after volleyball practice, fighting back wasn't such a good idea.

The fabric stuck to the grass as I squirmed, and I nearly wiggled myself out of them. My heart pounded so hard I couldn't breathe, and I couldn't grab for my waistband because he'd made certain I couldn't use my hands.

He liked that, too. His grin was twisted. His eyes wicked with glee. This was not the Robby I'd crushed on. The Robby who'd been my girl-friend.

I didn't know who this was, or why he was hurting me, and I wanted to yell at the top of my lungs: *Stop! Get off me! What's wrong with you? If my brothers don't kill you, I will!* But wasn't this all my fault for leading him on?

And that's when I heard Dakota call Robby's name. And I heard the word *pizza*. Thank good-ness Robby had left the back door open when he'd dragged me outside. I couldn't decide whether to warn him or wait. It didn't matter. He heard, releasing me and jumping up, then backing away as he jerked up his pants and ran.

I couldn't even move. I listened until I heard his car start, his tires screech on the pavement; then I finally managed to get rid of the dish towel, to fix my pants and sit up.

I swiped at my hair; it was a tangled mess of grass and dead leaves. My nose was running, and I could feel the smear of snot I left when I wiped it with my sleeve. I didn't think I was crying—it didn't feel like I was crying—but my eyes were watering, and my face was wet. It was too much to hide, so I didn't.

Dakota was standing in the doorway when I came back in. Tennessee was cutting the pizza. "Indy, what the hell?" Dakota asked, stepping back as I pushed inside. But then he grabbed me by the arm and looked me over, as if making sure I wasn't broken or bleeding, before looking at Tennessee and saying, "Robby."

"I'm fine. I'm okay." I wasn't either, but I would be. I just wanted to get back to my algebra, but Dakota was pacing the kitchen, his hands fisted, his face taut with rage. "I knew it. *I knew it*. That piece of—" He cut himself off, but under his breath cursed Robby, words I couldn't make out. Words I didn't need to. I understood.

Then he stopped and walked to the door where a baseball bat leaned in the corner. He picked it up. He popped it against his palm. He looked from me to Tennessee. My heart was racing when Tennessee nodded, and when Dakota nodded, too, my stomach tightened. I thought I was going to throw up. But I didn't say anything. I stood there while he made the decision. And then, along with Tennessee, I watched him go, too shocked to consider the consequences of what he had planned, too numb to stop him, and somewhere deep inside, rooting him on.

I wanted Robby to pay, to hurt. He'd betrayed our friendship. He'd broken our trust. Yet a part of me was convinced that I'd brought this on myself. Encouraging him, teasing him, tempting him. Yes meaning yes, and sometimes no meaning yes, too? How could he be blamed when I was sending mixed signals?

Tennessee and I were still sitting at the kitchen table when an hour later Dakota came home. I hadn't touched my algebra. Tennessee hadn't touched his pizza, or asked me what had happened. He hadn't needed to; wasn't it obvious? But he'd stayed with me the entire time, and I'd never been so happy not to be alone.

Dakota didn't say a word when he walked through the door. He set the bloodied bat back in its place and headed upstairs, cranking the volume on his stereo to full blast. The cops arrived at our house close to midnight. Our parents had returned earlier from the function they'd been tied up with. And that was the end of life as we'd lived it in the Keller household. The end of everything normal I'd known.

How many girls, how many sisters, could say without a doubt that their brother would go to prison for them? I'm not even sure I knew Dakota would until he did. Look out for me, sure. Tell me what to do, most definitely. Give me a hard time about my taste in movies, and music, and clothes, oh yeah. Brotherly things. He was good at brotherly things. But to literally put his life on the line in my defense? Without hesitation? No second thoughts? Because he loved me and as wrong as it was, it was the right thing to do?

I hope I would've made the same sacrifice for him.

A maiden in her glory,
Upon her wedding-day,
Must tell her Bees the story,
Or else they'll fly away.

—RUDYARD KIPLING,
"THE BEE BOY'S SONG"

INDIANA AND OLIVER
—ALONG WITH THEIR FAMILIES—
INVITE YOU TO WITNESS
THEIR EXCHANGE OF VOWS AND TO
ENJOY A BUZZING CELEBRATION
OF LIFE AND OF LOVE.

SATURDAY, OCTOBER 18, 2014
3:00 P.M.
THE GARDENS ON
THREE WISHES ROAD
GENEROUS FOOD, DRINK,
AND LAUGHTER TO FOLLOW

Epilogue

Indiana got married in her cowboy boots, though she doubted anyone noticed. Her dress had come from the same tony Austin boutique that sold Luna's Patchwork Moon scarves. It was the yellow of whipped butter, barely yellow at all, and the softest Indian cotton she'd ever encountered, with a fitted bodice, snug cap sleeves, a scooped neckline, and a lacy handkerchief hem that reached just below her knees.

Apple's Flowers & Gifts had been given free rein to decorate the lot on Three Wishes Road. Butters Bakery, in concert with Two Owls Café, catered the event, with next to no instructions from Indiana. All she wanted out of the day was Oliver.

Kaylie was the one who'd insisted Indiana would later regret not having a public ceremony. Kaylie and Merrilee Gatlin, though Merrilee made it clear she would've preferred the couple use Second Baptist Church where she and Orville attended worship.

Indiana mused with a bit of melancholia that it would've been nice to have her parents there, but getting back into rural China after getting out would've cost them a fortune emotionally, physi-

344

cally, and monetarily. They'd wired her cash instead.

How Kaylie managed anything with a five-month-old demanding her attention, Indiana didn't know, though she imagined Mitch and Dolly helped as much with the food as they did with babysitting Georgia May.

Indiana had her brothers and the Gardens on Three Wishes Road and the cottage demanding her attention. And Oliver. So much time with Oliver. She didn't care about invitations or registries, so she gladly let Merrilee—who had unexpectedly volunteered, an olive branch Indiana assumed and gladly accepted—handle those.

Neither did she care about cake flavors, but learned through Kaylie that Oliver had insisted Peggy Butters and Gail Apple use a citrus-flavored and citrus-colored theme. She couldn't imagine how he'd known of her love for grape-fruits and limes, until she thought back to that first breakfast they'd shared at Malina's, those two cups of Earl Grey tea, her chattering on about Ruby Reds and bergamot. The fact that he'd listened. And not only listened, but paid attention. And remembered.

She'd been unaccountably nervous that morning, a dirt-digging Keller breakfasting with the silver-spooned Gatlin heir. Then he'd ordered biscuits and gravy to go with his upper-crust tea. She'd probably fallen a little bit in love with him then. But she was completely in love with him now.

Standing beneath a cloudless blue sky, and an arch festooned with ribbons of orange and yellow and green and grapefruit pink—not summer pastels but the vibrant shades of zest and ripe fruit that brought her mouth to water—her hands in Oliver's as he held her gaze, she thought it truly possible that one could die from happiness. No part of her body was working as it should; all she knew was Oliver's voice.

"I saw you for the first time one year ago today. I think I said 'Excuse me' as I walked by, but the rest of the things I wanted to say I held back. Instead, I watched you. I wondered about you. And when a few days later I looked out the window and saw you standing across the road from here, I knew my life would never be the same."

His hands on hers tightened, and as he brought them to his lips to kiss, his expression grew more solemn, and the world around them narrowed and faded away until nothing else, no one else, remained.

"I didn't know what I was looking for until I found you. I didn't know I was looking for any-one at all. I didn't know what it meant to be in love. To want more for another person than I want for myself. To feel that need so deeply I can't separate it from the rest of who I am.

"You make me who I am because of who you are. I love you, Indiana, and with you I'll always be my best."

Behind her, Indiana heard Kaylie, her maid of honor, catch back a sob, and had no doubt that if she glanced to where her brothers, having both walked her down the aisle, were seated side by side in the row of chairs designated for family, their eyes would be as red as Oliver's, and filled with the same joyous tears as her own. Even Orville Gatlin, serving as his son's best man, was not unmoved, his head bowed, his fist to his mouth as he struggled for composure.

And then it was Indiana's turn. She knew by heart the words she was here to recite. She'd practiced them when harvesting green beans and summer squash, when pruning away sunbaked vines and leaves gone as brown as dirt. She'd refined them when celebrating seeds taking root, when transferring starter plants to their permanent homes, when unable to resist biting into a tomato fresh from the vine.

"One year ago today, you brushed by me in a crowded room. The feel of your arm against mine lingered for hours. I wished I'd introduced myself, that I had a reason to look you up, to call you. And when a few days later I sensed you at my side, I was certain that every dream I'd ever had for my future was about to come true."

A tear slipped past her lashes, over her cheekbone, and down to her jaw. Oliver's hold on her fingers kept her from reaching up to wipe it away, and she brushed her lips to his knuckles before going on.

"Finding you was like having the final piece of my life's puzzle click into place. I'd given up on that happening. Like giving up on a missing sock, or a lost earring. Or never knowing what happened to a note you wrote yourself, one guaranteed to make the rest of your days the best they could possibly be.

"I can't imagine them being any better than this. I didn't know being this happy was possible. But that's because I didn't know you, Oliver. Thank you for allowing me the privilege of knowing you like no one else."

After that, rings were slipped onto fingers, the words *husband and wife* spoken, a kiss to put all other kisses to shame shared while loved ones cheered and whistled. Indiana could barely keep her feet on the ground as she and her husband—*her husband!*—hurried down the grassy aisle, where Oliver finally tugged her to him, and lifted her, and twirled her around and around and around . . .

The rest of the afternoon was a blur of well wishes, and congratulations, and large bills slipped into her hand, which she then slipped into Oliver's pocket with the ones he'd been gifted.

Ten seconds after accepting a peck on the cheek or a hug, she couldn't have said for certain who had offered one, who the other. She wanted to leave, to find out the surprise of where Oliver was taking her, to know where they'd be spending their first two weeks as husband and wife.

Husband and wife. The two of them. Alone. Together.

She could not wait.

But there was dancing to be had, very little of it, sadly, with Oliver, and conversations to engage in, again sans her man. He was always there, however, catching her gaze, walking by and brushing against her, touching his fingers or his lips to her bare neck, sending shivers to coil like a spring at the base of her spine, in the pit of her belly, deep between her legs. She wanted to strip out of her clothes and crawl into bed, onto cool sheets, onto him.

She could not wait.

Husband and wife. The two of them. Alone. Together.

"Can we go?" she asked him scant moments later, having tugged him away from a circle of faceless men. Oh, she supposed she knew them all, had spoken to them all, would recognize them all given time to care, but she didn't. Not now when only Oliver existed.

He nuzzled his cheek to hers, the ends of his hair and the shadow of his beard tickling, and whispered, "I've been waiting for you to say the word."

Her chest swelled. Her stomach clenched. "I would've said it hours ago if I'd known."

"Then we'll have to work on you reading my mind."

"I have a few other things I'd like to work on first."

"Ah, see? You're catching on already." And then he kissed her, bringing his mouth hard to hers, his lips, his teeth, his tongue sliding deep, toying and playing and mating with hers, tempting hers, his hands on the swell of her bottom urging her close when she didn't need any urging at all.

In her lifetime she could never get as close to him as she wanted to. Skin to skin, limbs entwined, impaled . . . None of it would be enough. How had she ever lived without knowing this fullness, this completeness, this sense of being more than she could ever be on her own?

True love, this love, was of poets and musicians and artists who didn't need words.

"You ready for this?" her husband asked, and she nodded, not caring at all what he meant by *this*. She was ready for anything, for everything. She was ready for life to be an utterly brilliant adventure, perfect and blissful and wild because Oliver would make it so.

As they turned to go, she swore she saw

movement in the trees at the edge of the lot, a brush of black wings, perhaps, or the feral cat who kept the place free of mice leaping from a branch into the brush. But she couldn't be bothered with figuring it out. As much as she loved her cottage and the Gardens on Three Wishes Road and the birds and the bees and the wildlife, nothing mattered but life with the man at her side.

Laughing, giddy, her heart in her throat, her chest as tight as a balloon, she linked her arm through Oliver's as, together, they hurried through a shower of tossed birdseed for the car. Sending them on their way was a chorus of cheerful voices, those of friends, those of family, and the soft, constant hum of her bees.

Acknowledgments

Thanks to Susan Doerr and Oscar for my Oliver's Susan.

Thanks to Wendy Duren for the "man in training wheels," and to the chat group for the discussion that followed. You helped me pinpoint Indiana's fascination with Robby.

Thanks to Walt, as always, for everything.

Center Point Large Print
600 Brooks Road / PO Box 1
Thorndike, ME 04986-0001 USA

(207) 568-3717

US & Canada:
1 800 929-9108
www.centerpointlargeprint.com